After Charlie

After Charlie
Mucking Out and Tucking In

Jan Menell

Matador
9 Priory Business Park,
Wistow Road, Kibworth Beauchamp,
Leicestershire. LE8 0RX
Tel: 0116 279 2299
Email: books@troubador.co.uk
Web: www.troubador.co.uk/matador
Twitter: @matadorbooks

ISBN 978 1838593 162

British Library Cataloguing in Publication Data.
A catalogue record for this book is available from the British Library.

Printed and bound in Great Britain by 4edge Limited
Typeset in 11pt Minion Pro by Troubador Publishing Ltd, Leicester, UK

Matador is an imprint of Troubador Publishing Ltd

Dedicated to my life at the bottom end!

With sincere thanks to Jan Hurst, Cherry Coombe and Rosanna Ley for their patience and helpful editorial skills and to Carol Goodchild for her delightful art work.

Chapter One

A moment of passing
Little Fordham, Cambridge, late '70's

"'Ee'll be a dead weight, nurse."

Maggie Groves smothered the irreverent giggle welling up inside her as she bent over the dead body of the old man, Jack Newgate, spread-eagled on the carpet in the middle of his front room and surrounded by a group of his elderly friends. Dead weight he certainly was.

"It will take two of us to lift him, Annie, so I'll wait till the doctor arrives."

"'Ee'll take 'is time, never one to 'urry. Best make a brew now you've come," Annie Watson muttered, shuffling out of the room.

Watching Maggie's every move, the assembled gathering sidled closer together. It was early April, the evenings beginning to lengthen, but a chill wind crept through every crevice of the old cottage walls. Maggie, the local midwife, was unsure of all their names, recognising two of the women she had seen helping with the church flowers and one of the men who often tended the graves in the churchyard.

"Thank you, Annie," she said, as Annie returned clutching a mug of strong tea. "Can you tell me what happened? Did Jack say he was feeling unwell?"

"We'd been playing cards and dominos and some had gone back home to their beds. Jack'd just poured a drop of whisky, never said nothing and then just dropped on the spot." Annie was twisting a cloth curler in her hair. "Fact is, he'd won most of the games, artful bugger!"

"Annie!" Ethel Jones gasped. "Jack's just departed. It's not right to say that."

"'Ee won't mind me saying it. Still sorry to see our mate go so quick."

"Had he complained of pains anywhere before this? Had he been to the doctor recently, d'you know?" Maggie asked.

"No, never went to a doctor. Didn't believe in 'em. Just needed a drop of his carrot whisky and he was sorted."

"Has he got any relatives nearby?"

"His daughter moved to Cambridge a year ago. A couple of his cousins live in Waldersby and some of his wife Dora's family, live nearby. God rest her soul, she's been gone a year back."

"Thank you, Annie. I'm sure Doctor Southgate will want all the information you can give him."

A car door slammed in the yard, alerting them to his arrival. "Hello!"

"I'll go," Maggie said, relieved to hear the familiar voice, as she hurried out of the room and hastily opened the front door.

"Maggie! What on earth are you doing here?" Doctor Southgate exclaimed as she helped him out of his overcoat. "It's lovely to see you, my dear, but we normally meet at births, not deaths."

Maggie chuckled and lowered her voice. "Am I glad to see you; they call me for everything in the village," she whispered, hooking his coat up in the hall. "I don't mind, though; I love them all dearly. I'm a nurse to them because of the uniform. Poor Jack Newgate's passed away on the floor in the front room but I'm afraid I couldn't move him and there's quite an audience. Can I get you some tea? It's just been made."

"Thank you, *nurse*," Doctor Southgate smiled, squeezing her hand. "You get the tea and I'll sort out the old dears."

"It's so sad to lose another of that generation, Rob."

Maggie and her husband, Robert Groves, were sitting up in bed the following morning as Maggie recounted the event. Woody, their small terrier, curled up beside them; he had a habit of jumping on the bed at dawn and licking them awake, despite Robert's protestations. Robert, used to his wife's unusual comings and goings, had been fast asleep on her return.

"Pass your mug: there's enough for another," she said, checking the Teasmade on the bedside locker. "Jack was nearly ninety and the rest are well into their eighties." It had been bad enough losing their dear old neighbour, Charlie Watt. "D'you realise Charlie died nearly four years ago, darling? Now we'll probably see the demise of all his old friends."

"Hang on, Maggie, that's a bit depressing, isn't it? They aren't all going to drop dead in the next week."

"Hope not," she chuckled. "Come on. Charlie's waking up; he's chatting to his teddies," she said, throwing back the bedclothes. "Woody needs to go out so I'll take him a quick run round the meadow. I'm glad it's my day off: Angela and I plan to nip into Cambridge this morning to do a bit of shopping if that's okay with you still?"

"That's fine; you do that. I'll give Charlie his breakfast and get him ready for playgroup. The board meeting's not till ten o'clock. Just need to sort some papers out. Don't spend all our money on more clothes; this wardrobe's full…"

"Rob, would I ever?" Maggie said, yanking on her jeans. "I need to lose some weight," she said, grimacing at her reflection in the long mirror. "Look at me: fat! Daddy's getting your breakfast, darling, back in a minute," she called out, racing Woody down the stairs.

Later that day Maggie and her friend, Angela Farrow, chatted over tea. They were sitting in the next cottage up the lane, once owned by Robert and Maggie's deceased elderly neighbour, Charlie Watt. He had become a surrogate grandfather to their son, Charlie, who they'd named after him. Maggie had loved the old man dearly. He befriended them on their arrival in the village and supervised their every move into Nut Tree Cottage, which had been his cousin's former home, empty for several years and in a dilapidated state. The cottage and thatched roof had taken months to restore. He'd been prone to calling them "townies", teaching her his "country ways". She loved hearing his stories of how life used to be in Little Fordham. Once their cottage had been made habitable Maggie had held classes for the NCT – the National Childbirth Trust, much to the old man's curiosity. Angela had been Maggie's first client. Charlie Watt's unexpected death from a heart attack, alone, with his favourite chicken, Doris, nestled on his lap affected them all deeply. Maggie missed him still and made regular visits to the churchyard, where she and young Charlie put flowers on "G'andad's" grave. His empty cottage was now undergoing a major refurbishment as Angela and her new husband, Tom, had purchased it at auction. To their delight, permission had also been granted for a sizeable extension. They decided to name it Watt's Cottage.

"We're so lucky Charlie's cottage wasn't listed," said Angela. "The builders start soon so apologies in advance for what might be a rather messy few weeks. There'll be deliveries and it will churn up the lane a bit. Hopefully it won't be too bad, especially as I've told them you need to get away quickly if you're called out."

"Don't worry. I know the men quite well. One of them did some work for us last year. Can't wait till they've finished and you get stuck in. The ideas you had in your last house were extraordinary: colours I wouldn't dare to use. I think you could have been an interior designer, don't you?"

"Really? Maybe I'll think about it as a career when the children are off my hands," she laughed. "When will that happen now? I'm pregnant again."

"Early days. Let's hope you're not as sick as you were last time."

"Fingers crossed. I'm feeling fine."

"Good. Right, now the children," said Maggie, jumping up. "I'll go and collect Charlie from Dawn Creasey. She collected him from the playgroup for me at lunchtime. How about your two?"

"James has gone home with one of his school friends and won't be back till late. Our babysitter took Rosie home with her for the afternoon, so I expect they'll be here any minute," Angela said, helping Maggie separate out their shopping.

"We're so lucky," said Maggie. "Dawn's like a nanny to Charlie. She and her husband treat him as if he were their own grandchild. She won't take a penny from us and looks after him most days till I get back and is always on hand if I have to leave in a hurry. She's an absolute gem and I know she's been missing Kate sorely since she went off to university."

Maggie shuddered, thinking back to the shocking accident and Kate Creasey's amazing survival after she had been thrown from her horse in the village when a young teenager cannoned into them on his motorbike. The horse Kate had loved and owned for five years had died from its injuries. Maggie had been the first on the scene to help the injured girl.

"I think Dawn appreciates how much you cared for Kate then. You saved her life."

"I suppose so. I'll hide most of these from, Rob." Maggie said, hurriedly gathering up her bags and throwing Angela a fleeting kiss. "He's complained about me having too many clothes. I'll tell him I needed something new for Jack's funeral," she chuckled. "See you after the weekend as I'm on call and I know it's going to be busy: we've already had a lot of babies this week. Two of the mums booked for home births are overdue."

Maggie had achieved her ambition to work in the local area and delighted in having her own caseload, getting to know families intimately. Robert had been promoted and was enjoying running Suttons Scenario, the soft furnishing company in the nearby town of Waldersby. Charlie had finally been born after she'd suffered three distressing miscarriages and, although they did their best not to dwell on it, another recent miscarriage made their young son all the more precious. For now, both were enjoying their careers and Maggie was growing increasingly fond of her "mums". She didn't doubt, with her poor obstetric history and how long they had had to wait for Charlie, now four years old, that the amount of effort she put in to her work with pregnant women and their families, and the way she accumulated pets and fussed over them, was the extra mothering she needed for her own fulfilment.

Chapter Two

You had it last!

Maggie was off to an early start for her home visits when she arrived at the small council estate in the village of Bunston. She was looking forward to seeing this new baby. Maggie had looked after the family for the birth of their fourth child, but, despite her protestations, Mrs Atkins had had to be persuaded to give birth to her fifth in hospital. Back at home now their house was in full morning mayhem as Maggie could hear the children were being prepared for school and playgroup.

She listened at the door to the hubbub within before ringing the bell. As it opened a voice shouted, "It's the midwife, Ron. Tell her baby's upstairs."

Ron, looking harassed and holding two small odd socks, pointed Maggie towards the stairs.

"It's the one we 'ad before," he shouted in the direction of the kitchen. "She knows where to go."

"Thanks, Mr Atkins," Maggie said. "I'll go up."

"Right you are," he said, slamming the front door shut. "Come 'ere, Alfie. Get your bloody socks on," he yelled. "Put that cat down or I'll feed it to the dog next door."

The children raced around, giggling, infuriating him even more.

Maggie, searching upstairs for the new baby, was getting worried. There was no baby in any of the bedrooms, the Moses basket in the cot was empty and although there was evidence of a recent nappy change on the bathroom floor there was no sign of the new occupant.

Downstairs the two oldest children were being dispatched to the school bus and Mr Atkins was dragging a younger child and screaming toddler towards the back of his van.

"She can't find the kid," he shouted. "You had it last," he yelled, finally settling the protesting children before slamming the front door shut behind him.

Mrs Atkins looked tired and weary, slurping a mug of tea in the kitchen. "Want one, Maggie? I'll come back up now, love. Ron gets in such a lather so I came down to help."

"Well, I'd like to see the baby first, Norma. I thought you might like me to give him a bath this morning? Are you sure you had the baby upstairs last?" Maggie said, trying not to appear overly anxious.

"Well, I don't know what Ron did with him. He knows he had it last to change his nappy. We'll find him up there somewhere. I was feeding the little blighter all night long."

"I hear the birth was rather quick?"

"Quick? I should say. Ron got drenched. Daft 'apeth, he should have kept his head out the way instead of keep peering up my knickers to check if my waters had gone."

"I hear you didn't make the delivery room either."

"No: baby shot out on the bloody trolley in the lift!"

They were both laughing now, "Well, I'm glad to have you home," said Maggie. "Let's go and find the little one, shall we? Tommy, isn't it?"

Upstairs Norma shuffled round each bedroom. "Funny. Where's he got to?"

Just as Maggie was beginning to feel even more concerned she noticed a small bump move under the covers at the bottom of their double bed.

"Oh, goodness, Tommy's in your bed, Norma. Look: right at the bottom. Let's get him out quickly before he's smothered!"

The baby, curled up like a dormouse, stretched and yawned as Maggie lifted him out gently, appearing none the worse for being hidden under two blankets and an eiderdown.

Norma, totally unfazed, clambered gratefully back into bed. "See, I knew Ron had him last," she said, clamping Tommy to her breast. "No, p'raps best you bath him then I'll give him a good feed," she said, passing the sleepy baby back to Maggie. "I can get a kip before hubby comes back."

An hour later, satisfied that mother and baby were more settled, Maggie bade farewell with a promise to return in the afternoon.

Maggie recounted the tale to her colleague Susan as they lunched together at the clinic in Great Fordham.

"Apparently, Ron had put him there for safety! The bed covers were very light actually so I overreacted. Anyway, not only did Norma lose her baby in the bed but, when I got to Tracy Morgan at the other end of the village for my next visit, she was almost hysterical."

"Why? What happened?"

"She thought her baby had been stolen."

"What? How?"

"I found it under her bed!"

"Oh, my goodness! How on earth did it get there?"

"Well, it appears that Tracy fed the baby in the early hours. He was fast asleep and she decided not to change him in case he woke up. She popped him over the side into the carry cot, or so she thought, and went straight back to sleep."

"But how on earth could the baby fall out of the carrycot?"

"It didn't. She'd *thought* she was putting him in the carry cot. She actually dropped him in the gap between the carry cot and the bed."

"No!"

"Yes! I arrived just after she'd woken up and couldn't find the baby. Luckily as I walked into the bedroom I saw a little fist poking out from under the bed and found a very sleepy baby covered in carpet fluff, none the worse for a night on the floor."

Susan clutched at Maggie's arm, snorting with laughter. "Poor little mite; poor Tracy."

Maggie wiped tears from her eyes. "We shouldn't be laughing. Thankfully Doctor Southgate popped in and checked little Benjamin all over; no harm done. Tracy won't be making that mistake again. Poor girl: such an awful fright but she saw the funny side before I left," she said, gathering up the plates. "Come on, I'll make tea before the mums arrive. Doctor Southgate's doing the clinic today."

"I'll be off," said Susan. "I've got a half day. Can't wait to tell my student all this tomorrow."

Maggie spent the next two hours at the clinic. She enjoyed talking with the mothers, eager to discuss how their pregnancies were progressing, and encouraged those waiting to see Doctor Southgate to chat among themselves, knowing some would meet up in the parentcraft classes and gain valuable support from each other once their babies were born.

When the clinic ended at half past four she set off on her late visits and found Tracy fully recovered from her fright and Benjamin sleeping peacefully in his nursery. She popped in on Norma as promised and found her still in bed, baby Tommy nodding off on the breast. Norma was relishing the relative peace she'd enjoyed while her other children were at school, and kindly neighbours were now offering help and entertaining them.

As Maggie hurried up the path to their cottage she could see smoke puffing from the chimney, the windows misted from supper cooking on the Aga. Robert had already bathed and read to Charlie, who was fast asleep.

"Sorry, I had planned to get home in time, Rob. I hate missing out on getting him ready for bed and reading to him."

"He was dead on his feet – fell asleep mid-sentence telling me about lambing. They'd been on a farm visit."

"Ah, they're all out in the fields now. I love seeing them."

She went upstairs, to look in on Charlie before returning to the kitchen.

Woody stared at her imploringly, watching every mouthful she ate, until Robert reprimanded him.

"He's had a good walk. Darling, you must put your feet up. I've sorted out the rest of the menagerie. At least we're getting plenty of eggs now."

Maggie recounted her day and the tales of the missing babies and Robert outlined an idea that he'd had for the business to expand in Manchester.

"I'll have to miss the funeral unfortunately: I'm attending a conference. I'll need to pop up north for a couple of days in the next few weeks."

"You didn't know, Jack. That'll be fine. We can manage. I can rearrange my time off, if you can give me some dates."

"Okay. Do you and Angela have to do anything for the funeral?"

"No, Dawn and Edna Newbold have got the flowers sorted, so we're just going to help with tea in the village hall. I think it will be quite a small gathering for his funeral, very few relations and, as Annie Watson said, 'They're all popping their clogs.'"

"She sounds quite a character."

"She is. You know she and Charlie Watt didn't get on because he cut off one of her plaits when they were at school."

"That was a bit unkind."

"That's what I said. Her friend Ethel Jones also told me that he used to pinch the seat nearest the stove in the middle of their classroom when they were all cold and wet!"

Robert chuckled, "Why? Didn't the teacher sort the young bully out?"

"It appears that as they lived at the far end of the village they always arrived last and Charlie Watt grabbed the seat first for him and his best friend, Mary."

"He married Mary."

"Yes, he did and that's why we hardly know Annie and Ethel."

A silence fell as they remembered their old friend. "So sad he's not with us anymore," whispered Maggie, gently squeezing Robert's arm, "but we've got each other," she said, reaching up to kiss him. "Love you lots."

Woody, feeling left out and recognising the signs, retreated to his favourite place by the Aga in the kitchen. There would be no more treats for him today.

CHAPTER THREE

MAGGIE'S ARK

The rain was relentless as Maggie pulled into the lay-by. She had a pattern of stopping places on her rounds: pit stops to refuel when there was no chance of getting a lunch or tea break. The weather was making driving difficult and her thermos of coffee beckoned and she always had a stock of bananas or an apple to munch. She filled in a few notes and rechecked her diary as the rain eased off. Feeling energised, she decided to set off again; there were three new families waiting for her and a new parentcraft session after lunch. But, as she lifted the car boot to return the empty flask, she had an odd feeling of being watched. A sudden movement from the other side of the hedge revealed the dark outline of an animal. It was difficult to tell what sort – horse or cow, perhaps – but two sad large brown eyes held her gaze unflinchingly. Peering more closely, she found it was a donkey.

"Hello," she said, grabbing an apple, moving towards the field gate. "Here, look what I've got. You'll like this."

The donkey slowly joined her and chomped hungrily at the apple, licking her outstretched hand.

"That's all I've got, I'm afraid," Maggie said, patting it gently. "Sorry, little one, I've got to go."

The donkey's forlorn look stayed with her as she drove away. The next day Maggie made sure she took the same route for her visits and stopped at the field gate again, armed with carrots this time. The little donkey was standing by the hedge and Maggie, with more time, was shocked to realise how thin and unkempt it was. Its hooves were badly overgrown and its coat matted. She spent several minutes feeding and talking to it, telling it about their little boy, Charlie, and ruffling behind its ears, which it clearly enjoyed. Its loud "hee-haw" sounded pitiful as she made to leave and she was aware that she was beginning a habit she might regret. The donkey would now expect a daily visit, too. She had always loved donkeys for reasons she could never explain, however bedraggled they looked.

On her day off two days later she collected Charlie from playgroup and, with a promise that he too could have a carrot, she took him to visit the donkey.

"Can I ride it, Mummy?"

"No, darling, he's not ours."

"Can I have it, Mummy?"

"No, darling, he belongs to somebody else."

"Can I have another carrot?"

"Yes."

Maggie was endeavouring to explain to Charlie why she thought the donkey lived alone when a ramshackle van drew up behind her car, and a man in blue overalls approached them.

"Afternoon, lady. Seems to like your lad," he said, gesturing to the donkey having carrots thrust at it. "Here, son, I've brought him some more," and he produced two from his pocket. "He'll like these too," he said, holding out a packet of peppermints.

"I like them too, don't I, Mummy?" Charlie was jumping up and down now. "Can I have one?"

"Sorry, lady," the man said. "Started something, have I?"

"Charlie, hush, darling, you'll frighten the donkey."

Charlie, now happily munching the peppermints, turned his attention to the man's overalls.

"My daddy's got trousers with big pockets like yours."

"Well now, has he, son? Useful things, big pockets, full of secrets," the man said, chuckling. "Give the donkey one like this," he said, pulling out a large apple and placing it on his outstretched hand.

"D'you know who owns the donkey?" Maggie asked. "I'm a midwife and I've been stopping here on my rounds lately. It seemed a bit lonely."

"Well, it's mine at the moment but it'll be moving on next week."

"Oh, that's a shame. I'll miss him."

"I'm keeping it here for a mate of mine. He collects them up for the market and rents this field 'fore moving them on."

"Market?"

"Yep, sorry lass, but nobody buys them up and we get the surplus, 'fraid they usually end up as dog food."

Maggie was shocked and thankful that Charlie was preoccupied picking fistfuls of grass and buttercups. "Oh dear, that's terrible. I thought everyone loved donkeys. Surely you could give him a home? Move him to a sanctuary or something."

"Yeah, well, you don't know the half of it." He turned to go. "Bye, laddy, you see if your mummy likes butter with them flowers. Better just give the donkey the grass."

Maggie's heart was thumping, "Wait. I mean. I might be able to find him a home."

"For a price," the man grinned. "The right price."

"What would that be?

"Well, it ain't got much meat on it. It's a her not a him, by the way. It's a female. Twenty quid?"

Maggie drove home slowly, worrying. Had she really just agreed to have the donkey? She had no idea how she was going to tell Robert; he would be furious and where on earth would they put it?"

"No more animals, darling, please," he'd said, after their distress a few years before at nearly losing Woody to hare coursers. Woody had been found, but Charlie Watt's death meant adopting his ten chickens and Robert had been none too pleased when Maggie won two goldfish at the fete. Ebb and Flo resided on the kitchen shelf, swimming in never-ending circles around their plastic castle and green plastic fronds. Then there had been the guinea pigs, Midge and Mungo, left by a friend for their holiday and somehow still with them. They were found too often in Charlie's bed, having left telltale cigar-like droppings. Their rabbit, Lemmy, named after the Lunar Exploratory Module, had originally been a present to their son from Charlie Watt and had produced a litter of eight more baby bunnies one morning, following a secret love affair with a wild rabbit that had tunnelled into the run. Maggie never revealed to anyone that she had posted them all back in the woods when they had grown big enough to hop.

Maggie's overwhelming desire to get pregnant again had faded somewhat after her last miscarriage, as she now embraced her career, but she also discovered that she could not resist falling for any creature in need. Two cats and six more chickens being recent arrivals in need of a home, not to mention young Charlie's various worms, snails, slugs, ladybirds and dead bluebottles – but a donkey? That might be out of her league.

"So where do you propose to put a donkey, Maggie? In the front or back garden or maybe the spare bedroom? We haven't got a field and neither you nor I know a bloody thing about donkeys."

"Rob, sssh, you'll wake Charlie. I'm not that daft. I've spoken to Major Gibson, you know, he owns all the land round here. He's chairman of the parish council and keeps asking one of us to stand. I asked him about the meadow opposite Tom and Angela. He's dropped all ideas of building houses there and he was delighted when I asked if we could rent it for a donkey. He kindly said he'd have the small stable in the corner repaired; it's collapsed and an eyesore anyway, and he'd like to run some sheep with the donkey over the whole area first to get the grass down a bit. He was so nice about it and…" She hesitated. "Oh, yes, I agreed the rent too."

"What?"

"I agreed a rent of £10 a month, that's all. I was a bit naughty really – beat him down implying you, or I, might well cave in and join the parish council."

"So, you have it all cut and dried, Maggie, literally. Not much point in asking me whether I mind, is there?" Robert said, pushing past her angrily. "What's more, you've happily succumbed to blackmail! I'll take the dog for a walk and – I repeat – I'm not joining the parish council."

Robert called Woody and left, slamming the front door behind him.

Maggie was surprised the noise didn't wake Charlie as, near to tears, she decided to pour herself a rather large gin and tonic. When Robert returned she was in the sitting room, wearing a contrite expression and ready for bed.

"Darling," she said. "I love you so much. I thought you'd be pleased I'd bought you a little donkey." Giggling helplessly, she stood up and put her arms round his neck and kissed him. "Don't be angry, please. It's not as big as a horse."

Totally disarmed, Robert found himself making love to the wife he had felt ready to divorce barely an hour before.

News spread quickly once Edna Newbold, the village shopkeeper, got to hear about it. Collecting the donkey a week later went without a hitch. Edna, an old friend of Charlie Watt's, reminded the Creasey family that their daughter's unused horsebox was still parked on the allotments. The whole village was alerted to its arrival; Edna had even stocked up with more carrots than usual, forewarning all her customers that a "starving" donkey was about to arrive.

Maggie found it difficult not to tell her colleagues and all her mums as she went on her rounds and was beginning to collect second-hand bridles, harnesses, buckets, brushes, grooming kits and even a small saddle. The dilapidated stable was refurbished by the Major's handyman and Maggie was delighted to receive her first order of hay and straw, excitedly burying her nose in the sweet-smelling hay.

Angela hitched up the borrowed horsebox to a borrowed Land Rover and accompanied Maggie to collect the donkey, who calmly trotted up the ramp and was then delivered without incident to its new home. Weak as it was, it managed a brief wander around the meadow and seemed captivated by the cosy stable, refusing to move again. Maggie felt tearful and could hardly bare to leave it, wanting to comfort it. She brushed its bedraggled coat gently, stroked and hugged it, telling it that it was safe as it stood contentedly nudging and pulling the fresh hay from the net, its overgrown hooves disappearing into the thick bed of straw. It seemed to enjoy her attention and made no effort to shy away when Charlie, squealing with delight, rushed in with Robert to give it a handful of carrots and peppermints.

Maggie, in touch with a sanctuary for horses and donkeys, devoured the books they sent her on donkey care and hastily arranged visits from a farrier and the local vet.

The farrier was visibly upset at the sight of the donkey's hooves. "Wicked, it is, wicked," he muttered to himself. "There's some cruel bastards out there."

Trevor, the vet, called two days later when Maggie was out visiting a mother with breastfeeding problems. Trevor and she knew each other well as she had cared for his wife and delivered their first baby at home. He was happy to check over the donkey in her absence. On her return home Maggie was shocked to find a note pinned to the stable door.

Hi, Maggie,

Given donkey some wormer. Poor little bugger is lonely – get her a fella! Two donkeys better than one. Thought she was in foal but decided not, hence wormed.

Speak soon, needs teeth filed badly. Check out equine dentist with surgery.

Trevor.

Ps I'll check her over next week. Get louse powder – she's lousy!!! Go easy on the treats.

Chapter Four

In a bit of a rush

Maggie had just escaped to the toilet in the clinic when there was a loud banging on the door. Esther, one of the receptionists, sounded anxious. The afternoon sessions had finished earlier than expected and Maggie was planning to pop home before her evening visits.

"Quick, Mary Thomas just rang to say she thinks the baby's coming!"

Maggie had visited that morning to check Mary's blood pressure and deliver the box of home birth equipment. She'd had a feeling that Mary might be going into labour sometime soon, albeit two weeks before her due date as she'd been having more than a few twinges. She would have to hurry. Mary had only just made it to the hospital in time to give birth to her first baby so had wisely opted for this little one to be delivered at home.

"Coming," she called back, glancing at herself in the mirror. She looked and felt weary and was looking forward to her day off the next day. She had dark rings under her eyes and her hair was in need of a wash, the normal shiny black curls straining to escape a tight rubber band temporarily holding her hair back in a bun. She rinsed her hands and quickly applied a smear of lipstick – a habit she stuck to in all circumstances – before running down the corridor.

Esther had her coat and bag waiting as Maggie fumbled in the pockets for her car keys.

"Doctor Southgate's out on a call. Shall I let him know as soon as I can?"

"No, I'll ring when I've assessed her," Maggie said. "Thankfully they only live on the estate."

The front door to the small semi-detached house was wide open. Several of the small group of women chatting and smoking, now gathered on the garden path, were known to Maggie.

"She shouted out the window, Maggie, she's just had it, smashing little chap he is. Hubby's on his way and our Frances is in there with her."

"Thanks, that's good to know," said Maggie, hurriedly brushing past them.

Mary was lying on the settee in the front room. A

chubby baby boy lay between her legs, his head half cocooned in his mother's polka dot briefs.

"We wanted another little boy, Maggie. I daren't pick him up, 'cos of the cord, he just shot out. I didn't have time to get my pants off properly!"

"He's gorgeous. Well done, Mary. I thought this might happen."

Maggie wished she had a camera as she tore open a pack of rubber gloves. She could not refrain from chuckling while hastily cutting the cord and removing the baby's novel head gear, all the while instructing the next-door neighbour, Frances, to fetch warm towels and a blanket.

Frances, relieved she was no longer alone, gladly followed instructions before tightly holding the baby in its warm wrappings. As she rocked back and forth, she watched in awe as Maggie delivered the afterbirth.

"We must keep him warm, he's probably a little shocked too but none the worse for arriving so quickly. I'll bath him in a moment and we'll see what he weighs. I think you might have an eight-pounder here, you know, judging by those fat little legs. Doctor's calling in after his surgery; he'll be sorry he's missed out again."

"He's hardly cried, just blinking at me with those big eyes." Mary clutched at Maggie's arm. "He's so beautiful," she said, tears of relief and joy streaming down her face. "Raymond will be so shocked. I'm sorry he missed it but I couldn't hold on." She was laughing now, mopping away the tears. "I'm glad it's all over. I've been worrying I'd drop him in the street. I was just watching something on telly when the pains took hold. You warned me this morning; you knew I'd be quick again, didn't you?"

"Yes, but not that quick. I'm sorry you were alone."

"Lucky the phone was just near enough and my mates came quickly. Frances was here almost at once."

Frances, relieved of the baby as Maggie prepared to bath him, was happily making tea and passing round the biscuits when Mary's husband, Raymond, tripped up as he ran through the front door fifteen minutes later, panting with anxiety.

"Too late, love," Mary said, reaching up to hug him. "He's your double."

Maggie returned to the clinic and gave a brief report to Dr Southgate. Amused and glad that mother and baby were safely delivered, the doctor promised to visit, regretting as always that he had not been there for the birth. He still maintained that babies were better off being born at home and disliked the current move to hospitalise all pregnant women. Maggie had great respect for him and relied on his knowledge and advice. Now, happy and stimulated by the events of the afternoon, she drove home with one aim: to soak in a bath and wash her hair before going out again.

Later that evening, feeling fully revived, Maggie arrived at the hospital in Waldersby to attend to a group of parents awaiting their refresher course in preparation for births a second and third time. Robert had taken charge at home, which, as always, made her feel guilty.

"I won't be gone long, Rob. Sorry to leave everything, I should be back by nine o'clock."

"Look, don't be silly, darling. We both agreed that you should do this job, so please stop apologising. We knew there would bound to be a few problems, but nothing we can't sort out together."

"You know Mum's coming to stay over the bank holiday?" Maggie said. "We might persuade her to stay a few days while you sort things up north?"

"Excellent; that'll be a big help."

Maggie knew four of the couples, having cared for them during their first pregnancies and subsequent births. The other two, new to the area, were already mingling happily when she arrived. It always gave her pleasure to see them getting on well, developing that special bond which would continue after the birth. For some it would be all the support they needed.

She started the session with a discussion of their previous experience of birth, which enabled her to find out what, if anything, was causing them concern. Memories of a difficult labour and the dread of it happening again filled one of the couples with fear. The presence of other men talking through their experience too unlocked a fierce debate.

"Maggie, why can't you midwives admit it's bloody painful?"

They were laughing now but Maggie understood that it was probably the first time that these fathers had really been able to talk about their feelings and discuss the apprehension they felt, knowing that they were once more expected to support their loved ones in distress or pain.

The session continued with a reminder of the breathing exercises to cope with contractions – "not pains" – and Maggie's constant reassurance that a second or third birth was inevitably going to be so much easier than the first.

"Now, I don't wish to alarm any of you," she said, during the tea break. "But I will just explain that some babies don't want to hang around anyway, and decide to come fairly quickly."

"That's great," said one of the women. "I hope it happens to me. Being in labour for three days last time was no fun."

The consensus was that a quick birth would suit them all nicely, as Maggie outlined the principles of a "precipitate labour".

"This is the baby that can't wait to meet you," she said, trying to sound light-hearted. "For some glorious reason a few lucky women manage to outdo the rest of us and give birth with comparative ease, and in some cases rapidly. So, a word of advice, ladies. If you know this is about to happen to you, *lie down* – your uterus will be contracting strongly and trying to push the baby out quickly."

Without naming names, Maggie described how one baby had performed a bungee jump on a short cord as the mother, shocked at the cascade of her waters breaking, remained upright. The short cord and a shag pile carpet kept that baby from harm. Warming to her theme, she told of the father desperately searching for a parking space instead of stopping at the hospital entrance, as his frantic partner was shouting that the baby was coming, the result being a "Carry On" display with the hospital staff having to race to the car parked yards away, where his abandoned wife lay on the back seat, clutching their newborn.

Maggie hastened to reassure them that babies born in this way were usually in great shape, a little surprised maybe, but they usually yelled robustly and quickly got on with the job of living.

Following the tea break, when more stories were swapped, Maggie spent time playing mood music to relax the group. Incredibly, all six couples fell asleep, some snoring softly as she left them briefly to make a phone call and check for messages. When she returned the couples were still sleepy but awake and relaxed, so she left them chatting together for a few more minutes. She wanted them alert for the drive home and was pleased to hear them planning to stop at a pub, cementing their friendship further.

"Don't forget those pelvic floors," she chorused as they left. "Boys too!"

It was dusk by the time Maggie stopped by the field gate. She could just make out the little donkey, standing in the stable entrance as she walked across the meadow with the last carrot of the day. The Major's sheep were cordoned off; unperturbed by her arrival, they gave her a brief glance and carried on with the job of cropping the grass.

Maggie was touched to see that the donkey seemed to recognise her, and, though eager for a carrot or apple, it also registered pleasure at the sight of her, snorting and snuffling before raising her head high in the air, baring its teeth and braying "hee-haw" loudly.

"So, what are we going to call you?" Maggie said aloud, offering a last mint. "I'd better get Charlie to choose a name tomorrow," she said, pausing. "I'm glad to see someone's mucked you out today." Maggie was smiling to herself as she noticed the freshly turned bed of shavings that Robert had prepared earlier.

"Bless him. I'm not sure but having two donkeys might just be the last straw," she mused, leaving the meadow to hurry home.

It would be best to wait till after Robert had sealed the deals up north.

CHAPTER FIVE

A SEVENTY-YEAR ITCH

Maggie's mother, Elizabeth Edwards, was anxious to see her oldest daughter and catch up with her news. Her first grandchild, Charlie, was growing up quickly and she wanted to see as much of him as possible before school took over later in the year. She was tired after the long train journey from her home in Kendal, and grateful to find her friend and Robert's ex-boss, Frank Sutton, waiting at Waldersby Station to taxi her to Nut Tree Cottage.

Frank was now the retired owner of Sutton's Scenario, having promoted Robert to managing director of the company. He had encouraged and supported Robert from the time the firm moved from London to Waldersby. It was well known that Frank and Elizabeth had developed a close friendship that started soon after Robert and Maggie had married, but just how close was up for debate. Elizabeth had last been down south at Christmas. Frank Sutton had last been up north only the week before.

"Well, he's a very nice little donkey, dear, but what do you do with him?" Elizabeth asked, standing in the stable entrance.

"It's a she, Mum."

"I got on him, Nana," said Charlie. "Mummy lets me brush his fur."

"Coat, darling."

"Does the donkey have a name?"

"He does lots of poos."

"Yes, so I see." Elizabeth stepped back just in time as the donkey spread its back legs and a rapid stream hit the ground, followed by a steaming pile of dung. "Good heavens!"

Charlie, giggling, pretended to canter round the field. "Come on, Nana, I can race you!"

Elizabeth was already moving away heading towards the field gate.

"Nana will come back and see him tomorrow, Charlie. Mummy's going to get your tea ready now."

"Mrs Queesy gives my donkey ginger biscuits and he eats the packet," Charlie said, placing a grubby hand in Elizabeth's. "Mummy says we can have two donkeys."

"I take it he means Dawn Creasey?" Elizabeth said.

Maggie gently tugged at Charlie's arm. "Yes. Charlie, sssh, it's a secret."

"Did you mean that, darling?" Elizabeth said, startled. "Why on earth d'you want another?"

"The vet suggested it. He thinks this donkey's lonely and says they're much happier in pairs, but I don't want Rob to hear about it yet."

"Can you manage to look after two?"

"Yes. Oddly, I rather like mucking out, and one of the lads in the village is coming every Saturday morning to help out."

"Well it's your decision, dear, but I can understand Robert being concerned – after all, you are working full time now."

"Mum, it's alright really, now don't nag. Come on, let's get Charlie's tea and get him to bed. Robert will be home any minute. He likes to take Woody out after being cooped up in the office all day, but he's prepared something nice in your honour for supper."

"Right, come on, little man. Nana will read you a story before bedtime, but you'll have to have a bath first," said Elizabeth, walking rapidly away.

After Elizabeth had congratulated Robert on his culinary efforts and Maggie had pointed out that the lemon tart for dessert was down to her, she managed to turn the conversation to her mother's relationship with Frank Sutton.

Robert recalled the departure of Frank's wife the year before and the breakdown of that marriage.

"It was common knowledge at work that they didn't get on, always rowing, and she was often away, either at a golf match or playing bridge. He's been so much happier since they separated, and no doubt she is too."

"We know you two have been getting on well together, Mum. You seem to have kept in touch quite a bit…"

"Yes, darling, we correspond," said Elizabeth, not meeting her eye.

"Eleanor says you and he seem to be chatting on the phone every day."

"Darling, how would your sister know what I was doing when she isn't living at home anymore? Just because Frank was talking to me when she called the other day."

"Well, come on now, spill the beans. What are you two up to?"

Maggie was intrigued. It had become a worry to both the sisters after the death of their father that their mother lived alone, and they were secretly delighted at the thought of her having an affair.

Robert poured them both another glass of wine. "You don't have to say anything, Elizabeth. Your daughter's just winding you up."

"Thank you, Robert. Well, I suppose it won't remain a secret for much longer that Frank's divorce is going through, and, yes, we have kept very much in touch but that's all I'm saying."

"You can't leave it there, Mummy."

"I can, and I will."

"Okay. I didn't mean to pry. You can tell us about Eleanor, though. How is my sister getting on?"

"Very well; she's really settled down with Martin. He's such a nice chap and I know he's as keen as she is to start a family."

"What's stopping them?"

"They want to buy their own place. They're both fed up with renting and his company are thinking of moving down this way, nearer to London."

"Eleanor didn't tell me that."

"I think they've only just heard about it."

"She thinks she can get a teaching job down here more easily and he's keen to stay with the company as it's expanding."

"He can get a job anywhere as a chartered surveyor," Robert said, wafting the wine bottle in the direction of her empty glass.

"No, no more, thank you," Elizabeth said, easing herself out of the armchair. "Yes, you're probably right. Goodness, I'm stiff. Old age creeping up. Now, it's bed for me please. It's been a long day and I'd like a shower too, Maggie. I can still smell that donkey, you know," she shuddered, leaving the room and blowing them both a kiss.

Robert filled Maggie's glass with the remains of the wine and slumped back on the settee, putting his arm around her. "How long is Mum staying? I don't think she's too taken with our donkey, is she?"

"She'll come round. I hope she'll stay on after half term and spend a few days with us."

"That's good. Can we ask her to babysit one night next week? I'd like to go to the Arts Cinema; there's Robert Powell in the *The Thirty-Nine Steps*. We could have a meal at that nice fish restaurant first. D'you realise it's a month at least since we had an evening out?"

"I'm sure she won't mind at all; she loves looking after Charlie. I just wish she lived a little nearer."

"Yep. That would be really handy, and she and Frank could see even more of each other."

"Now, careful, Rob. She'll get annoyed if we start interfering. They're good friends but that's about it, don't you think? Very, very good friends according to my sister," she chuckled.

"Stop it, Maggie; you sound tipsy. Come on: it's bedtime and Woody needs to go outside again."

"Can you let him out? I didn't shut the chickens in either."

"One night the fox will get the lot. We shouldn't leave it this late."

"I know, sorry. Don't forget to put Doris on her perch. She's getting old and lazy."

"Whatever next? Perhaps she should sleep with us?"

Maggie laughed. "She's a very precious chicken."

Robert left as Maggie reflected on the day their old friend Charlie Watt had died with Doris in his lap. It still brought tears to her eyes. She dragged herself up and had managed to clear the dining table and do the washing up by the time Robert and Woody returned.

"Just come with me," he said, leading her towards the front door. "Look."

It was a clear moonlit night and they watched shooting stars scudding and fizzing among the tiny glitter of millions. Small dark clouds temporarily blocked their view before moving quickly on. The beauty of the night sky was revealed again as the light of the moon beamed down on them. There was not a breath of wind, just the call of owls in the wood beyond the meadow, accompanied by the bark of a fox seeking its mate.

Robert wrapped his arms round her tightly. "Darling, it's at times like this that I know how lucky we are to live here."

"Our Charlie Watt's up there watching over us, I'm sure," said Maggie. "It was Charlie who taught me to be more aware of our surroundings. So different to our life in London. It's better than watching telly and—"

She was glad Woody interrupted her with a whine and a big yawn as she dabbed her cheeks. Remembering their old friend, his teachings and his appreciation of the natural world made her weepy.

"Right, come on, it's bedtime," Robert said, shooing the little dog back inside.

Next morning Maggie was woken by the delicious aroma of bacon cooking and made her way downstairs.

"It's a bank holiday, so we have to spoil ourselves," said Robert, throwing more sausages into the frying pan. "Charlie's had a whole sausage already."

"I slept very well," Elizabeth said. "So are there plans for today, as we're all at home?"

"Charlie has a birthday party to go to in the village hall. Fancy coming along, Mum?"

"That'll be fun, as long as it's not too noisy."

"Dawn Creasey and Edna Newbold will be there overseeing everything. They're both on the village hall committee now. A couple of the mothers have organised the food and party games. We could drop Charlie off and go for a walk through the woods. It's mild out and not too muddy."

"How is Edna? Still a bit of an old battleaxe?"

"She's still the village gossip; after all, she misses nothing running the village shop. But since Charlie's death she's got really involved in the village hall activities and the over-sixties club. She doesn't boss everyone quite as much as she used to and Dawn is a calming influence. They've become very good friends, in fact."

"Well, she'd better not boss me about, although it'll be nice to meet them both again."

"If you two are going for a walk later I'll pop into Waldersby to do a bit of shopping. I want to meet up with Gordon anyway; he's got some ideas for me for business."

"D'you mean Angela's first husband, Gordon?" Elizabeth asked, surprised.

"Yes. They were our first friends in the village and although the marriage failed Gordon and I still meet up. He's got a good business head on his shoulders and comes up with some really clever suggestions. He's been a good mate."

"Is he still living with the woman he had the affair with?"

"Yes, not married but they're living together quite happily."

"Does he see young James?"

"Not a lot. Tom is much more of a father figure to James now, but Gordon and his girlfriend take him out occasionally. It's all very amicable. James adores Tom as well, so it's worked out well for the little boy."

"That's good. I'm glad he hasn't suffered from their break-up. It seems so hard on the children sometimes, doesn't it, or am I just a bit old-fashioned?"

Elizabeth wanted to hear about the village and listened with interest as Maggie told her more about the people she'd got to know and about the rift that Charlie Watt had apparently caused all those years ago among some of the older generation, and how she hoped that could be mended.

"It's extraordinary, isn't it, how something like that can make enemies for a lifetime?" Elizabeth said. "I'd like to meet these old dears, Annie and Ethel, whilst I'm here."

"Right, Mum, if we have time. Now, would you like to come with me and Charlie? We'll check on the donkey and then take Woody that walk."

"You check on the donkey, dear. I'll just tidy up first."

"Nana, I'm going to call my donkey 'Stinker,'" said Charlie when they were all back in the cottage.

"Oh, did Mummy say you could?" Elizabeth tried to look serious as Maggie walked in.

"No, Charlie. We have to choose a nicer name."

Charlie's face crumpled. "You keep saying stinky poo when we do the stable."

Elizabeth grabbed a biscuit tin. "Here, Charlie, I think you deserve a chocolate biscuit for helping Mummy," she said, winking at Maggie. "Your donkey's brown like a biscuit, isn't he, so why not call him Biscuit?"

Charlie, grabbing two biscuits, pondered the suggestion, as Elizabeth and Maggie hid their crossed fingers.

"Biscuit," Charlie jumped up and down. "Our donkey's called Biscuit, Mummy."

"Well done, Nana. Let's have a cup of tea," Maggie said, looking relieved. "That was inspired, Mum, I like that," she said quietly. "So clever of you!"

"Stinker is probably more apt."

"Not after tomorrow. I've got some proper horse shampoo. Biscuit will be transformed."

"I believe you; thousands wouldn't. Come on, Charlie, let's go in the sitting room. I want to hear all about your party, and you can show me what you got in that party bag."

Better not to mention that the horse dealer had left a message and Biscuit could soon have a companion after all, Maggie thought, as she poured the tea.

CHAPTER SIX

THE UNEXPECTED VISITOR

"Hi, Maggie. You're on call tonight, aren't you?" Her colleague Susan was on the phone. "I'd better tell you how to find Jane Curtis. She's not due for a couple of weeks, but you never know. The cottage is quite easy to find. Got a pen?"

"Right." Maggie was used to Susan's detailed directions and grabbed a notepad. "Ready."

"Take the first turn into the village of Skimpton, follow the road down the hill, pass a duck pond at the bottom – mind the ducks; they are always waddling about in the middle of the road – pass four council houses (two pairs of semis), carry on for roughly half a mile, the road bears left and comes to a crossroads. Take the left turn, pass about four cottages –vicious-looking dog in first, looks as if it will jump the gate – look out for a rough track on the right about a mile further on. You can't miss it. There's a plum tree on the corner. Hundred yards down there is a row of white thatched cottages (the thatch is in a bad state, mind you). Go through the side gate and round to the back – none of them use a front door. Knock very loudly. Jane never seems to hear the bell when I visit. You'll need to get there quickly as it's her third and she doesn't hang around. Hope you got all that. You'll be well fed. She makes the best cakes. I shall be really sorry if I miss out on her but it's Mum's sixtieth birthday and we're having a big family get-together. Anyway, must dash, really hope she doesn't have it while I'm gone. Thanks, Maggie. Bye."

Maggie put the notes in her delivery bag with a smile. She wasn't sure Susan had even paused for breath before hanging up.

"Are you on call again, darling?" Robert asked, as she prepared dinner.

"'Fraid so, but I don't think I'll get called out. That was Susan on the phone; she's off to a family 'knees-up'. One of her mums is booked for a home delivery, but she's not due for two weeks. Susan really wants to be with her as she delivered her last two, so she's asked her to keep her legs crossed."

Robert laughed. "You always tell me that there's no stopping a baby if it wants to come."

It was midnight when the phone rang and she heard the voice of Jane Curtis.

"Can you come, Maggie? They're quite strong and every five minutes."

Drugged with sleep, Maggie dressed, gulped down a glass of milk and hurriedly put her delivery bag and gas cylinders in the car boot.

Halfway to the village she stopped in a lay-by to go through Susan's instructions for Rose Cottage again. She was cross with herself for not having checked the route earlier as she normally did.

She passed the pond, but there were no waddling ducks, no street lights, just the moon and the stars. She was beginning to feel concerned until she saw with relief that she was approaching the crossroads. All the houses were in darkness. She drove up and down the road several times trying to locate the track. It had been over half an hour since Jane had rung and she kept remembering Susan's warnings about Jane being quick.

She stopped at the telephone box near the crossroads to ring Jane, but there was no reply. Seeing a dim light on at the back of one of the cottages, Maggie ran towards it; remembering at the last minute about the vicious dog Susan had warned her of, she slowed down warily. Peeping through the window of the conservatory, Maggie saw a young couple enthusiastically engaged in making love. Without hesitation, she tapped on the window. The young girl screamed as her young man scrambled up, clutching the nearest item of clothing to cover himself. In the background the "vicious dog" started barking, scrabbling ferociously at the adjoining door.

Apologising profusely, Maggie hastily explained the reason for interrupting them and the urgency of finding Jane. She was relieved when their shock turned to laughter and she left them giggling with a cheery "See you in nine months!" as she hurried away.

Afterwards Maggie reflected that it was probably her uniform that had prevented them and maybe their dog from tearing her to pieces.

Arriving at the Curtis family cottage, anxious and apologetic, Maggie was greeted by Jane.

"I'm really sorry to have called you out, Maggie. It must have been a false alarm; I haven't had any contractions since I rang you, not even a show, no waters leaking, nothing, so I went back to sleep."

Maggie's disappointment was mixed with profound relief: the panicky night-time search had left her wobbly and shaking. She knew her colleague Susan would be delighted as she would probably now get to deliver Jane's baby after all. Before leaving she checked Jane over, listened in to the baby and enjoyed a cup of tea and a large slice of delicious cake. Tired and weary, she made her way back home, to wrap her cold feet round Robert and fall asleep immediately.

Maggie met with Susan to discuss this episode at the clinic the next day and Susan vowed to provide a simple route map in future. The two midwives worked well together and felt a personal obligation to "their" mums, and remorse if they missed out on delivering one of them. Susan did not have long to wait for Jane to deliver as she went into labour the following week. Susan just made it to the house in time as the baby arrived two minutes after she stepped over the threshold. The supply of delicious homemade cakes at the clinic increased until Susan reluctantly handed over Jane's care to the health visitor.

At Nut Tree Cottage, Maggie and Elizabeth were still enjoying each other's company and Maggie had asked her mother to consider staying another week. Elizabeth loved hearing about Maggie's mums and the babies she delivered and cared for. The idea of returning to Kendal and her large, empty house held no appeal. Maggie knew her mother's joy of caring and getting to know her grandchild made her feel useful and loved. Maggie was also certain that the relationship her mother had with Frank Sutton was not a passing phase. They had met each other in Waldersby several times, and talked on the phone every day.

"Do you think you'll stay in Kendal, Mum? I know you didn't feel you could leave Daddy, or rather his grave."

The two women were in the kitchen preparing supper.

"I know you think I'm silly, darling."

"We can always visit his grave. I could take you there. It's just that you seem much happier here with us."

"I'm going to watch *Blue Peter* with Charlie; perhaps we can talk about it another time."

"Okay. He's having his tea in there at the little table," Maggie said, refilling the kettle.

"There, scoffed the lot," said Elizabeth, reappearing moments later with Charlie's empty plate. "He certainly loves fish fingers. He's watching John Noakes with his lovely dog, Shep."

"He's everyone's favourite," said Maggie, putting a bowl of fruit salad in the fridge. "That's ready for later. I've sugared it," she said, pushing a fresh mug of tea across the table.

She was determined to continue the earlier conversation.

"If you sold up you could buy a small place near here. You'd be nearer both of us if you moved down south. Eleanor would like it too."

Elizabeth sighed. "Okay, darling. I've a lot to consider but it would be lovely to be nearer to you both. I miss your father, you know."

"So do I. Eleanor and I worry about you. We realise you must get lonely; after all, you and Daddy shared so many interests."

Elizabeth looked uncomfortable. "Let me tell you what Frank and I have been discussing: he also wants me to move down here and be near him."

"Really? Good heavens!" For once Maggie didn't know how to respond.

"We're very fond of each other, you know. I know he's a bit 'flamboyant' for you, but he's good fun and makes me feel young again, so I've told him I'll consider it."

"You dark horse, Mummy," Maggie said, seeing her mother's discomfort and noticing her blush. "I didn't realise it had got that serious. Does Eleanor know?"

"Not yet. I was going to discuss it with you both next week after I'd got back home and could put my mind to it better. You know, talk to my friends up there, and, yes, even Daddy."

At that moment Woody started barking as he and Charlie ran from the sitting room to greet Robert as he opened the front door.

"Daddy, Shep did a wee on the telly!"

Robert laughed and lifted his son up into his arms for a hug, before reaching out to give Maggie a kiss.

"Daddy, come on, come and watch *Blue Peter*," said Charlie, wriggling from Robert's arms and pulling him towards the sitting room.

Elizabeth poured an extra mug of tea and lowered her voice, "Take this for Robert and let's leave this conversation for now, darling. We'll discuss things another time."

Chapter Seven

A Lonely Biscuit

Maggie had just finished clearing the donkey droppings from the field, and mucking out the stable, when Trevor, the vet, drove down the lane, tooting for her attention.

"Hi, Maggie, thought I'd visit the old girl as I was passing. How's she been?" he called.

"I hope she's put on a bit of weight. What d'you think?"

Trevor parked his car in the lea of the hawthorn hedge and pushed open the gate.

"She certainly has. Don't overdo the treats; donkeys get overweight very quickly."

"She has quite a few visitors," Maggie chuckled. "I'll put a politely worded notice up to discourage too many treats. Carrots, apples, but no more ginger biscuits?"

"Good idea. You know she would love to munch on some small branches of that willow tree hanging over the hedge there. Donkeys are browsers rather than grazers – not too much: it's got salicin in it, which converts to aspirin."

"Won't that harm her?"

"No. The bark's been used for centuries for pain relief. She'll enjoy the taste and you said she's a bit stiff when you let her out. Now, have you thought any more about getting her a companion?"

"I have, especially now the sheep have gone to a new field. I've spoken to that dealer and he's going to let me know if one comes by him," she said, gently rubbing the donkey's ears. "Mind you, I have to get round Robert."

"Well, you didn't the first time," Trevor chuckled. "Best just to get one and tell him it's on my advice."

"I've already said that, but he's not convinced."

"I promise you, it'll make the world of difference to this old lady."

"How old d'you think she is?"

"Looking at her teeth I'd say she's in her twenties at least. They're looking much better for being filed down."

"Yes, the horse dentist you recommended came yesterday. He thought about twentyish. Not sure I liked him much – very brusque, in such a hurry. Anyway, he said they weren't too bad. How long do donkeys live, d'you know?"

"These guys are few and far between but, as long as he did the job, you're not likely to need him again for a while. I visited a really old donkey the other day in its late forties."

"Good heavens, she could outlive me! By the way she has a name now, Biscuit."

"Ha. That's different. I like that."

"Charlie's choice, helped by my mother."

"Well as long as the next one isn't named fruit cake."

"No, it's going to be Cookie or Crumble, I think."

"Great. Keep looking and let me know when you find one. Perhaps I could look it over before you actually buy it?" he said, patting Biscuit. "Bye, old girl. I'll pop by anyway in a couple of weeks, Maggie."

The following day Maggie made a point of visiting the village, and parking by the field in which the dealer had kept the donkey. She was surprised to see several horses, including a carthorse and two Shetland ponies, but no sign of a donkey. It upset her to think that any of them could be destined for slaughter. She wished she could persuade Robert to visit the field with her and felt sure he'd be moved by their plight then. He might even be persuaded to take a Shetland pony.

"Pull yourself together," she muttered to herself, before driving off to continue her morning round. "We do *not* need a pony."

Elizabeth was packed and waiting to be taken to the station by Frank Sutton when Maggie called home at lunchtime.

She was sorry to see her mother go back up north. They'd enjoyed their time together and Charlie would certainly miss her.

"Sure you've got everything you came with, Mum? Checked the bathroom? You usually manage to leave your toothbrush, or something."

"Yes, darling, but it makes more sense for me to keep a few toiletries here, if that's okay. Saves me having to pack them each time I visit. I promise to come to some decision in the next month as to whether I should move or stay put."

"No hurry, Mum. You must think it all over very, *very* carefully."

"I'm taking a trip to Kendal to see your mother next month, Maggie. I'll help her decide," Frank said, picking up the suitcase and carrying it to the car.

Maggie knew that it was Frank who would be the real influence on her mother's final decision. Elizabeth became quite coquettish in his presence, which amused and comforted her. She did not want her mother living a lonely existence so far away. Frank may not have been her choice for her mother but he made her happy, and, what's more, had the means to keep her in comfort. He'd twice mentioned that he'd like to take her on a cruise next year.

Maggie kissed them and waved them off, before quickly making herself a sandwich and taking a short walk to the village green. A couple were feeding the ducks by the village pond; otherwise, it was deserted as she approached the shop. The door was propped open, and Edna Newbold was sitting outside in the sunshine, reading the *Waldersby Gazette*.

"Hi, Edna," Maggie said, as Woody, wriggling with excitement, tried to jump on Edna's lap. Theirs was a friendship that had always mystified Maggie and Robert. Edna, with her sharp tongue softened of late, had been more distressed than anyone when the hare coursers had stolen Woody and had since formed a close bond with the dog.

"Your mother's gone, then?"

"Yes, Frank Sutton gave her a lift to the station as I have a clinic this afternoon."

Edna gave Woody a hug and stood up. "He still fancies her, then?"

"They get on well, keeps Mum out of mischief."

"Well, he's not short of a penny or two, that's for sure," Edna sniffed. "I've got your order boxed up. Couldn't get that strong cheese you liked so put in a mild one; nice ham this week."

"Thank you," Maggie said, inwardly bristling at the insinuation that her mother might be interested in Frank Sutton's money. "I'll ask Robert to pick it up later, if that's okay. You're open till six tonight, aren't you?"

"Yes, only 'cos the fish man comes after five from Grimsby with my month's order."

"Could you add his fish pie mix to mine? I'll make one tomorrow."

"Can do. By the way, I was going to tell you about the girl that's moving into that empty council house by the gravel pit."

"Jacky Richards's old house?"

"Yes, where all those good-for-nothings lived. Can't think what made you get friendly with that rotten lot."

"Oh, Edna. Jacky was a lovely person. She's very happy living in Spain now and her son's doing well in the clubs. Her husband, Len, seems to have disappeared, though; no idea where he went after leaving prison."

Edna pursed her lips. "That's as maybe. Anyway, there's a young girl moving in there next week. She's another one for you, pregnant, quite far on."

"Really? Well, that is news. Nice news, too, to have another baby in the village."

"Shocking I think. No father."

"It happens. We mustn't judge her, Edna. There'll be a reason, I'm sure, it's not always the woman's fault."

Edna made no reply as she bent down to give Woody a treat.

"You can leave him here. I'll drop him back at yours later. Shame to shut him in."

Maggie hurried back to the cottage. Why was it that Edna, whom she'd grown fond of, despite her acid tongue, still managed to unsettle her? After all, she had changed a great deal since Charlie Watt's death. She had become more involved in church and village activities, and seemed to be making a real success of the village shop. She just couldn't contain that hard streak that made her appear so embittered, making hurtful comments without thinking. Charlie had kept her in check and his influence was sorely missed.

She shook off her irritation and thought again about Jacky Richards, the woman she had befriended after Jacky's youngest son was killed colliding with Kate

Creasey's horse. Len Richards, an unpleasant bully, had been jailed for beating Edna up in her shop and violently turning on Jacky, which caused her to escape to Spain with their oldest son. Maggie often thought it would be nice to get in touch with her again. Her spirits rose as she saw Biscuit grazing contentedly in the meadow as she hurried past. She left Robert a note in the kitchen reminding him to collect the groceries, before grabbing her diary and bag and driving quickly back down the lane.

The clinic finished earlier than usual, which enabled Maggie to spend more time on her second round of visits. Mary Thomas had already been discharged but had left a message that she wanted Maggie to call if she had time. The baby was thriving and feeding well and Mary had had no postnatal problems, so Maggie was curious to know why she wanted to see her. She found tea and a large slice of Mary's best fruit cake also waiting.

"I'm so glad you've come, Maggie."

"Is everything alright, Mary? I know the health visitor was very happy with you."

"Yes, we're all fine. Baby's a contented little chap and he's doubled his birth weight. Our little lad wants to hold his baby brother all the time; he's being spoilt rotten. I wanted to give you something, that's all."

Maggie was immediately on her guard, knowing Mary was not that well off.

"I got this for you," Mary said, reaching behind her. "Hope you like it."

Maggie unwrapped the tissue paper carefully and let out a delighted "Oh, how sweet, a donkey!" as she turned the silver charm over in the palm of her hand. "Where did you find it?"

"Couldn't resist it. My husband saw it in that antique shop in Waldersby, by the marketplace."

"You really shouldn't give me anything, you know, but I'll treasure it."

"It's not much. We're so grateful you helped me out. It's just a little something, knowing how you love that little donkey you keep telling us about, and you mentioned you were going to get your husband to give you a charm bracelet like your mother's, didn't you?"

"You remembered? Yes, I'd love one. Now I've got my first charm he can't refuse, can he?"

"There's a book and a toy donkey in the other packet for your little lad."

"Oh my! That's very naughty but thank you so much. I'll keep it wrapped, shall I? Charlie loves opening presents."

"Good idea. Luckily the toy's a biscuit colour too."

"Thank you, Mary; you've been so thoughtful."

Maggie was getting ready to leave when the baby started to stir.

"Now, I need a cuddle. Has he got a name yet? You were both undecided."

"We've called him Jimmy, after Grandad."

"I love that," Maggie said, cradling the baby in her arms. "I bet Grandad's proud of you, little one."

"You can have as many as you like as charms," Robert chortled when he examined the little silver donkey after supper that evening.

"That's not funny."

"I'm only teasing, darling. I'm certainly getting enough hints for your next birthday present."

"You've seen Mum's one. It positively jangles. I love them."

Luckily Robert was fast asleep on the sofa when the phone rang later that evening.

"Is that the midwife?"

"Yes, how can I help?"

"I've got another donkey for you."

"Oh, really?" Maggie lowered her voice to a whisper, recognising the man's voice. "Where?"

"It'll be in the field if you come by in a couple of days. I'll need to know if you want it by next Wednesday, otherwise it'll go off with the rest."

Maggie could feel her heart pounding. "Okay, thank you. I'll go and see it. Is it old or young? Boy or girl?"

"No idea, love. It's a donkey. I can't tell you if it's been gelded or not. Just let me know soon as—"

The phone went dead.

CHAPTER EIGHT

NEW ARRIVALS

Maggie could hear a child crying as she approached the house at the end of the track past the old gravel pit that had once housed the infamous Richards family. It was a small terrace of older council houses and Maggie's new elderly friends, Ethel Jones and her husband, lived in the middle of the row. She had parked at the top of the lane to walk down the track, reflecting on the day Woody had been found in the pit after escaping the hare coursers, shuddering again at the memory. She was enjoying the warm sunshine following a heavy downpour overnight; wildflowers peeped through the long grasses and the gentle hum of bees gathering pollen reminded her that Ethel's husband kept several hives near the top end of the gravel pit.

She waved to Ethel, who was peering out of her front window. Maggie and her mother had had tea with Annie Watson and Ethel during Elizabeth's stay and they too had mentioned the possible arrival of a new neighbour. Maggie had received a message asking her to call at the house and visit the young girl, who had been temporarily housed by the council and was pregnant. She had no other information, but was anxious to meet her, keen to know more than Edna's gossip about the poor girl.

Knocking twice, she heard an inner door slam and the cries of a child coming close to the front door.

"Hello, can I come in?" said Maggie, smiling at the toddler, who peered timidly around the narrow gap in the opened door.

The toddler, tear-streaked and snotty-nosed, stopped crying as the young girl pulled back the door, muttering, "Yeah, alright."

"I'm sorry I didn't warn you I was calling, Alice. I live in the village. We were notified that you'd moved in and I was asked to visit you."

Alice, thin and wary, had the toddler perched on her prominent bump. "That's okay. The council bloke said someone would come."

"Here, may I?" Maggie put her bag down, removed her cardigan and stretched out her arms. "I'm going to be your midwife. He's a strong little chap." She rocked gently as the little boy, now quietly snivelling, studied her face. "What's his name?"

Alice was looking more relaxed. "It's Bobby," she said. "He's not mine."

"I understood you're expecting your first baby. Who does Bobby belong to?"

"My sister. I look after him when she's working."

Maggie sat down on the same old couch that she and Jacky Richards had once shared and told Alice about her previous connection with the house.

"Yeah, the council left some bits and pieces as I haven't got much. It's only temporary."

"So baby's due soon I guess?"

"Yeah, end of September, I've been told," Alice said, producing a packet of cigarettes out of her pocket and lighting up. Maggie had been aware that the she smoked as soon as she'd entered the house and was waiting for the right moment to advise her.

Bobby, now relaxed and sleepy, sucked his thumb as Maggie sought as much information as she could before laying him down beside her to fill in her notes. Alice made her a mug of tea and explained how her boyfriend had "done a runner" when she'd told him she was pregnant and had not been in touch since. She was a hairdresser and still had a few clients in Waldersby. She'd been living with her parents but her father ordered her out when she became pregnant, saying they needed her room. Her sister worked in a beauty salon in Waldersby and was married to a soldier from the nearby barracks.

Maggie examined her and checked her blood pressure before discussing when and how the baby might be born, emphasising the care she needed to take, especially with her diet. The girl looked undernourished and despite being a hairdresser her hair was lank and greasy. Maggie mentioned the possibility of a home birth and was concerned that Alice seemed totally unprepared for motherhood. Alice was adamant she wanted to go into hospital, citing her sister's caesarean birth for Bobby as reason, plus her fear of birth itself.

It was a sensible decision as it was difficult to know if she would be getting any help afterwards. It appeared that her father worked nights on the railway, her mother worked in a local dress shop and there were still two of her younger brothers at home. Alice was going to need a lot of extra care. After finishing the interview Maggie helped carry Bobby to the sitting room and tucked him up on an old armchair.

"Now, I'll be calling again, probably about the same time but I can't be definite as we have two home births due and they always scuttle our plans."

"That's okay. I won't be going far. Thanks for coming though, Maggie – can I call you that?"

"Of course. It's been lovely meeting you, and thanks for the tea. Just one thing, Alice. D'you think you could try and give up the cigarettes? They're not good for your baby."

"Yeah, I've tried. I only have them when Bobby's asleep."

"Try and cut them out altogether if you can. Good girl. See you next week, then."

Maggie was pleased that their meeting had gone so well and determined that she would keep a close eye on

Alice. It also struck her that Ethel Jones might take an interest. Ethel was a kindly soul and would probably love having the new baby nearby. Maggie would broach the idea when she met Annie and Ethel the following week. A surrogate granny or two could be the best way of helping this young mother.

Ethel was still at the window as Maggie left, hiding a smile as she hurried back to her parked car. Ethel would tell Annie and Annie would tell the village and finally Edna would add on extra titbits, until the whole village would know exactly what was going on. Nothing would be missed but Maggie rather enjoyed the fact, feeling safer for it. Some called it nosiness, but Maggie valued the way they cared for each other.

Her afternoon visits over Maggie had a brief chat with Dawn Creasey, who'd once more agreed to collect Charlie, knowing she'd arranged to go and see the second donkey with Angela. Excitedly, she stopped at her friend's cottage in the lane.

"Hi, Angela. I'm ready; can't wait."

"This place is such a mess. I can't wait to get this sorted," Angela said. "We'll take my car if you like. Tom's taken the children to Waldersby in his."

"Okay, thanks, saves me rearranging all my stuff."

Within the hour they'd parked in the lay-by next to the field. This time several horses of all shapes and sizes were grazing together.

"I can't see a donkey anywhere, can you?" said Maggie, scanning the field.

"He's having you on. I told you not to trust him."

"No, he was quite definite. Is that a piebald pony over there?"

"A bit funny-looking. Its ears are a bit long for a pony. It might be a donkey."

"Really? Piebald?"

"Don't they come piebald, then?"

"I've no idea."

The herd of mixed ponies and horses looked across curiously at the two women pointing and laughing.

"They're coming over. I really like that carthorse, Maggie. Why don't you have that one?" Angela was getting giggly. "Let's take them all home."

"It is, it is. It's a donkey."

A small piebald donkey was now heading straight towards them, its long ears proof of its identity. Maggie's heart was thudding and she started to cry.

"What on earth are you crying for?"

"You don't seem to realise: they're all destined for dog food!"

The donkey tucked into the carrots they offered, as the other animals jostled each other for attention.

"We'd better go. We're upsetting them all."

Angela was already moving away, looking nervously at the gathering herd. "Come on, let's go. I've run out of carrots now."

They sat in the car, watching the animals drift away, all except the donkey.

"I must admit, he's a bit odd looking, but I'm sure Biscuit won't mind."

"Sounds as if you've decided, then? To have it, I mean?"

"Of course. That's got to be Crumble."

"Maggie, you're incorrigible. Have you told Robert about the little duckling yet?"

"Oh, no. I'll tell him tomorrow. That wasn't my fault – it dropped out of the sky."

"He sounded very pleased with the results of his trip so strike while he's happy?"

"I always choose my moments."

Chapter Nine

The dear departed

"What is that, for heaven's sake?"

"A duckling."

"I can see that. What is it doing in the washing-up bowl?"

"Hydrotherapy."

"Who does it belong to?"

"Doctor Southgate."

"So why is it in our sink?"

"He asked me to look after it."

"Maggie, what on earth are you going to do with it? Are there any more?"

"No, it fell out of the sky!"

"I thought you said it was the doctor's."

"Well, it was. He was out on a visit and suddenly this little chap landed on his car bonnet. He thinks it might have been dropped by a crow. Possible."

Robert sat down heavily, audibly groaning. "Any chance of a cup of tea?"

"There's some in the pot, darling. I'll just put Danny back in his box."

"Danny? It's named already? Has Woody met it? He might like it for his tea?"

"That's not funny. Woody likes it; he's nosed it round the floor and gently licked its bottom," Maggie said, amused by Robert's look of disgust.

"Ugh, pity."

"Charlie's been cuddling it and wants it in his bed."

Robert poured the tea and wandered off into the sitting room, as Maggie patted the duckling dry and put it back in the cardboard box by the Aga. Picking up her mug, she followed him.

"So, how's things? Any more problems in Manchester?"

"No, it's all going well. Couple of decent reps there."

"Oh, good. That's encouraging."

"Where's Charlie now?"

"He's at Dawn's. He went to play with a little friend from playgroup. She'll bring him back in a minute for his tea. I thought I'd do us a curry later?"

"Nice change. D'you mind if I pop up to the Dog and Duck? The darts team want to plot the strategy for our next match."

"That's fine, darling. You go and I'll settle Charlie, then we can have supper about eight?"

"Right, see you later." Robert stopped by the door. "I could put it on the village pond; there're other ducks for it to play with."

"Certainly not. How cruel."

Robert enjoyed playing with the local darts team and after a couple of beers was soon regaling them with more tales of his wife's uncontrollable desire to look after all God's creatures.

"I mean, how many of you have come home to find a duck swimming in the washing-up bowl?"

"She's a midwife, isn't she? Motherly, I suppose," said Ben, one of the players. "You've just the one little lad, haven't you?"

"Well, yes. We've had problems."

"Sorry, mate. Didn't mean to cross a line."

A round later Robert patted Ben on the shoulder as he was leaving. "See you all next week. Not to worry, Ben. I know what you meant."

He walked back across the green deep in thought, before sitting on the bench by the duck pond, idly watching the mallards chasing midges in the gathering dusk. His friend had a point: perhaps they should keep trying for another child to satisfy Maggie's mothering instincts. Their distress after the last miscarriage had stopped them thinking of any more children in the near future; losing babies was heartbreaking for them both. Maggie was enjoying her job and he didn't think she was ready yet to consider trying again. Perhaps he should show a bit more understanding and allow her to fulfil her apparent dream of having an animal rescue centre. He got up, picturing the mini Woburn developing in Little Fordham. Bypassing the cement mixer and other heavy machinery parked at the top of the lane in readiness for work on Watt's Cottage, he made a mental note to get some hardcore for the developing potholes in the lane, before stopping by the field gate. Biscuit saw him and ambled over, eyes alert, for a treat.

"Sorry, old girl, no carrots, I'm afraid," he said, rubbing behind the donkey's ears.

Biscuit hee-hawed loudly as he moved away and Robert remembered that the vet had suggested to Maggie that the donkey might be lonely. Looking into the donkey's sad, mournful eyes, he had to agree.

Back in the cottage, Charlie, now tired and sleepy, nodded off with kisses and cuddles from both parents. The job of settling all the other members of the growing menagerie was shared, before Robert and Maggie sat down to enjoy their meal.

"The cats spend all their time mousing up at the stable now," Maggie said.

"Good. I'd much rather that. I hate the way they prey on birds, always hanging round the bird table. By the way, is Charlie cleaning out Lemmy and the guinea pigs?"

Maggie laughed. "After a fashion: they're almost buried under hay. He'd love to keep them in his bed given the chance."

"I see Edna's selling our eggs at the shop. There's an advert in the window."

"Yes, she offered. I meant to tell Charlie that little Doris laid an egg yesterday. Poor thing: she's really looking her age. Did you notice Edna's other sign about old carrots suitable for donkeys only?"

"Yes, that's good of her. She's a funny one, kind as anything with our animals. Perhaps that's it: she prefers them to people," Robert said, coming to his own conclusion as Maggie busied herself washing up. He put a hand on her shoulder to distract her. "Now, darling, leave the dishes. Come with me; I need to say something."

"Sounds ominous."

Settled on the settee, Robert put his arm round her and hugged her close, restraining Woody, who wanted to join in. "I'm sorry I've been a bit awkward about things. I think the vet was right. That donkey – Biscuit – is a bit lonely, I think. Perhaps it would be kinder to get a companion for him."

"Oh, really, Rob, oh—" Maggie seemed lost for words. Laughing, she hugged and kissed him. There was no getting out of the situation now.

"I thought you'd be pleased," he said, as Maggie smothered him in kisses.

"Thank you, darling. Now, how can I put this? I know you'll love Crumble when you see him," she whispered in his ear.

"Who on earth is Crumble?" Robert said, looking stern, holding her at arm's length.

"Can't you guess?"

"I get it. I thought you were up to something, you little minx. Okay, confess, now tell me you've already got another donkey?"

"'Fraid so, darling. I'll explain." Maggie said, making a poor attempt to look contrite.

They were both laughing as she described the piebald donkey, becoming more thoughtful as she went on to tell him of the plight of the others and the horse dealer that was only interested in money. Saddened by the story, Robert promised to accompany her to the dealer's field the next day to see for himself.

"So, you see, he's unusual, being piebald, and I've only offered twenty pounds again. You'll love him; I know you will. D'you think Crumble's a good name? I'm sure Charlie will."

Holding her in his arms, Robert felt overwhelmed with love for his impetuous wife, equally determined that one other donkey was all that they would be collecting, despite her moving description of the bedraggled mixture of equines and their uncertain fate.

Having overcome that hurdle without all the difficulty she had imagined, and finding Robert surprisingly sympathetic, Maggie took no time in making the final arrangements for Crumble's transfer. Trevor the vet had agreed to look him over and Angela arranged to borrow the horsebox and organise the transport.

Nobody had foreseen the antics that would take place when Crumble and Biscuit were introduced to each other. It was worthy of a circus act. Clods of mud and grass flew in the air as the pair raced each other round the field, braying loudly, noses held aloft. Sliding to a halt in one corner, they reversed and tore round the field in the opposite direction.

Maggie could only hold her breath as the once-frail Biscuit skidded and almost collided with the field gate.

"Well, he may have been gelded but that's not holding him back," said Angela, now helpless with laughter. "I could swear that Biscuit was grinning then."

Finally, the donkeys calmed down and sank their noses into a patch of grass, moving forward in unison as though they'd been friends for years.

Chapter Ten

Memory Lane

Maggie had been intrigued by the older people she'd met at Jack Newgate's funeral. They were a hard-working, stoical group of men and women who'd spent their whole working lives working in and around Little Fordham. Many had been employed at the big house now owned by the Major; others had worked the estate lands or cared for the horses and other livestock. Charlie Watt had told her many stories of those earlier days. He had walked geese to market in Waldersby along the drovers' routes, some of which were now overgrown and thick with brambles, others surviving as bridle paths. Foreign holidays were unknown to them and for many a trip to Waldersby was the highlight of their week. They worked long hours and had little time for recreation. Many of the men, like Charlie Watt, had survived the war as members of the Home Guard and the women the Land Army, while those who had perished were listed on the memorial in the churchyard. Maggie was touched to see them all dressed in their Sunday best for Jack's funeral. Sombre dress, rigid white collars and black ties, hats and gloves, shoes that shone from spit and polish, the men's hair tamed with Brylcreem, faces close-shaven and pink cheeks. The women, some veiled, all in mourning black from head to toe.

It was at the tea in the village hall after Jack's funeral, with the customary egg or salmon and cucumber sandwiches, Swiss roll, jam tarts and Battenberg cake, that Maggie had arranged to call again on her new friends, Annie and Ethel. Annie's cottage, retained by the Major's estate, overlooked the village green, a few yards from the Dog and Duck, four doors from the Creaseys.

Annie, despite widowhood, had been allowed to retain her cottage for her lifetime. Annie and Ethel had known each other since working together as housemaids. With the new over-sixties club now being eagerly promoted by Edna Newbold and Dawn Creasey, this age group were rekindling those earlier friendships. The monthly bingo was proving especially popular with the ladies, although the men still preferred their darts and dominos in the pub.

When Maggie arrived, she found the two older women were very keen to get to know "the nurse" better. It was several days since Jack's funeral and their meeting with Elizabeth, and they had been busy preparing for her arrival. Annie had produced her best china cups for the visit and Ethel had brought a freshly baked ginger cake. As they chatted to Maggie over tea, an elderly and very small Yorkshire terrier called Sammy stayed curled up on Ethel's lap, apparently to avoid Annie's equally elderly cat.

"Never could stand the sight of each other," informed, Annie, ruffling the cat's fur. "Too old to hide from 'im now, Socks, aren't you?"

The very name, Socks, produced a tiny snarl from Ethel's lap.

Maggie enjoyed the sense of being cosseted by the two women. They were well into their eighties, mentally alert but physically showing the wear and tear of years of hard work, small grimaces evidence of arthritis in Annie, and both complained of poor eyesight and hearing loss.

"Cataracts, dear, just cataracts," Annie had said in a matter of fact way as the vicar had caught her mid-tumble in the churchyard, after Jack's funeral.

Annie was as thin as a stick and all no-nonsense, whereas Ethel was as round as a bun in contrast and had a much softer character. Their deafness enhanced the conversation with comical answers to misunderstood questions.

Despite the long-held rancour that Maggie learnt had prevailed between them and the now-deceased Charlie Watt, the pair had had a similar upbringing. They reminisced, eager to tell her more of their school days, chuckling now at the tale of being last to reach the classroom in the mornings, cold and wet when they finally arrived to find the other children basking in the warmth from the boiler, not allowing them near. It transpired that Ethel had rather fancied Charlie Watt when they were at school and had been very jealous of his sweetheart, Mary. Now they had both passed away the two old ladies could talk more freely. Ethel blushed, confessing her youthful desire. The death of their friend, Jack, had been a shock, but they weren't grieving but rather envied his rapid exit, having witnessed, and dreaded, many friends' long-drawn-out illnesses, reflecting on the good hard-working life that he'd enjoyed.

"Best way to go," Annie declared. "Sooner go that way than get bloody daft. The district nurse found my hubby dead in the bed ten years ago. Surprised he did that 'cos he hadn't had his breakfast."

Maggie endeavoured to look sympathetic, stifling another fit of giggles. Ethel stated that she envied her George's bees. He paid them far more attention than he did her – but he was, after all, ninety-two now. Not the frisky young thing she'd married.

Maggie finished her tea and two slices of cake before broaching the subject of Alice, Ethel's new neighbour. Ethel said she would be happy to get to know the young girl. Maggie was amused – young Alice, first shunned by them because of her unmarried status, was now to become their new project. Ethel had already spoken to her, but had not been aware that the little boy, Bobby, was not Alice's own son. Having been assured that Ethel would indeed befriend Alice, Maggie could now convey the good news to Doctor Southgate.

Before Maggie left, Annie showed her the garden and pressed her to take home some fresh vegetables picked from her allotment behind the Dog and Duck. The allotments were well used by the older generation and plots seldom became free. Ethel gave her two pots of honey.

Delighted with her old friends, and the support she hoped Alice would get from Ethel, Maggie thanked them and was ready to leave when she realised that Ethel would have quite a walk back home. She offered her a lift.

"Me and my Sammy may look decrepit dear, but he likes his walks and so do I. George will be waiting at the end of the lane too; he can still manage that. He's an old soldier; they made 'em tough. Besides, I need to call at the shop and see Edna now she's a bit friendlier."

Maggie thanked them both and left, stopping her car at the top of the lane to Nut Tree Cottage. It was less trouble parking there rather than squeezing past the workmen and all the equipment surrounding Watt's Cottage. Angela, hanging out some washing, beckoned her over.

"Where've you been? I was hoping we could have lunch out?"

Maggie picked her way round the muddy tyre tracks and told Angela about her successful visit.

"They both love knitting too. Knitted squares and blankets everywhere and as soon as I had persuaded Ethel to keep an eye on Alice she said she would hunt for patterns for baby's cardigans. Isn't that wonderful?"

"It'll be more than cardigans then. You and your old dears. You'd be as happy working in an old folks' home as you are with mothers and babies. I'd forgotten you were going there today."

"They've so much to offer. I love hearing about this village and I think they love reminiscing about their good old days. I feel so sad that they didn't get on with Charlie, though. He kept that secret, didn't he?"

"He certainly did. You've more patience with them than me. How about lunch tomorrow?"

"I can't unfortunately. I've got a study day and lectures in the afternoon. Think of somewhere we could go next week."

"Okay. Perhaps we can persuade these chaps to finish here by then. They're nearly done; just the kitchen and bathroom to finish off. The new Aga is in, red again."

"Great. I loved your other one, as you know."

Angela gathered up her basket. "Watch out; we'd better let this one in," she said as a white van appeared at the top of the lane. "It's the electrician."

"Right. I'll see you later," Maggie said, hurrying away. "I need to walk Woody. Call me."

Maggie stopped to talk to Biscuit and Crumble, who came to the gate as she was passing. She was delighted that they had settled down together so well. Her concern that the shed cum stable would be too small if they needed to shelter was unfounded. Every day they stood side by side inside it, facing the lane and watching all the comings and goings of the workmen who also found time to chat to them.

She had developed their daily routine and managed to dissuade people from giving them too many treats with her polite notice. Trevor the vet had decided they were similar ages – teenagers, in his view – and warned her that, although gelded, Crumble might be a bit skittish occasionally. A warning she quickly forgot about.

Maggie collected and boxed up the eggs and took Woody for a short walk, stopping to let him nuzzle the donkeys through the bars of the field gate to get them used to each other as the vet had suggested. The last thing she wanted was their dog chasing them. Several nuzzles later Maggie dragged him away and headed for the village shop, pleased at how much she had managed to fit in before Charlie came home.

CHAPTER ELEVEN

DEPRESSION

Maggie sat in the lecture room, the same room in which she held her parentcraft classes, in the cottage hospital on the outskirts of Waldersby, and studied a small herd of cows grazing in the meadow beyond the window. The building itself was part of the old workhouse and had three wards, a small X-ray department and a minor injuries unit. The wards on the south side overlooked well-kept lawns and an outstanding herbaceous border maintained by George, the cheery hospital gardener who had tended the garden lovingly for many years. He told Maggie, when she had first visited the hospital, that he had taken the job on in memory of his mother, who had passed away there.

Maggie's wandering thoughts of owning a cow were halted as soon as Miss Thomas, the tutor, walked in the room. Maggie had attended her lectures before and found them interesting, though Miss Thomas was not well liked. She was small, sharp-eyed and in the habit of snappily reprimanding anyone whose mind she felt might be wandering. She had been a midwife since before Maggie and her colleagues were born, a point she made often.

Listening intently, Maggie heard her describe in detail the danger of postnatal depression. Not the "blues" described in the immediate postnatal period, but the more worrying psychosis that occurred when women, so distressed and depressed, were sometimes capable of harming themselves, and their babies. Maggie's mind wandered to the time she herself had experienced overwhelming sadness following her third miscarriage, before giving birth to Charlie. The grief and utter despair she and Robert had experienced remained a deep and painful memory. She was thankful that Robert had been such an observant husband, quickly getting her the help and support she'd needed.

Miss Thomas, hawkishly observant, rapped the lectern sharply – aware that Maggie's mind was wandering.

During the lunch break Maggie met with her colleague, Susan, reflecting on their caseloads, and considered whether any of their mothers were at risk. They discussed the young girl, Alice. She'd not managed to stop smoking, despite Maggie's advice, and repeatedly told Maggie how unhappy she was and how she was dreading having the baby. She was taking good care of Bobby, her sister's little boy, but he was proving quite a handful for her. They decided to discuss this worrying situation with Doctor Southgate and pay special attention to Alice, before and after the birth of her baby.

"I'm so glad that Ethel Jones lives nearby. She's such a motherly soul and has already started knitting baby clothes. She's agreed to keep an eye on Alice for me."

Susan frowned. "Are you sure Alice wants her to?"

"She's lonely and her mother can't give her the attention she needs. She gets on well with Ethel. Her sister expects a lot of her and young Bobby's on the go all the time while he's with her. Doctor Southgate knows Ethel. He told me that she and her husband were his oldest patients and he's very fond of them, so no qualms. He visits the old man every couple of weeks for a chat, and free pots of honey."

"Does he? Cheeky man."

"You have to admire him, don't you? So caring; he visits all his older patients regularly."

"Old school, as they say. A dying breed."

"We're lucky to work with him. He's got so much experience, makes me feel safe as houses."

"Yes. Now, are you staying for all the lectures this afternoon? Serious stuff today: postnatal depression and cot deaths later."

"So I believe. I'm just nipping home to let Woody out, and pop Danny the duckling in the sink. I'll be back in time."

"Maggie, you're incorrigible. How is the little chap anyway?"

"He's doing really well. His damaged leg is nearly better so I'm giving him hydrotherapy three times a day."

Susan burst out laughing as she stood up and pulled her coat on. "What a crazy animal lover you are. Right, I'll see you back in an hour, then. I'm going to the Co-op. The lecture starts at half past two. Don't be late! She'll report you."

"Okay. By the way, I have a new student coming out with me next week."

"I know; he's a man! I've got him for two days the following week. I've met him; he's very nice and really keen to be a midwife. He told me there's going to be a change in the law."

"Really? Wonder if the women will accept a male midwife? Should be interesting. Bye."

The afternoon was hard to take. While Miss Thomas stressed that a baby's death was distressing, it was in her experience rare. Maggie had first-hand experience of how devastating it might be and was asked to tell the group about an incident that had nearly ended in tragedy. Maggie recalled the day she visited a young mother who'd parked the pram in her hallway after a shopping trip.

"The baby was still fast asleep as the mother unpacked the shopping before making herself a cup of tea. The danger lay not in the amount of clothing the little one had on but in the covers: a quilt and a rain cover on inside the house meant that her baby had become dangerously overheated.

"I arrived and thankfully managed to rouse the baby just in time. I'll never forget the anguish on that mother's face. We were both distressed and upset. The baby recovered quickly and we both learnt a lesson. Now I always make a point of reminding new mothers of this danger when I visit and I always bring it up at my parentcraft sessions. It had been such an easy thing to do."

"Thank you, Maggie, a very disturbing tale," Miss Thomas said. "Susan, I think you have a report of a baby who did not survive. Can you tell the class the background to the tragedy, please."

Sadly it had not been possible to revive another little boy, born prematurely to one of Susan's mothers, who had been a heavy smoker. Susan described how the distraught father had rushed the baby to the clinic when they found him lifeless, but it was too late to save him.

Miss Thomas thanked them both before updating them on the latest research, assuring them once more that it was indeed very rare in her experience. There was a stigma attached to cot deaths and parents had been wrongly accused of causing the death of their baby. It was known that almost two thousand babies died suddenly and for no obvious reason in the United Kingdom in their cots every year. Research at Bristol University was receiving funding to examine some possible causes: prematurity, sleep patterns, feeding regimes, the environment. In time it was hoped these studies, headed by Professor Peter Fleming, would help to reveal the most likely cause for such a distressing event.

Clustering together for a tea break afterwards Maggie and Susan chatted with colleagues they normally only encountered in the hospital. There was a lot of interest in the experience that those working in the community had, and some envy. Maggie knew she had been lucky to get her job and how easy it was for her to fit her home life around it. She knew it was far more than a job – it was a vocation and she would go to endless lengths to make a difference, caring deeply about all mothers.

That evening she and Robert reflected again on the good fortune that had brought them to the village, and how settled they had become.

"I really feel we belong here, Rob," Maggie said, spooning another helping of fruit crumble on his plate. "Custard?"

"Yes. What was that expression Charlie Watt used when we first arrived? 'Townies', that was it."

"I think he would agree we'd earned the right to be called 'locals' now, don't you?"

"Just about. How are all your old dears, by the way? The real locals?"

"Don' t call them old dears."

"Okay, Ethel and Annie."

"That's better." She grinned. "They're not mine either." Maggie piled the plates up and took them through to the kitchen. "I'm sure they're all fine. I don't visit them every day, you know." Robert gave her a hug. "I know. Anything good on the telly?"

"Before you fall asleep in front of the box there's something I want to show you."

Peering into the gloom in the chicken shed, Robert could just see the yellow fluffy bottom of Danny sticking out under Doris, Charlie Watt's old chicken. "How did that happen?"

Maggie told him how Doris, who was tame enough to wander in and out of the kitchen, had found Danny in his box and simply sat on top of him, as if she'd hatched him herself. The duckling, snug and warm, was unaware that his new mother was a chicken.

"I thought you wouldn't be too pleased to find poo all over the floor, so I put them both in there, and now Woody is pining. He loved the little chap but he resents Doris, although she's definitely won this time." Robert sighed, the long-suffering sound that emanated from him frequently when Maggie talked animals. "Come on, let me hear about Charlie's day, darling, before I watch the news."

"Oh," she said, "I meant to tell you, I saw some lovely cows today."

Chapter Twelve

An accident waiting to happen

"This is nice, just the two of us and a chance to catch up."

Maggie and Angela were trying out the new tea rooms in the Market Square in Waldersby.

"Nice décor and I'm told the food's good."

"Sorry I couldn't make lunch: I was up most of the night and Robert didn't wake me when he and Charlie left this morning."

"That's okay. I had a check-up with Doctor Southgate this morning and he told me you'd been busy. Gave me a chance to have a browse in the new furniture store round the corner. Some really nice stuff: a set of dining table and chairs that Tom would love. We can pop in there afterwards. Was she the woman you told me about?"

"Yes, I delivered her last two. She called me a bit too early, though, as she was worried it would be quick, so we were both marching around the garden in the moonlight."

Angela laughed. "Poor woman! What happened?"

"It was a lovely delivery in the end. A little boy." Maggie smiled. "Well, hardly little: he weighed just under ten pounds. They were thrilled as they already have two little girls. They're calling him Noah."

"That's different. Ooh, let me, I'll be mother." Angela arranged the teacups, expressing delight at the variety of sandwiches as the waitress removed her tray. "Scones and real Cornish cream too – yummy. You first, you're hungry. I'll let the tea brew a bit."

Maggie yawned. "I'm really going to enjoy this. Was everything okay? Your blood pressure?"

"Don't yawn; you'll start me off. Yes, fine, I'm booked in with you next time. I thought I heard you go out last night. I was up with Rosie again, trying to wean her off night-time milk, but she refuses water and then starts crying so much it makes me feel awful. The cruel mother."

"I seem to remember having that trouble with Charlie. Took me ages. When are you going down to Cornwall?"

"Well, Tom decided we should leave it till the beginning of September and get the workmen out of the house, which is sensible. Then we can come back just before school starts and get all the furniture sorted. He phoned them yesterday and we can have the same cottage for a week as they've had a cancellation."

"Gosh, that was lucky."

"It was. Now, more news." Angela smiled. "It's a bit soon to be telling you as I haven't even told Tom yet."

"Let me guess. Can't. Go on, tell me." Maggie looked bemused.

"We were so relieved that work on the cottage was going so well, you know, after waiting for all the planning permission and the rest, it was so good to see everything coming together, our dream home now it's been such a relief – anyway, we got a bit carried away. Tom asked Major Gibson if he'd sell us the field behind the cottage."

"You never told me you wanted more land."

"Well, as I said, it was Tom's idea. Major Gibson rang this morning and offered it to us."

"Wow. Lucky you, but you don't even have any animals. What d'you want a field for? Football pitch?"

"Tom's always been worried that the Major might start thinking about building more houses and being selfish we don't want them surrounding us."

"I'd have thought it very unlikely. He gave up the idea on the meadow we rent."

"Yes, I know. Tom was still a bit worried. We thought you might like to have more grazing for Biscuit and Crumble?"

"Really? D'you mean that?"

"Of course! You're our best friends and we'd be more than happy to let you use it."

"You never told me you were so rich."

"We're not; it was a bargain. Tom's aunt left him some money. I don't think he expected it at all. She was a favourite of his and died last year without any immediate heirs."

"So he decided to buy land?"

"Yes. Tom was flabbergasted when he was told he'd been left so much but we kept it to ourselves and then he had this idea of investing in another property: a holiday cottage or some such. Actually, it was Gordon who suggested the land behind us and it increases the value of this cottage quite considerably."

"Not with my donkeys in it."

"We could buy some more of those poor discarded creatures." Angela grinned broadly. "We could fill it with your animals and have a proper sanctuary."

"It's really kind of you to offer it, thank you. Tom might not like it, though…"

"Here, have another cup," Angela said, adding the hot water to the teapot. "It was his suggestion."

"Gosh." Maggie couldn't hide her surprise. "Just a half. I've got to get back. I'll have another scone, though. I'm so pleased for you both. Can I tell Robert?"

"Of course. Oh, and also I meant to say I'll be here for the village fete before we go away and I can still help you with the donkeys."

"Eh? They'll be okay, all penned up."

"Edna told me you would be giving donkey rides."

Maggie spluttered, spilling her tea. "Donkey rides?"

"Well, aren't you?"

"Certainly not. That's Edna's idea, not mine. I don't want Crumble bolting off with some poor little kid on his back."

"Well, I thought you'd agreed as she's printed the notices and there's a picture of a donkey giving a ride – apparently she got a picture from Blackpool."

"The artful old bat," Maggie said, spooning clotted cream onto the scone. "I thought she was getting better. She's so bossy and anyway she should have asked. I'm not sure I want to risk them giving rides."

"She's also arranging a dog show and said she would be showing Woody for you, as you would have your hands full."

Later that evening Maggie shared Angela's news and she and Robert raised a glass to them and their generous offer. Maggie was still feeling cross with Edna and keen to tell Robert what she'd apparently planned for the donkeys.

"That's your third glass, darling, I know you're angry but no need to get drunk. Here, sit down and tell me all about your delivery last night," Robert said, patting the seat beside him.

"Edna can be so irritating with all her interfering," Maggie said, feeling the wine take effect, starting to find the whole thing funny.

"What you need is a holiday," said Robert, looking thoughtful. "Tom and Angela have got the right idea with their holiday cottage in Cornwall. I could introduce Charlie to rock pooling, crabs in buckets, sandcastles, burying Mummy. What d'you think? We could take Woody along."

"Maybe we could take the donkeys too, darling, give rides on the beach – why not take bloody Edna as well?"

Maggie stared up at the bedroom ceiling, making a list in her head of everything she had to do. Major Gibson had seemed genuinely excited at the fete committee meeting when he'd announced that the parish council had agreed to hand over some cash from the precept for village activities, adding that he was happy to allow full use of his gardens. He had also put Edna in charge, which Maggie suspected might be a stroke of genius, despite all the disagreements with the parish council decisions he'd clashed with Edna over. Better to keep your enemy close, she supposed, and with Edna at the helm the fete committee would feel obliged to ambush every last soul in the village into providing cakes, bottles and raffle prizes. She picked up the note by her bedside, reminded yet again of how lucky she was to have Robert. He had left her to have a lie-in, it was almost midday and the note let her know he'd fed and watered all the animals and that Dawn Creasey was looking after Charlie, while Edna Newbold was going to walk Woody and then keep him at the village shop. She stretched luxuriously, her thoughts once more turning to her friends Angela and Tom and their good fortune, before picking up the phone as it rang.

"Hello, darling."

"Mum? Hi, how are you?"

"I'm fine. Is it alright if I pop down next week?"

"Of course, are you alright?"

"Yes, yes. I have something to tell you."

"Spill the beans." Maggie could hazard a guess. "Anything to do with moving house or getting married?"

"No, darling. I'll let you know what time I'll be arriving. Tuesday, if that's okay?"

"Meany! I want to know now," said Maggie, smiling to herself.

"No, I need to talk to you and Eleanor face to face. You sound tired, dear."

"I'm still in bed. Robert left me asleep as I was out in the night."

"A new baby?"

"Yes. Also a false alarm and a mother with very sore nipples."

"Oh, poor thing."

"Poor me."

"You chose to be a midwife, darling. You must see to your mums when they need you."

"Okay, but it was a bit tiring just getting to sleep and then having to crawl out of bed again. Anyway, I've recovered now."

"Good. How's my grandson?"

"He's fine. Bit of an upset at playgroup the other day. Apparently Charlie tried to sit on a little girl and she fell and hurt her lip. He told the teacher that she was pretending to be his donkey."

"Oh dear."

"The teacher said her lip bled all over her dress and the little one's mother threatened to take her away because of the lack of supervision."

"Oh dear."

"Charlie refused to go the next day."

"Oh dear."

"He kept crying so Robert took the morning off and stayed with him. He's fine now."

"Good."

"Robert enjoyed it too. Lego building together."

"That's nice, dear."

"I'd better get up. Can't stay in bed all day. Does Eleanor know you're coming?"

"Yes, she might join us at the weekend if that's alright? She's quite bothered that she hasn't seen you all for months."

"That'll be great."

"Bye, darling. Don't work too hard."

"Bye, Mum. See you Tuesday."

Maggie took a long lingering bath before she dressed. She was plucking up the courage to go and see Edna before the village shop closed.

She walked up the lane, stopping on the way to check the donkeys, who were busily grazing together at the top of the meadow. Angela was in the garden in conversation with two of her builders. Maggie waved, not wishing to interrupt but wanting all the same to put off seeing Edna.

Turning into the main road at the top of the lane she was startled to find three caravans parked on the verge either side of the road, and a mixture of cars and vans. Two lean dogs tied to stakes barked at her approach, pulling at a restraining chain.

Maggie, fearful of the dogs, hurried past two men chopping wood, who ignored her approach. She smiled at a small child and noticed a baby in a pram. She couldn't wait to get to Edna; she would be sure to know that the gypsies had arrived the village.

Chapter Thirteen

On the Move

Maggie was relieved to find the village shop empty when she arrived. It was near closing time and Edna was in the backroom totting up the sales for the day, a job Maggie knew she detested. She looked up, frowned and gestured to Maggie to wait.

Woody jumped up eagerly to greet her. "Down, Woody, down," Maggie said, offering him one of his treats before sitting beside the counter. "Have you been a good boy or has Edna been spoiling you?" She tugged at him playfully. "Please don't hurry, Edna, I'm not in a rush."

"I won't," came the terse reply.

Maggie got up and began browsing the shop, pleasantly surprised to see that Edna was stocking other local produce beside her own eggs. Honey from Ethel's husband, George, jams and chutneys from Dawn Creasey and other members of the over sixties group. Edna's niece, Jennifer had hung up some of her own paintings of local scenes in pastels and watercolours in the shop, as well as some attractive seasonal cards. Fresh vegetables from the allotments and some potted plants stood on a stand by the door next to the donkey carrots.

Edna bustled out. "Bring that lot in," she said, pointing to the stand. Maggie did as she was told.

"He's had a long walk. Jennifer was here today, so she took him."

"Thank you; he loves coming here." Maggie paused. "Edna, d'you know anything about the gypsies?"

"Gypsies? What gypsies?"

"Well, three caravans are parked at the end of our lane. They weren't there last night, so I imagine they arrived this morning. They've got children and two rather fierce dogs are tied up."

"Fruit pickers. They're early."

"D'you know them?"

"Yes, if it's the usual lot. They've been coming for years. Usually park up at the Major's, if it's them. They go hop picking in Kent and then come this way, cherry pick mainly and then the apples later on." Maggie felt relieved; she had read and heard so many differing reports regarding the gypsies and she found Edna's reaction reassuring. "PC O'Sheridan will move them on. He'll not let them stay on the verge," Edna said, looking puzzled. "Strange, I wonder what's made them park up there. Word gets round fast; I expect he knows by now."

Edna was rearranging the displays, ready to shut up shop, but Maggie had something else on her mind.

"Edna, Angela thinks you want the donkeys to give rides at the fete."

"Well, that's what they're for."

"Not mine. They're not ready for that sort of thing and Biscuit is still a bit frail, you know. I can let people stroke them, but that's about it."

"That won't be much of an attraction, will it? Donkey rides are always popular."

"They could walk a little way and get brushed; children will like doing that. I hear that you're having a dog show too?"

"Major Gibson put me in charge."

"That's good; you know Angela and I will help you all we can."

"Right, now let me lock up. We've got the church flowers to do. I'll probably cross the donkeys off the list."

"Oh, don't do that." Maggie could sense the older woman's irritation, but at least donkey rides were off the agenda for now. "Don't cross them off completely. They'll love seeing all the people and I'll smarten them up." Edna patted Woody, turned the shop sign to "Closed" and, with a briefly muttered "Right then, I'll be off", off she went.

"That's us dismissed, Woody," Maggie said, putting his lead on, relieved that one hurdle had been dealt with without too much aggravation. "Come on; it's your teatime."

The caravans were still at the end of the lane as Maggie walked past. Woody whimpered, frightened by angry barking and the shouts of a man walking towards them.

"Wait a minute, Miss. I think we might need your help," the man said, gesturing to his dogs to be quiet. "You're the nurse round here, so we're told," he said.

"Midwife, not nurse," said Maggie, feeling more than a little apprehensive.

"Yeah, well, that's even better. You see, I think my missus is about to have it."

"It?" Maggie dreaded what she guessed was coming next.

"She drops them quick, always has."

"D'you mean a baby? She's in labour?"

"Not yet, keeps telling me not to fuss. Any day likely. Can you have a look at her for us?" the man asked, gesturing to the caravan behind him.

"You should really call the doctor, you know."

"Yeah, well, you have a look and I'll take it from there."

Maggie could sense his agitation and was becoming concerned herself now, for a pregnant woman she'd never seen.

"Has anything happened?"

"Yeah, she's wet the bed. Her sisters with her."

"Sounds as if her waters might have gone. Look, I need to get my dog home; if you wait I'll just pop him down the lane to my friend. It's not your first then?"

"Not bloody likely. It's our sixth, well, seventh if you count the one we lost a year back."

Maggie felt her heart stop. "Sixth?" she said feebly. "Oh, my goodness, here: hold onto Woody," she said, slipping past him up a rickety pair of steps to the caravan.

Ten minutes later, surrounded by women from the other families, Maggie held a very cross baby boy in her arms. He was born almost the instant she entered the caravan. She barely had a second to say "hello", slip through a circle of helpers and lift the mother's skirt, before he arrived in the world. Maggie had never felt so unprepared and without any of her equipment to hand was wondering how to separate mother and baby.

"I've got a ball of string, love."

"Don't worry, love, my scissors are clean, used them for her last baby."

"Perhaps we could sterilise them quickly?" Maggie said, placing the baby boy on the mother's stomach as the afterbirth slithered out into her waiting bowl.

"I've put a pan on," said one of the women.

"Boil them for two minutes, they'll be fine," Maggie said, relieved to see that there was very little else filling the bowl. The awful thought of the woman bleeding in these circumstances filled her with fear.

The baby found his mother's nipple and was sucking eagerly to the "oohs" and "aahs" of the small crowd now filling the caravan as Maggie unravelled the ball of string and cut the cord with the still hot scissors, adding to the delight of the women.

"You're on your own now, kid," they chorused as Maggie, enjoying the unexpected drama, examined the contents of her bowl.

The husband beaming with pride and relief shooed the women out and busied himself pouring large mugs of strong tea for Maggie and his wife when there appeared a flashing blue light outside the caravan, and a burly shadow crossed the window.

"You can't stay here," said a familiar voice. PC O'Sheridan banged on the door and marched straight in.

"Meet Turpin," said Maggie, chuckling at the policeman's astonishment.

Maggie couldn't wait to relate the incident to Doctor Southgate, who she knew would be sorry not to have been on duty.

"I was wondering how on earth I was going to cut the cord when one of the women handed me a ball of string and a pair of scissors," she told him the next day. "I had nothing sterile. We did manage to boil up the scissors in time."

"Worse things can happen, dear. I've resorted to string many a time. No harm done. It will have been fine."

"Yes, but you've had so much more experience. I admit I was panicking. It all happened so quickly. I was very nervous, to be honest. Thankfully our policeman arrived and got my bag, then I felt more in control. He was wonderful, took Woody home and came back, cuddled Turpin and told them they could stay there for two more days."

"Interesting name, Turpin."

"After Dick Turpin, highwayman – you know, born on the highway verge etc. The father, Doug, said they name their children according to where they are at the time. A lot of them are named after rivers, apparently, as they are their favourite stops."

"Good idea."

"They've moved onto the Major's land now so I can still do my visits."

"I'll call tomorrow. What's interesting, Maggie, is that they knew you lived nearby."

"I asked Doug and all he said was that they find out all they need to know if they're on the move – canny lot." She laughed. "That's forward planning for you."

Maggie enjoyed her visits to baby Turpin and was struck by the closeness of the three families, the women eager to share the care of mother and baby and all the other children. Their vans were kept scrupulously clean and the ornaments that adorned them gleamed in the light. They told her of their own concerns now that more immigrant labour was taking over the hop picking in Kent and how they felt their own way of life was being sullied by new travellers giving them a bad name. They received abuse wherever they went and were not tolerated well, as of old. The reason was the litter and mess that they claimed the newer travellers left behind. They were aware that the illegal stops upset local communities and were careful to keep to regular stops, except on this occasion. It was a sad tale of dying Romany traditions, but for the moment they were happy to be made welcome once more by the Major, and intensely proud of their own three families.

"I'm surprised you weren't more frightened, darling. Gives me the shudders to think of you in that situation." Elizabeth was unpacking her things in the bedroom.

"I'm really glad I've had that experience, Mum. I'm sure they wouldn't mind you meeting Turpin. He's such a bonny little lad."

"I'm sure he is, but I'd rather not."

Maggie smiled to herself; she knew exactly how her mother viewed the idea of meeting the gypsy family. She had to admit she had harboured similar misgivings, but that was before Turpin's dramatic arrival. Her feelings towards the family were quite different now and she was glad of that. That was why she loved Doctor Southgate, a man who had experienced so much and was fazed by nothing and no-one.

"We'll go and collect Charlie, and then you can meet Biscuit's new mate, Crumble. Charlie has to see them before his tea and I'm sure he'll want to show you our duckling," she said, ignoring her mother's raised eyebrows.

Chapter Fourteen

A little premature

"Gin and tonic?"

"Thank you, Robert. No lemon."

"Cheers, dears." Elizabeth smiled. "Now, look, I told you I've already spoken to Eleanor and she quite understands how I feel."

Maggie sighed. "We all know how you feel. What we really want to know is what you're going to do about it, Mummy."

"Well, it's a little premature, darling, I think. Frank hasn't been divorced that long really and although we get on very well I'm not sure that we're ready to actually live together."

"So, you're not going to move down here?"

"Frank's thinking of arranging a wonderful cruise when we'll be together all the time; obviously, if it works out, we can move onto making the bigger decisions."

"I thought you were lonely at home."

"True. Its moved on a pace. Frank has been popping up about once a fortnight – and, much as we get on, I'm not sure I'm quite ready for anything more just yet."

"I think that sounds very sensible," Robert said, holding aloft the bottle of gin. "No need to rush into things at your age."

"Thank you, Robert. I'm not as old as you think, you know, but at least you understand. My girls don't seem to," she said, passing him her empty glass. "Just a small one, thank you."

"That's not really fair, Mummy. Eleanor and I understand; we just want you to be happy and not lonely."

"Good. So I hope you agree that we're being sensible about all this."

"Very sensible." Maggie started to giggle. "Too sensible in my opinion."

"Maggie," Robert said warningly.

"It's alright, Robert, my daughter has had one too many, I think."

The next day Maggie and Eleanor commiserated with each other over the phone for not having sorted their mother's future.

"I'm being selfish," said Maggie. "I just hope that they get on so well on this cruise he's planning that they decide they can't live without each other, don't you?"

"They will, I'm sure. You know we're hoping to move your way – next spring, possibly."

"That'll be good. Any sign of a baby yet?"

"No. We haven't been trying. We're going to wait till next year."

"Well, don't leave it too long, sis. Come and see us soon. Charlie's growing fast. Primary school in September, can you believe? He asked where Auntie Elly was the other day. Mum's here for a week, maybe two if I can persuade her to stay. It would be so nice if we could get together more often, good for Mum too. She still needs us, you know."

"Maggie, come down quickly, darling, the police want a word."

It was early the following morning and there had been a sudden series of loud knocks on the front door. Maggie thought the blue flashing lights and heavy bangs were part of a dream she was having, until Robert stumbled from the bed to go downstairs.

Leaning over the banister and straining to catch what was being said, she made out the words "word with your wife, please" and crept towards the stairs, chilled by the cold air coming from the front door and a feeling of dread. Behind her, her mother was reassuring Charlie, who had been woken by all the noise, and below Robert was restraining Woody from whining and barking loudly.

Hurrying down the stairs, heart pounding and pulling her dressing gown tightly around her, Maggie stood trembling in the hall, confronted by two policemen.

"Sorry to disturb you, young lady, but we're told you are the owner of a donkey, or donkeys, I should say. Would that be correct?"

"Yes, yes, why d'you ask?" Maggie was shaking now as Robert put his arm round her. "Has something happened?"

"Perhaps you can tell us where they might be?" said the policeman.

"In the field, just down the lane; you've just driven past the gate."

"Er, yes. Could you describe them, madam?" Maggie, still half-asleep, had no idea what the policeman was talking about and wished it had been PC O'Sheridan who had turned up at their door at dawn. "They're very old, one's piebald and the other's lightish brown," said Maggie.

"Thank you, that suits the description we're after nicely. Well, Mrs…?"

"Just call me Maggie, please."

"Well, your donkeys didn't strike me or my officers as old, I must say. We've been trying to catch the b— the two of them all night."

"You can't have, officer, they're in their field," said Maggie, shivering in her nightwear.

"Were in their field, my dear, but they've been cavorting, for want of a better word, half the night. My men finally caught the brownish one halfway to Waldersby and now we've got them both tied up in the children's play area on the green by the pub. I might add that they're in a bit of a lather, specially the piebald one – he's been trying it on all night!"

"No!" Maggie thought she was going to faint. "Really?"

"Er, yes, really."

"Look, can I offer you a cup of tea, officers?" said Robert.

Maggie couldn't understand how Robert could be so calm. He even sounded like he was beginning to find the whole thing slightly funny.

"Strong black coffee, if you will. Two sugars in both. We need to get these animals back in that field so I suggest you arrange that pretty smartish. I shall also need a statement from you, missus, as the owner of the runaways."

Maggie managed to stop shaking, relieved to know that the donkeys were safe and no harm had come to them or anyone else.

"What do you want me to say?"

"Names first."

"Biscuit and Crumble." The two policemen suddenly burst out laughing. "That's not what we'd call them, I can tell you, love."

Maggie, thankful that her mother was able to help Robert with Charlie and the rest of their growing menagerie, gathered together the harnesses, two packets of mints and a haynet and headed for the village play area.

Biscuit and Crumble, crestfallen, stood disconsolate together tied up with ropes. Two more police cars, blue lights flashing, drew an early-morning crowd as Maggie untied them, telling them how naughty they'd been, much to the enjoyment of the locals on their way to work.

"Sign 'em up for the Grand National, love," one shouted to the amusement of the others.

"Donkey derby you mean, mate," called another. "Ride them back, love." Declining offers of help, Maggie persuaded them to return home, lured by the peppermints she'd brought with her.

Once the donkeys were back in the field she tried to work out exactly how they had got out in the first place. It didn't take her long to realise it was down to her mother. Elizabeth had made a reluctant visit to see the donkeys, pulled along by Charlie just before his bedtime. The catch on the gate was loose and always needed an extra yank to secure it. It had not had the extra yank. Two donkeys simply saw an opening, pushed the gate open and nosed their way out of the field, tempted by the thick hedge and greener grass in the lane. Buoyed by this new freedom, Crumble must have become more frisky and the two were soon off on their jaunt.

Maggie decided not to tell her mother but fixed the gate with a new chain and padlock. The donkeys, chastened and exhausted by their night on the tiles, spent the rest of the day in the stable, too tired to move.

Next day the *Waldersby Gazette* rang Maggie twice. They wanted to find out more and a photographer appeared in the lane taking pictures of Biscuit and Crumble for the local story of the week, letting Maggie know they'd make the front page. A couple of amateur photographers turned up as well. The donkeys were fast becoming local celebrities and Maggie suspected it wouldn't be long before Edna latched onto the interest they'd created. They'd be billed as the star attraction of the fete, she was certain.

Chapter Fifteen

A Foot in the Dark

The stairs were freezing again beneath Maggie's bare feet two nights later, as she crept as quietly as possible downstairs, instinctively avoiding the ones that would creak. She had no idea why her heart always beat a little faster than normal on these night-time forays – it wasn't as if it was out of the ordinary. But it was a relief to reach the kitchen all the same, to place her feet on the Aga-warmed tiles, ignoring the wall clock that let her know it was three in the morning. Robert seldom woke when she crept out of bed. He was used to it by now, but her mother was a light sleeper and if Charlie woke he would call out for her and expect her to join in a night-time chat and then wouldn't be able to get back to sleep. Woody, accustomed to her habits, lifted his head briefly from his basket by the Aga, wagged his tail and went back to sleep. Relieved that Charlie and her mother had not stirred, knowing she could leave them all snoring happily, she gathered her nursing bags before heading in the direction of Great Fordham.

The call had come unexpectedly, given the baby was not due for a couple of weeks. The woman had thought her waters had gone and was having pains regularly. Moira was unknown to Maggie, having just moved to the area to stay with her mother. Maggie had met her only briefly at the clinic, where she had been examined by one of Doctor Southgate's partners, and so she knew very little of her background, apart from the fact that she'd insisted that she was having the baby at home, whatever anyone else might think. Maggie was intrigued: a mother in her early thirties, very defensive and with a history of one normal birth five years before. It was raining hard as she strained to see the road ahead, eventually finding the house down the winding lane, set back from the road. Every light in the house was ablaze.

Maggie was ushered in by Moira's mother, whom she recognised as a shy but keen member of the over-sixties club.

Escorting Maggie to the bedroom, she hastily disappeared to make tea. Moira was looking relaxed, quite different from how she had been at the clinic, and she seemed pleased to see her, so Maggie delayed an immediate full examination and settled on just turning back the covers and checking the baby's heartbeat first. She wanted to know how and when labour had started and more about her previous birth experience. It appeared that five years earlier Moira had given birth in a military hospital. Her husband was still stationed abroad and sadly they had separated. She had not had a pleasant experience giving birth the first time, blaming the doctor who had carried out a forceps delivery; this had made her determined to avoid a hospital birth second time around. The child, a boy of six now, was still with his father and his family, in order not to disrupt his schooling, and would return to Moira and his granny in England later in the year. However, this baby, she confessed, was not her husband's.

Having got to know Moira a little better, quietly observing her as she dealt with a couple of strong contractions, Maggie was keen to examine her internally and see how far on in labour she was. Moira was beginning to get distressed, requesting the gas and oxygen Maggie carried with her.

Preparing her equipment, she gently pulled the bedclothes right back in readiness for the internal examination, freezing at what she found. Nestling between Moira's thighs was a baby's tiny blue foot, an emerging footling breech. Maggie, her heart pounding, tried to calm herself, breathing slowly. She had witnessed breech births, but had never dealt with one alone and she was well aware of the controversy that raged over whether it was safer for the baby in a breech position to be born by caesarean section. It was just at that moment that Moira's mother appeared with a tray of tea.

"Mrs Simmonds, may I use your phone, please?" Maggie heard the squeakiness in her voice, felt how parched her throat was. "Moira, I need to phone the doctor at once. Baby has decided to arrive feet first."

Moira, now enjoying the gas and oxygen, was blissfully unaware of Maggie's concerns. "What fun," she said. "The little tinker."

Wrapping the little foot up to keep it warm, Maggie grabbed the phone, willing the doctor to answer straight away, commanding herself to stay in control. The doctor on call answered sleepily, assuring her he would try and get to her as soon as possible, instructing her to summon an ambulance.

A little calmer knowing that the doctor and ambulance were on their way, Maggie steadied her thoughts and grabbed two chairs. If no-one came in time the baby was going to be born in this house and she was going to make sure it was born safely. Moira, breathing the gas deeply, was happy to oblige when Maggie dragged her to the bottom of the bed, instructing the silent and bewildered Mrs Simmonds to add her support, as she prepared the way for the baby to be born.

"Baby's nearly here, Moira."

Maggie felt a wave of calm engulf her as she took control. A recent lecture on how to cope in any emergency came to the forefront of her mind and she almost smiled. She could do this; she was getting used to emergencies. Outside was silence, no ambulance sirens or the sound of a doctor pulling up in his car, while inside the sound of three women taking deep breaths filled the room. Maggie, slowly, with great care and total concentration, delivered the baby girl who had decided to walk into the world. Overwhelmed with relief as the head finally emerged, she noted the baby's healthy cry and with the cord clamped and the baby separated she placed her gently in Moira's arms.

Moira and her mother were both crying with joy, unaware of the challenge and fear Maggie had just experienced and whose tears were also tripping off her chin with relief. She was lightheaded and proud at what she had accomplished, saying little as she made Moira comfortable, taking in the gratitude that shone from both Moira and her mother's eyes. The baby had already attached herself to Moira's breast and was sucking contentedly.

"I fed my little boy for over a year; it's one thing I can do well," Moira said, hugging the baby close.

Maggie retreated to the kitchen and collected up her instruments. Standing by the sink, she noticed how much her hands were shaking and her body still trembled. She took some deep breaths to compose herself before returning to the bedroom.

The doctor and ambulance arrived together ten minutes later. Mrs Simmonds, unable to stop smiling, produced tea and a plate of jam tarts. She had found her voice and was eagerly telling the doctor and ambulance crew in great detail how Maggie had delivered baby Constance.

"We may need to have Constance seen at the hospital tomorrow," the doctor said after examining them both. "Need to check out baby's hips – it's all routine."

All signs of Moira's earlier resentment towards doctors had vanished and she listened carefully before thanking them all for coming and urged her mother to feed them more tea and tarts.

"We'll take you in, love, and bring you back," said Bill the ambulance driver as he left. "Don't you worry about a thing. That little mite will be fine."

As she drove towards home through the quiet lanes, a soft pink dawn heralded the start of another day. Before she had left, Maggie had bathed and weighed baby Constance. There had been no need to supervise her feeding. She yawned and smiled, relieved now and feeling pleased with herself. How could she not love her job?

"Hello, is that Miss Thomas?"

"Yes. May I ask why you're calling me at this hour?"

"Yes, it's Maggie Groves, one of your students. Well, I just wanted to thank you for saving my life," said Maggie, twiddling the cord on the phone.

"I beg your pardon?"

"I don't mean literally, but—" Maggie took a deep breath to calm the elation bubbling up inside her. "I got called out to an undiagnosed breech birth. If you hadn't emphasised the importance of using the chairs and reminding us how to suspend the baby and conduct the delivery I'm sure I would not have been able to deliver baby Constance safely. I've never been so scared in my whole life."

"Well, that's rather a sad admission."

"Honest one, Miss Thomas. You see I've witnessed them, of course. I saw several in London, where I trained, but actually having to conduct a breech birth myself came as quite a shock. I just wanted to tell you how grateful I am for your lecture last week."

Miss Thomas was silent. Maggie could tell she was taken aback. "Very well, I'm listening."

It was a relief for Maggie to tell her how she'd managed to deliver baby Constance and despite the tutor's offhand response to her call she felt the need to confide in her.

"Well, I'm-I'm glad I proved helpful," Miss Thomas said. "It appears that you do listen after all," she said, replacing the receiver with a firm click.

Maggie's friend and colleague, Susan, wanted to hear all about the birth at lunchtime and Maggie was only too happy to oblige, sensing her friend was relieved she had missed it.

"Glad it wasn't me that didn't suspect it was breech before she gave birth," she said.

"It happens, though. Her last birth was abroad and the young locum we had in last week can't really be blamed. Doctor Southgate has been giving him a bit of advice."

"I bet he has. Michel Odent, the trendy French obstetrician, thinks this tendency towards caesareans is dangerous. He thinks women should stand up and deliver normally for a breech birth. He was on the telly last week. He's dishy as well."

"I heard that. I think we should go to one of his lectures. He's coming to Cambridge soon," Maggie said.

"Now, I'm off to see Moira and baby Constance after the clinic and I'll tell them you'll call tomorrow?"

"Yes, you can have a lie-in. Constance. That's a sweet name, isn't it?"

"Yes, but don't say Connie. She doesn't want it shortened."

"Thanks, Mummy, for doing everything today." Maggie was washing up after their evening meal. "Did you shut the chickens in?"

"Yes, but I must say that duckling looks rather too large to be sitting on top of that old hen."

"I know. It used to be underneath her. I'll organise a proper run for Danny next weekend. Robert's made him a little duck house."

"I was pecked by that horrible cockerel you call Paxo."

"Were you? I'm sorry. He's alright with me."

"Charlie's a good helper, isn't he?"

"Yes. Did he make you read for a long time?"

"We're working our way through *Wind in the Willows* again."

"Thanks, Mum. It's so lovely having you here. Tomorrow we need to go and see Edna and discuss the arrangements for the village fete next week."

"That'll be interesting."

"Let's take our coffee through and watch the news before I fall asleep. Robert said he'd be late and I feel shattered."

"I'm not surprised," said Elizabeth. "But you do know what you do is very worthwhile, don't you?"

"Do you know, I think I do," said Maggie, giving her a hug.

Her mother wasn't one for paying outright compliments, but when she did you could be certain she meant them.

Chapter Sixteen

Bottoms up!

Edna Newbold was in a flap. There were only three days to go before the village fete and Edna, in charge of all the arrangements, had mislaid her lists. The site plan for each stall was also missing.

"Hello, Edna. How nice to see you again," Elizabeth said as she and Maggie walked into the shop.

Edna barely acknowledged them, muttering that she had lots to do. "Jennifer's out the back; she'll serve you," she said, pacing back and forth, repeatedly turning things over on the counter.

"We've come to talk about the arrangements for the

donkeys. Mum's staying on a few days and she'd like to help on the day," said Maggie. "What've you lost? Can I help?"

"Dawn could probably do with extra help in the tea tent," Edna said, turning over papers by the till for the third time. "I need to check where everyone's going. Oh, where is the damn thing?"

"Shall we bring something with us? More cakes? Biscuits?"

Edna, exasperated, didn't answer.

Elizabeth was mouthing, "Let's come back later," just as Edna pounced on a notebook hiding under a pile of old newspapers.

"Found. Thank goodness. Now then, you'd best ask Dawn. She'll tell you what's needed. How long did you say you were staying?" she queried, finally acknowledging Elizabeth's presence.

"A week, maybe more, I'm not sure."

"Unfortunately I can't keep her forever," said Maggie. "We'll be seeing Dawn later so we can find out what extra help she might need. D'you know where you plan to put the donkeys? Angela and I'll spruce them up and she's happy to look after them until after the dog show so that Charlie and I can show Woody off."

Edna's whole demeanour changed at the mention of Woody.

"He's booked in the 'smartest dog' class, and he'd better win."

"Charlie wants to lead him round so let's hope he behaves."

"He always behaves with me," she said, tartly.

"Charlie not Woody, Edna."

"Right, now the donkeys. The Major's lad is arranging a pen for them in front of the Dog and Duck. They've got 'star billing' on the programmes. Jennifer's done a lovely job on that and the local press are coming."

"She just rattles me," Maggie said later when they were busy fulfilling Dawn's request for scones and jam sponges. "She might have asked whether I want star billing and reporters frightening them with their cameras flashing. She's so bossy. One day I might say something I'll regret."

"She means well, darling. I know her bark's worse than her bite and she is a big help to you remember? Looking after Woody among other things." Elizabeth put another batch in the oven. "Pass me the flour. Remember the walks she took with Charlie in his pram?"

"I know you're right, but she can still get my back up."

"It's not like you to be unforgiving. Make a fresh pot of tea. I'm parched; aren't you?"

"Yes. Forget Edna, I've got some good news from my friend up the lane, Angela."

"Oh, really? How old are her children now? It doesn't seem long since they had the last little one."

"Rosie's two and a half and James is nearly nine and you know she's expecting another one, don't you? Now, it's still a bit of a secret but Major Gibson's letting them buy that two-acre field at the back of their cottage."

Elizabeth poured the tea. "It's none of my business," she said. "Here, d'you put cream on the scone first or jam? But why? Do they need more land?"

"So I can fill it with more donkeys," chuckled Maggie. "No, it's an investment, but she did say I could use it."

"Don't you buy any more animals; you can't cope with what you've got."

"Thanks, Mum. You sound just like my husband," Maggie muttered, cramming another scone in her mouth.

The donkeys wore smart red-and-green harnesses, their coats shone and their small hooves glistened as they stood in the small enclosure, looking as if they were wondering what all the fuss was about. A small crowd had gathered and Angela had quite a job dissuading them all from offering treats.

"Please don't. It makes them pushy, you see," she said, trying to stop one young lad from plying them with carrots.

"My mum said to give them to the donkeys," he said, ignoring Angela and giggling when Crumble yanked the whole bag out of his outstretched hand.

There was also a new attraction confined in a small pen next to the donkeys. Major Gibson had arranged for a fat piglet to be used in a "Guess the weight of the pig" competition. Angela hastily turfed the carrots into its enclosure when she thought no-one was looking.

Large crowds milled round the green, encouraged by the sunshine and the cloudless blue sky perfect weather for a fete. The Waldersby Majorettes strutted their stuff, accompanied by the town band raising money for the local hospital.

Maggie left Angela in charge while she went to find Robert and Charlie. She had brought Charlie a clean T-shirt for the parade, noticing on the way that Elizabeth was enjoying herself helping in the tea tent.

"I simply love this, Dawn. Such a wonderful sense of the community working together. It's just not like this in a big town," remarked Elizabeth. "Thankfully Frank's got the urn boiling again."

"We'll have to persuade you to live down here. You'll get roped in for everything, if Edna has anything to do with it."

"You never know, it just might happen one day," Elizabeth said, blowing Frank a kiss and looking coy. "You're doing a grand job, Mr Sutton," she called out.

Maggie found Robert and Charlie sitting on a straw bale near the entrance, both licking the last remains of chocolate ice creams slithering down their fingers and dripping onto their clothes.

"Here, darling, put this on, you can't parade covered in chocolate," she said, swiftly changing Charlie's shirt. "I'm glad you've brushed Woody nicely."

Charlie showed her the two goldfish in plastic bags he'd won. "Just what we need," muttered Robert. "I had a better win," he said, holding out two coconuts. "We did avoid the candyfloss, just. If you take over I'll join the lads in the pub. We're having a friendly competition with the guys from Great Fordham later. They've got quite a crack darts team now."

"Okay, hang on a minute, though," Maggie said as Major Gibson's voice calling dog owners to the ring boomed over the loudspeaker. They both looked on proudly as Charlie, the only child and smallest handler, walked slowly past the Major's wife, a well-regarded dog trainer who was judging them. Fifteen dogs of various sizes were pushed and pulled by their owners, with Charlie managing to avoid a few skirmishes as they finally lined up. A very sleek red setter was given first prize. A Labrador and cocker spaniel were then placed second and third. Charlie, crestfallen and trying hard not to cry, perked up when Woody was announced runner-up and the Major's wife pinned a smart rosette on his collar.

Edna, who had stopped supervising events in order to see Woody in the parade, was annoyed by the result, convinced that Woody deserved second place at least. Crossly, she returned to chivvying the stall holders and checking that they all had adequate cash in their floats. She and Dawn would enjoy totting up the takings when it was all over. Judging by the throng of people on the green they would do very nicely this year.

No-one was quite sure how it happened. Angela suspected the young lad with the carrots, but couldn't be sure. She recalled hearing a very loud squeal from the piglet, which appeared to spook the donkeys, before she was almost knocked to the ground by Crumble. Luckily Angela's husband, Tom, and James had joined her and just managed to hang onto the two agitated donkeys and stop them stampeding as the piglet hurtled out of its pen and careered into the crowd. Annie and Ethel, manning their bric-a-brac stall, watched in horror as the squealing piglet raced towards them. It managed to avoid their stall but caught the drapes of the vicar's wife's plant stall and sent it flying. Now the screams became human as it took a short cut through the tea tent. Catching its tiny trotters in a guy rope, the piglet caused the tent to slope precariously to one side, before collapsing finally, burying the table laden with cakes and their hungry customers in its folds.

Robert, standing in the garden of the Dog and Duck, choked on his beer at the sight of the piglet streaming from the collapsing marquee at speed and heading towards the main road. He chucked his glass onto the grass verge and called to the other members of the darts team to give chase, hoping to direct it towards the playground.

Edna, tutting at what she thought were the squeals of overexcited children, carried on delivering loose change to her stall holders and walked straight into the path of the fleeing piglet. As soon as she saw it she braced herself, lunged at the last second to catch the animal and fell sprawled in the only muddy bit of field, bumping her head on a hard stone in the process. Stunned, unable to move, she was vaguely aware of a crowd gathering around her.

Maggie, running to help rescue the cakes in the tea tent with Charlie, witnessed her fall and rushed over, issuing instructions to Elizabeth to call the St John's team. Edna, in considerable pain, swore and cursed, urging Maggie to pick up the loose change scattered around. Charlie and Woody were both alarmed by the sight of Edna on the ground. Charlie started crying and, hanging onto Maggie tightly, he whispered, "Is Edna going to die?"

Edna, despite her pain, managed a retort.

"No, I am bloody well not going to die. You help your mother pick up all them pennies."

Woody stopped whining, reassured by her voice. Charlie, eager to please, gathered up the scattered coins.

"Don't you miss any. Not one, d'you hear?" she said, wincing with pain. "Good lad."

Maggie urged her to stay still, anxiously waiting for more help.

"Don't let them see my undies," Edna muttered to Maggie, aware of the growing crowd of curious onlookers.

"I'm sure you've nothing they haven't seen before, Edna. Please, you must stay still. The St John Ambulance is on its way. What a good thing you asked them to attend our fete. I'm sorry we're calling them for you!"

The crowd moved aside as Major Gibson pushed through breathing heavily. He leant to grab Edna's hand. "My sincere apologies, Mrs Newbold," he boomed. "Dreadful mistake. We've caught him, the little varmint. He's gone straight back to the farm."

"I hope you roast the little bugger," she said, her face a twisted smile.

The gathering crowd waved and cheered as the ambulance approached, light flashing and siren sounding, much to Charlie's delight. Protesting and in obvious pain, Edna was put gently on a stretcher and driven away.

Maggie, now in possession of the "float" and copious lists of instructions Edna had insisted she take, was not quite sure where to start. The Major made a reassuring announcement on the loudspeaker as order was restored but not before several onlookers expressed disappointment that they were not going to have a pig to take home. That competition, he announced firmly, was cancelled. Dawn and Elizabeth rearranged the tea tables and scooped up as many undamaged cakes as possible while the town band restored a little gaiety into the subdued crowd pounding out "When the Saints Go Marching In".

Charlie, awarded a few pennies on Edna's instruction, went with Maggie to Annie and Ethel's bric-a-brac stall and chose some marbles and a jigsaw while Maggie reassured them both about Edna's accident.

"Nearly gave me a heart attack," said Annie, "and Ethel wet her knickers!"

"There's no need to broadcast it," said Ethel as Maggie, laughing, gave them both a hug.

By late afternoon the crowds thinned as people dispersed and made their way home. Edna had organised a team from the village to clear any rubbish up, much to Maggie's relief, and each stall holder tidied their own patch. The darts team were instructed to dismantle the tea tent and were taking chairs and tables back to the village hall as Maggie, aided by Charlie and James, walked the donkeys back to their stable.

It was dusk and Maggie was clearing the table after a light supper when the phone rang.

"That was the ward sister. We'll know more tomorrow. She might have a fracture," Maggie said, replacing the receiver and rejoining them at the table. "She's being transferred for X-rays. I expect she'll be in the hospital for a while and of course she'll hate that."

"I would think she'd be a difficult patient," said Elizabeth.

"More than difficult, Mum," Maggie said, gathering up the dinner plates. "You can get down, Charlie. Daddy'll help you finish your jigsaw."

"Good idea," said Robert, leaving the two women to gossip as he and Charlie went back to the sitting room.

"Thank goodness Angela's alright, though. She was so nearly pulled over. I'd not forgive myself if anything had happened," Maggie said, making up a fresh pot of coffee. "I'm so relieved Tom and James were with her."

"Yes. That could have been very worrying," Elizabeth said. "By the way, will the village shop have to close?"

"No. You've met Jennifer, her niece. She'll keep it open. She's very capable and I expect Dawn will probably help her."

"That's a blessing anyway," she said.

Suddenly there was a loud shriek from the sitting room and Charlie reappeared, tearfully dangling a plastic bag and the squashed remains of a goldfish. "Daddy stood on my fish and broke its leg."

"Oh, my goodness! Fin not leg, I think you mean, darling. Poor fish," said Maggie as Robert poked his head round the door.

"I didn't see it," he muttered, trying to look contrite.

"I thought you'd put them in the bowl?"

"Sorry, we meant to. 'Fraid the carpet's a bit damp. Hope you don't mind but I said I'd join the team in the pub to celebrate our win today."

"Daddy's sorry, darling. It was an accident," said Maggie, pulling a face at Robert. "That's all I need," she said, as Elizabeth grabbed a dry cloth to mop up the carpet. "Where's the other one?"

"In its bag on the coffee table. Can you deal with it? I'm really sorry, Charlie," Robert said, hugging him. "Mummy'll put the fish in with the other two now."

"Goodbye," Maggie called out crossly as the front door shut. "Come on, Charlie, let's put it in with Ebb and Flo for company. It's way past your bedtime."

"I'll take you up while Mummy puts all the animals to bed," said Elizabeth. "We've got a story to finish, haven't we?"

Charlie reacted by crying and running into the sitting room and slamming the door shut.

"My goodness, I've never seen him do that before."

"He's very tired, Mum. He's been worried by Edna's accident even though he got some extra pocket money. He didn't get a red rosette for Woody either and Rob hasn't helped by standing on the fish!"

"Oh dear, now what? He sounds so upset." The child's sobbing got louder as Maggie left her mother to finish washing up.

"I'll handle it, Mum. D'you mind shutting up the chickens and all the others? I'll sort the donkeys out later."

Maggie was hoarse by the time she'd finally settled Charlie. She'd allowed him to play in the bath till his skin got wrinkly before cuddling up next to him to read a Richard Scarry book he loved. As soon as his eyes closed she crept back downstairs.

She flopped exhausted onto the settee as Elizabeth handed her a large gin and tonic. "I think you need this. Frank's coming round in a minute if that's okay. He'll not stay long."

"Poor little chap. It's been quite a day, hasn't it? All a bit too much. I feel absolutely shattered. How about you? You've been such a help, Mum. Thanks."

"It's certainly been a long day. Charlie had too many sweets and ice creams, d'you think?" Elizabeth said, as they clinked glasses. "Cheers. Let's wish Edna a speedy recovery. By the way, you should change the water in the fish bowl. It's green. They seem happy together but unfortunately I do have some bad news."

"Bad news?"

"Yes, darling. That old hen, Doris. I found her dead on the floor beside the nest box."

"Oh, no!" Maggie suddenly cried out. "Not Doris. Where is she?"

"I put her in the peg basket by the back door and now Woody's taken her out and won't let me near her. He's put her in his bed."

Robert tottered and tripped down the lane, having celebrated the victory with the darts team. He could see clearly by the light of the full moon as he stopped to pat the donkeys by the field gate, vaguely wondering why they were still in their fete attire. Frank Sutton's car was parked on his drive and he heard Tom's laugh as he made his way to the cottage door and put his hand on the latch, surprised to find a party going on. Woody welcomed him back eagerly as loud voices greeted him from the sitting room.

"Ah, there you are, Robert," said Frank, holding out a tankard. "These two are ahead of us. One too many, if you ask me."

"Sorry, Rob," Maggie giggled, swaying as she stood up to greet him. She raised her glass. "I've just buried the fish you squashed," she hiccupped, hanging tightly to his sleeve before suddenly bursting into tears. "And, darling, here's to the best hen that ever lived. Poor little Doris has just died."

Chapter Seventeen

Little boy lost

Maggie was grateful that her mother had decided to stay for an extra two weeks. September was nearly upon them bringing with it the annual baby boom. The result of past Christmas parties and New Year revelry created a lot of extra daily visits and an increase in home birth requests. Maggie had managed to get two extra days off, which enabled her to visit Edna in hospital, but Edna had discharged herself and was coming home. Elizabeth, settled into a relaxed granny role, was proving invaluable giving Charlie the extra attention he needed following the unexpected death of Doris, the elderly hen.

"My goodness. She's the most difficult patient I've had to manage for many a year," muttered the ward sister to Maggie when she arrived to collect Edna.

Back in her own home Edna coped with extra help from Dawn and her niece, Jennifer, who had loved being left in sole charge of the village shop and was rather sorry to have Edna back. Edna turned the district nurses away, petulant about "being fussed over", and only allowed the doctor to call. She had fractured her left wrist and ankle and was encased in plaster, but she'd avoided more serious damage to her hip. Luckily she was still able to use her right hand.

The fete had proved a big success, despite the dramatic departure of the Major's piglet and Edna's accident. They'd counted the takings and found they'd doubled the amount made in previous years. Dawn told Maggie that you could almost believe from the look on her face that Edna thought it was worth it, piglet, accident and all. The town band and majorettes had been a big draw, keeping half their takings for the local hospital, but the fete and stalls, teas and donkeys had made a handsome profit in their own right. The village playground would be enhanced with a roundabout and see-saw once the fete fund had been added to the money local families had raised on the village recreation committee. The Major was so delighted with the result that, despite her accident, he assured Edna she would be in full charge every year and Edna told him she expected that anyway.

In Nut Tree Cottage Charlie's reaction to the death of Doris, the elderly chicken, upset them all. He cried at the drop of a hat and hardly touched his food. He kept asking if Maggie and Robert were going to die too, if everyone was going to die. He wanted to be with Woody all the time, checking his breathing and checking on all the animals far too frequently. He seemed frightened to go to sleep in case he didn't wake up again. Maggie and Robert were relieved when Elizabeth agreed to stay on as they were getting concerned. Charlie, such a bright, happy and energetic little boy, had never reacted like this before. His attachment and fondness for animals matched Maggie's own and this had been his first real encounter with death. The fish had not concerned him quite as much as Doris, who was more personal. The family decided it might help if Doris had a special ceremony and could be buried with Charlie Watt. The vicar was consulted and decided to overlook the problem of disturbing consecrated ground and even said he would allow a small plaque to be placed by Charlie Watt's gravestone. The chicken's funeral was conducted with great solemnity, though Frank Sutton excused himself. Maggie shed a few tears and helped Charlie read a poem that she'd written for the occasion. Woody sensed something was amiss and whined continuously. Even Danny the duck appeared to mourn the absence of his surrogate mother, pottering around the garden as if seeking her out. The brief ceremony over, the family returned to the cottage, where Frank joined them to indulge in some of Elizabeth's special cakes, their solemn procession watched by the donkeys, whose forlorn looks lent sadness to the occasion.

Maggie was surprised that it hadn't seemed ridiculous, that it was more than playing a part for Charlie's sake somehow. She and Robert felt it had been the right thing to do. They didn't want him growing up terrified of life and death. She restrained herself from hitting Frank, who repeated once too often "She was only an old hen". It had been a strange day and Maggie found herself thinking back to the time she'd spent with Charlie Watt, surprised at how often she still thought about him and the companionship they'd once shared. He would have appreciated the concern for Doris and her fitting end.

When it came to Charlie's bedtime Robert and Maggie stayed with him. It was a clear night and Robert pointed at the stars from his bedroom window.

"Look, Daddy. Look, Mummy, look. I can see G'andad's star," Charlie was standing on tiptoe and pointing at a lone star when a shooting star whizzed across the sky. "Look at that big one; it's got sparklers."

Maggie blinked away a tear. It was perfect. It helped to bolster the story she had often told him of G'andad in the sky.

"I keep saying we never saw anything like this when we lived in London. Too much light pollution," Robert murmured.

Maggie nodded, stroking his hand.

"Doris is up there too. She's back with G'andad in the sky. Perhaps she's sitting on his lap again," Maggie said, hugging Charlie tightly. The image seemed to satisfy him as he snuggled up to her before climbing into his bed.

Elizabeth popped her head round the door. "Shall I tell you a special story, Charlie? The one I promised you yesterday?"

More settled, he nodded sleepily as Elizabeth took over, giving Charlie a story out of her head and drawing him close to her. "How about the worm that wanted to be a shoelace?"

As Maggie and Robert stood outside the door, listening, Charlie giggled. Maggie remembered the story being told to her by her mother, remembered how it always sent her straight off to sleep. She felt blessed as they went downstairs as quietly as they could.

"What a day," Maggie said, wrapping her arms round Robert when they too were in bed. Elizabeth had wanted an early night while Robert and Maggie stayed up to watch the late news. "Charlie was brave, wasn't he?"

"One of my reasons for not wanting to get so attached to all these animals: it's so traumatic when they have to be put down, or die," Robert murmured.

"I thought you'd say that. At least we can let them go knowing they've been loved. I know Frank and other people think we've been quite silly but it really helped Charlie."

Robert turned to her. "I can't win, can I?" he said, holding her closely and whispering. "Well, wife, let me put it this way, I'm more than happy to have more children 'cos we wouldn't have them put down. You know I quite fancy having another baby. That would help Charlie too, wouldn't it? A little brother or sister to love rather than a mangy old chicken?"

Maggie made no attempt to answer as she found herself tearful, engulfed by emotion and a longing to make love. Robert, encouraged by Maggie's closeness and warm response, murmured, "You see, darling, I watched our little lad today and decided then and there that I wanted more little Charlies."

"Oh, Rob." Maggie felt more tears welling up at the memory of miscarrying so many babies. "But I mess things up, don't I? I can't hold onto these little Charlies."

"You can and you did. It's a risk we take together," Robert said, wiping her tears away. "Come here. I have you and that's all I want at the moment."

Chapter Eighteen

Making babies

"Frank and I will pick Eleanor up from the station as she's arriving late this afternoon and you'll be in the clinic."

"Thanks, Mum. It'll be great to see her; it's been an age," Maggie said, delighted that her sister had at last decided to stay with them for a weekend.

"It seems a while since I had them to stay with me too. We'll have lots to catch up on. Pity Martin had too much on this weekend," Elizabeth said.

"I'm sure we can have a girly gossip tomorrow morning if we go into Waldersby. Rob will take Charlie and Woody out."

"Oh good; he'll like going out with Robert on his own. I'd like to get you two girls on your own too," Elizabeth said, "just the three of us, like old times."

"Ah, hah, that's interesting."

"Don't be silly, Maggie. It'll do us good to have a chat."

"Okay. You know Eleanor and I have been dying for you to tell us what's what with you and Frank."

"Yes, well. Let's wait till we're on our own and I'll tell you what's what, as you put it, then."

"You do know Frank's taking me to the Arts Theatre in Cambridge tomorrow night? He arranged it before we knew Eleanor was coming. He's booked a table for dinner so we might be back quite late."

"You deserve a night out. Rob and I are so grateful for your help, Mum," Maggie said, giving Elizabeth a hug. "Eleanor and I need a chance to really catch up too."

"I thought you were on call?"

"Tonight, not tomorrow."

Maggie was finishing the clinic when the call came. Ethel Jones was with Alice Peters and looking after the toddler, Bobby. She had rung to say she was worried about Alice and thought she might be about to have the baby.

Maggie was surprised she'd contacted the clinic as Alice had insisted that when the time came she would go straight into hospital, but when she checked her notes she realised that Alice wasn't due for another two weeks.

"Has she rung the hospital labour ward, Ethel? Baby's coming a bit early if she's in labour."

"No. She won't. She wants to see you first."

"Oh, okay. I'd better pop in and see her. Are you happy to stay there?"

"Yes. Bobby's having his tea."

Quickly rearranging a postnatal visit she'd booked in earlier, Maggie reassured Ethel that she was on her way.

Arriving at the end of the lane she saw another car parked outside the house and was relieved to see the toddler being carried out by a young man in soldier's uniform, Bobby's father.

Ethel stood at the door waiting for Maggie, waving to Bobby as the car drove off.

"Am I glad to see you? His dad didn't want to stay as you were coming. She's in the sitting room, leaking."

"D'you mean her waters might have gone?"

"I think so. Looks that way and she's getting them pains."

Maggie hurried through to the sitting room to find Alice bent over the settee, tears streaking her face.

"I don't know what to do," she sniffed, wiping her face with the corner of her blouse. "Bobby was playing up a bit this afternoon. I caught him running out the front door and grabbed him and that's when it happened."

"You mean the pains started or the waters went?"

"Both. It started to trickle down my legs and then I got these pains."

Ethel hovered in the doorway. "Like a cup of tea, Maggie?"

"Thank you, Ethel. That would be lovely."

Maggie's quick examination surprised her. Alice was definitely in labour and her contractions were getting stronger.

"Alice, we'll call an ambulance and get you into hospital. You'll be having this baby before long and I know you don't want to be at home."

"I'm not leaving here."

Maggie half expected this reaction. "But you'll be happier in hospital, love and—"

"I'm staying here with you and Ethel," she said, crying as she clutched her stomach. "I don't like these," she broke off, her voice reaching a shrill pitch. "Can you give me something? I don't like it."

Ethel hurried in, setting two mugs down. "There there, lovey. Don't you get upset. Our midwife's here and I've put a hot water bottle in the carry cot all ready."

Maggie smiled. "Thank you, Ethel. We should be in hospital but I'll rearrange things. Alice doesn't want to leave now."

"I reckon she's better off here with you," Ethel said. "My hubby's getting his own supper so I'm here too. I've got towels warming and covered up the bed."

"Wonderful, thank you. Could you find a plastic sheet? She's in a bit of a puddle."

"I'll use the plastic cover off the kitchen table. The kiddy's crayoned all over it, just needs a quick wipe over. Make do and mend," she said cheerfully.

Maggie was relieved on ringing the clinic to find her colleague Susan still there. She was happy to join her and informed her that Doctor Southgate was delighted Alice was having the baby at home and would get there as soon as the baby was born, if not before as it was a little premature.

"Shall I phone your mother, Alice?"

"Yeah, but she probably won't come. My sister'll come if Bobby settles early," she said, grabbing at Maggie and letting out a high-pitched scream.

In no time Alice was hanging onto the gas, getting more and more giggly.

Maggie was thankful that she had asked Ethel to keep an eye on Alice. It was obvious that the two got on well. Ethel was unfazed by the drama going on around her, clucking like a broody hen, stopping to reassure Alice and supplying cool flannels and water and patting her reassuringly until Susan arrived.

"You don't know how happy it's made me looking after Alice," she confided, during a brief lull. "It's like having a daughter."

"I'm so glad, Ethel. Does your husband mind?"

"'Course not. He's happy playing with his bees and says looking after this young girl is keeping me out of his hair!"

"I'm sure he doesn't mean it."

"'Course he doesn't and you mark my words: he'll be one of the first wanting a cuddle."

Three hours later Maggie was back home tucking into a supper of cottage pie, one of her favourites, and describing the evening events to her sister, Eleanor, who was hanging onto her every word.

"What I really love is that she's called the baby Honey."

"Honey? That's different."

"Well, Ethel's husband keeps bees and he kept saying 'It's a little honey' when he saw the baby, so it sort of stuck."

"Literally." They both chuckled.

"It was quick but a perfect birth. Honey only weighed six pounds but she'll soon put on weight and Alice wants to feed her herself."

"Did you think she wouldn't, then?"

"She'd said she was going to bottle-feed. I don't pressurise them but the odd thing was her mother turned up after all and said she'd stay for a few days and told Alice that she'd fed all of them and it was easy."

"That was a nice one. Tell me some more. Mum says you had one baby born feet first. Is that what you call a breech baby?"

"Another time. I'm going to have a bath and go to bed. I'm still on call. You and Robert can have a good natter as Mum won't be back for another hour at least. There's some wine open. It'll be good tomorrow, just the three of us. Thanks for reading to Charlie, by the way."

"Loved it. He calls me Eminor. We had great fun before Mum had to go out."

"Did Mum tell you how he'd been a bit unsettled?"

"Yes. I'm sorry I've seen so little of you all lately. I seem to have missed out on Charlie's growing up and I can't believe he's starting primary school."

"Me neither. I find it hard to think of my baby as a schoolboy." Maggie felt herself welling up. "Don't make me cry, now; it's only 'cos I'm tired."

"How time flies," said Eleanor, "and we're getting old."

"Well, you'd better hurry up and start a family before

you're an ancient," Maggie said. "Here, I need a hug and then I'm off to bed. Rob's poured you a drink. Oh dear, it looks as if he's nodding off too."

"That's okay, I'll read my book."

Chapter Nineteen

Moving on

Elizabeth looked at her two daughters, deep in conversation, as they had been for most of the morning and felt overwhelmed with sadness. If only her husband had lived long enough to enjoy the pride she now felt in their children. One a successful midwife and mother and the other fast following, wanting her own family, while happily engaged in a teaching career. The two sisters had been quite inseparable when little and although they had not seen each other for some months the bond seemed as close as ever as they chatted non-stop over coffee and sandwiches in the little Waldersby cafe. Her own sandwich remained untouched and her stomach was fluttering with nerves. She hated to interrupt them but needed to get it over with before she changed her mind again. She had not found it easy to come to this decision and was pretty sure neither of her girls would find it easy to accept what she intended to do.

"Okay, you two, if I can get a word in—" She had their immediate attention, their eyes on hers, but her throat felt dry and she was having trouble carrying on. Maggie and Eleanor remained silent, glued now to every word their mother was uttering.

"Frank and I are very fond of each other, as I'm sure you know." Her daughters both rolled their eyes like ten-year-olds, putting her off her stride for a moment. "What I'm saying is that it seems only sensible for me to move down here and be nearer to you all, and my grandchild." She stopped and sipped her coffee, giving them time to respond, but they stayed silent, waiting for her to carry on, unsure of what she was about to tell them. "I know you won't feel happy about it but I'm going to sell our home in Kendal." The expression on both their faces changed and a lump came to her throat as she looked away from them, out of the window to the market square.

"I've got loads of friends up there and so have you, Mum," Eleanor said quietly.

"We grew up there. You said you'd find it hard to leave Daddy. His grave, I mean," Maggie said quietly.

"I know," she said. "But I'm going to buy a little place in Waldersby."

"I don't understand. You're not going to live with Frank?"

"No, I'm not. We're both set in our ways. I've had time to become independent since your dad."

"Is this a permanent thing?" interrupted Eleanor.

"Frank wants me to move in with him, but I think we just need to be able to see each other more easily, for now at least. Like I said before, we can decide if we wish to live together later on."

Now it was out in the open she knew she'd made the right decision; it felt like a weight had been lifted from her and once her girls had reconciled themselves to saying goodbye to the family home and its memories she suspected they'd be relieved she wasn't going to move in with Frank for the time being. She knew they weren't as keen on him as she was; he was no replacement for their father. Elizabeth took a large bite from the sandwich on her plate. She was hungry, after all.

"You could move in with us," Maggie blurted out.

"I'll certainly not do that, darling. That wouldn't be fair on Robert. I've thought this through and seen a very nice two-bed cottage on the outskirts of the town. If you two agree, I can put our house on the market and could move down here early fairly soon. They're keen to sell."

"It's your life, Mum. You must do what's best for you," Maggie said.

"I agree," said Eleanor. "It'll be sad to say goodbye to our home but if it happens we'll both be thankful that we won't have to worry about you so far away, and all alone."

"Thank you both. It's such a relief to get that off my chest. I know you're not that fond of Frank but he's very kind to me and I think we can grow old quite disgracefully together," she chuckled.

"That's a bit naughty," Eleanor said, screwing up her face in mock disgust.

"We love you," said Maggie, getting to her feet with Eleanor and hugging her. "You don't have to worry about us. Our lives are sorted out and we just want you to be happy, not lonely in Kendal. Daddy would want that too, wouldn't he? We can still visit and see to his grave, and meet up with old friends."

"Yes, and we'll come round to Frank in the end," said Eleanor with a laugh, picking up her coat. "I don't know about you two but I think this calls for a few gin and tonics in the Dog and Duck later."

"I'll arrange it," said Maggie. "I'll get Robert to book a table."

"I'm so relieved," said Elizabeth. "I was dreading telling you about selling the house."

"Mum, don't be silly; we just want whatever's best for you. Now, come on, we've shopping to do and I want to explore that new boutique," said Maggie, getting up and moving to the counter to settle the bill. "Later on, we can take you to Marks and Sparks in Cambridge, your favourite haunt!"

"Perhaps, if there's time before I go back, we can see the cottage you mentioned?" Eleanor queried. "No time like the present."

"Good idea," Elizabeth said, stretching out her arms. "Let's have another hug."

The woods that skirted the village were dark and dreary, rain dripping through the trees from a sullen sky. Woody kept close, seeming to sense Maggie's mood since her mother and sister had left. She was missing them both so much, reflecting on their time together, just the three of them. Giggling like naughty schoolgirls they had spent far too much time shopping in Cambridge, buying almost a complete wardrobe for the cruise that Elizabeth and Frank were planning. The love they felt for each other had cocooned the sisters throughout their childhood and comforted them after the sudden death of their father. It would never alter; having a sister to love and share with had always been a vitally important part of Maggie's life and always would be. And maybe her own son deserved the same; maybe it was important to consider the joy a brother or sister would bring to him. Tearful, she stopped by a fallen tree and hugged Woody as the memories of babies she had lost flooded back. Sadly, making babies was not her problem; losing them was.

They stopped at the village shop on her way back to buy a few treats for Charlie. He had been reluctant to go to playgroup but she was relieved to see him chatting with his friends before she left. The death of Doris had been a full-blown tragedy for him, and one that had taken him a while to get over. His recovery had been helped by Woody, who had been allowed to sleep in a bed in his room. Robert was not in favour but with the promise that it would only be for a few nights he'd given in. Maggie did not tell him that the little dog had crept out of his bed and onto Charlie's bed, a habit that might prove difficult to stop now started. Woody had lost no time after all in learning to jump onto their bed every morning, despite Roberts protestations.

Edna seemed to be recovering well from her injuries after her collision with the Major's piglet at the village fete. It would be some weeks before she was back in charge, but she was not one to dwell on her own problems, keener instead to keep an eye on her niece, Jennifer, and her running of the shop. She still fussed over Woody and Maggie was grateful when she insisted on him being left with her and Jennifer if she was unable to get home or Robert was away. Maggie always found herself armed with more treats for the dog than for Charlie whenever Edna had had him.

It was warm and sunny as she walked across the green, keeping Woody on a tight leash after collecting him one lunchtime. Several of the ducks he loved to chase were waddling around the edge of the pond, squabbling over bits of bread. Maggie was delighted to see Annie and Ethel sitting together on a bench by the pond.

"Hello, ladies. How's your little dog, Sammy?" she asked, turning to Ethel as she joined them. "Can I sit here for a moment before I collect my little boy?"

"'Course you can, dear. Sammy's fine. Glad you told me to see the vet the other day. He thinks it's just old age and his bladder's a bit weak."

"He has my sympathies," said Annie. "Give me a cup of tea and I'm leaking like a sieve." Maggie laughed; she was used to the old ladies' banter now. "Sammy doesn't drink tea, though, does he, Ethel?"

"'Course not, but little puddles everywhere is a bit of a nuisance. He's got some tablets I mix with his food in the morning and I must say he's piddling less."

"That's good. How's your cat, Socks, Annie?"

"Old. Sleeps all the time now, cosy on top of the boiler. We're all getting to that stage now, aren't we, Ethel?"

"You're as old as you feel, they say. Some days I feel pretty ancient," Ethel said. "Mind you, our little Honey keeps me going."

"That was my next question, Ethel. How's Alice getting on? I know Brenda, the health visitor, has called a few times, hasn't she, and she tells me Honey's putting on weight."

"So she says."

"She really couldn't take to feeding her herself, but she tried, bless her. Honey seems to be taking to the bottle well now."

"I don't think her sister should bring Bobby back, do you?"

"No. I hope they're not suggesting it?"

"He's back already. Her mother's stopped coming and her sister collected him last night. It's asking too much of her, I think. He's up to all sorts."

"Really? That's a shame. She needs more time but I know she liked the extra pocket money. Perhaps Brenda could have a word with them."

"It'd be better coming from you."

"I don't think I should interfere," Maggie said.

"You could make a neighbourly call. She'd like that. Stop by when you're walking the dog? She's let me feed him a couple of times and my George might be in his nineties but he can still hold a baby nice and tight."

Maggie patted her hand. "Am I glad she lives next to you Ethel! You've been such a help, especially at the birth – you were marvellous. By the way –" Maggie got up to leave "– Have you both seen Edna?"

"Yes. We just bought some cards at the shop; she's looking well, isn't she?" Ethel said.

"Still a bit sharp," said Annie, tossing some more bread to two ducks that were eyeing them from a distance, wary of the dog. "Ordering her niece around when she was supposed to have put her in charge."

"Leopards don't change their spots," said Ethel, "and Edna's never going to change. It'll take more than a few broken bones to shut her up."

"I'm very glad you two didn't get hurt or lose your stall at the fete. That little pig caused chaos, didn't he?" said Maggie, changing the subject.

"What a laugh that was," said Annie. "Not for Edna, mind."

Maggie got up to go. Woody, eager to get at the ducks, was straining the lead. "We'd better be off," she said, pulling him back. "Lovely to see you both and I'll see you in a few days' time, possibly, Ethel?"

"Good girl. You stop by, like I said."

Chapter Twenty

Lollipops to the Rescue

Her pulse began to race and her chest grew tight at the sound issuing from the direction of Alice Peters's house when Maggie paid the promised visit a few days later, while walking Woody. There was nothing more distressing than the sound of a child in pain, she thought, as she hurried past the gravel pit and down the lane towards Ethel's husband, George, who was gesturing for her to come as quickly as she could.

Once inside Alice's kitchen it took Maggie a moment or two to work out what was wrong over the sound of baby Honey's crying, Ethel's loud attempts to comfort her and

Alice's efforts to get Bobby, yelling at the top of his lungs while frantically clawing at his arm,

to stay still for a minute.

"Bee sting," George said, leaning in and pointing at the sting protruding from Bobby's arm.

"Let's have a little look, shall we, Bobby?" Maggie said in the voice she used for panicky mums. The boy stopped jumping around and looked at her with big tearful eyes. It would be like taking a thorn from a lion's paw, she thought.

"Good, that's got it," George said, watching Maggie expertly scrape the sting away. "Bobby, let Maggie wash your arm, now. The naughty bee's gone," he said tenderly. "Uncle George had a sting this morning but its better now, lovey," he said, gently stroking the little boy's head.

Maggie bathed Bobby's arm quickly with soapy water and, noting how rapidly the little arm was swelling, asked Alice to search in the fridge for ice cubes.

"Will this do?"

Maggie laughed. "Thanks, Alice, just the ticket," she said, wrapping an ice lolly in a tissue. "Let Alice put the lolly on your arm, Bobby; it'll stop the 'hurty'."

George was still visibly upset. "Must have brought it in with me," he said. "I was sorting out the hives this morning."

"Don't be daft," said Ethel, passing Honey, who was now happily sucking her tiny thumb, back to Alice. She patted George's hand. "You weren't to know a bee would follow you, love."

Bobby's sobs subsided when Alice gave him another ice lolly to suck. Maggie agreed to stay for a while as George and Ethel were leaving to catch the bus to Waldersby. They never missed market day, George told her with a sheepish grin.

"I've got some baking powder and can make a paste and put that on it like my mother used to do if it doesn't go down," said Ethel as they left.

"Well, glad I decided to take my dog a walk, Alice," Maggie said, lifting Bobby onto her lap and holding the remains of the ice lolly pack in place. "I'll wait till this swelling subsides a bit. No official visits anymore but it's good to see you. I bet it gave you a nasty fright, didn't it?"

"To be honest, it scared me stiff," Alice said, putting the baby down. "I'll do her a feed in a minute. Fancy a cuppa?"

"Yes, thanks, half a mug. Tell me how you're getting on. I didn't realise that you would have to look after Bobby so soon."

"My sister couldn't get anyone else and Bobby played up at nursery so I said I'd have him. He's alright if we walk or go to the park and that keeps Honey quiet too."

"George and Ethel think the world of you, you know. It's so nice for them to have you next door."

"Yeah, they come every day for a cuddle. They're just like my real nan and gramps, only they live in south London – too far away to just pop in."

Maggie wiped Bobby's face as he scrambled to get down again, distracted by his train set. The inflammation and swelling were subsiding. Just a raspberry redness lingered from the lolly.

"At least he's not had too bad a reaction to the bee sting. That's a relief as you're so near the hives. It could have been worse, so we'll not be needing Ethel's paste."

"I'd a friend at school that had to inject herself if she got stung. By the way, d'you know anything about the buses here? How I can get to the clinic?" Alice asked. "The health visitor isn't visiting for a couple of weeks and I need to get Honey weighed."

Maggie told her about the regular bus service that stopped on the green.

"I'm sure they'll pick you up at the end of the lane if you ask. The drivers are usually helpful if they see you with a baby and they always stop for George and Ethel."

"That's good," said Alice, handing her a half mug of tea. "Ethel said she'd help me. Sugar? Biscuit?"

"No, no thanks, trying to lose weight," Maggie said, patting her stomach. "I expect Brenda wants you to join the group of new mums at the clinic, make some more friends with babies the same age."

"I might. It's a bit difficult with this little one running about," said Alice as Bobby launched himself across the room at her.

Maggie blew Bobby a kiss as she untied Woody and made her way back up the lane, much to the dog's disappointment. It was a favourite walk for them both, leading past the houses to the woods, despite Woody's previous capture and the awful state he was in when they found him in the gravel pit. Robert could take him out again later, she thought, hurrying now as Charlie would be on his way home. Carpets of violets fringed the lane and among the tangled, straggling clumps of bushes ripening blackberries clustered like jewels waiting to be gathered. She made a note to come back and pick them and some of the wild strawberries she could see on a grassy bank in the pit, before too many other people had the same idea. The village and lanes attracted hordes of visitors every autumn. Robert had collected many recipes from old Charlie Watt that would later guide the transformation of elderflowers and their berries, not to mention the sloes for gin. She quickly gathered some sprigs of wild honeysuckle and violets to make a posy, breathing in the scent as she watched some blue tits playing chase, reflecting on the changing seasons. She loved each one, but there was something magical about early autumn, the glint of gold and beauty of leaves changing colour, and the harvest waiting to be gathered in.

Maggie could see the workmen, backs bent over, absorbed in finishing various odd jobs, painting and plastering, as she passed Watt's Cottage. Angela, Tom and the children were in Cornwall and wouldn't be back for a few days. She stopped to talk to Crumble and Biscuit, who were standing by the gate. Woody was quite at ease with them now and licked their noses through the bars. Not content with that, they raised their heads for Maggie to scratch behind their ears. Both had been given a thorough check-up by the Trevor the vet on a recent visit and Maggie was delighted when he praised the condition they were in, even suggesting they should enter a show. Not an idea Maggie fancied after the amount of preparation she had been involved in for the village fete. The sound of a car coming down the lane cut short her thoughts. Charlie was in the back, shouting at her and waving excitedly as they drove past, on their way to the cottage. Maggie hurried after them, eager to greet the mother who had invited Charlie to play with her son, Alex, and was now bringing them back for tea. She raced Woody home and by the time she got there Charlie was already showing his new friend the animals, starting with the goldfish. Maggie left him to it, inviting Alex's mother, Harriet, to join her in the sitting room while keeping a watchful eye on the boys. The family had recently moved to Great Fordham from Scotland and Maggie guessed she must be at the "getting to know everyone" stage.

"Make sure no-one escapes, especially the donkeys, darling. Just let Alex talk to Biscuit and Crumble through the gate. I'll be calling you in for your tea in a minute," she called out, seeing the two boys wanted to run back up the lane. "Woody stay," she added firmly.

The water turned muddy brown at bath time that evening, while Charlie described the tumbles he'd taken racing round with Alex. They'd had fun together and Maggie finished off his bath and bedtime with his favourite stories, struggling not to yawn herself. She read until he fell asleep and she could finally creep downstairs to Robert.

"What a day," Robert said when she flopped down onto the settee next to him. "I've been chasing reps, chasing customers. What about you?" Maggie told him about Charlie's new friend and then described her call on

Alice and Bobby's bee sting and how grateful she felt to the old couple now caring so much for Alice and baby Honey.

"She's finding it tough with such an active little boy and her mother isn't helping much now, so Ethel and George have been a godsend."

Robert perked up more when Maggie mentioned the rich pickings they could have from the gravel pit later in the year. "I'm really looking forward to a good crop of sloes and my elderflower cordial wasn't bad last year, was it?"

"You make the booze and I'll make the jam. Mind you, we've still got several jars and bottles left from last year. D'you think we'll ever finish Charlie Watt's carrot whisky?" Maggie asked, topping their glasses up. "We must keep it in memory of our dear friend; we'll never drink it. Well, I certainly won't," she said.

"It would probably blow your head off now, darling."

"You could be right." She laughed, tucking her legs under her as she settled into an armchair nearer the fire. "Supper will be another half hour, I'm afraid. I'll finish telling you about Alex's mother, Harriet. She was telling me that they moved down from Scotland a year ago. She spent five years teaching in a primary school in a village near Glasgow. It was very different up there, I imagine. I'm not sure what her husband does; we'll have to invite them round one evening. By the way, have you heard of test tube babies?"

"Are you asking me or telling me?"

"Both, really. I know there's a lot of research going on in Cambridge and she and her husband are taking part in trials. She's never been able to conceive and Alex was adopted; they are desperate for a baby of their own."

"Well, that's not a problem we have, darling, is it?"

"No, it's certainly not," said Maggie wryly. "It made me realise that others can have a worse time than us and at least Charlie is all ours," she said, getting up. "I'll get the table ready and I also think it would be nice to invite them to supper with Angela and Tom."

"Good idea," said Robert, gulping the last of his wine. "Let's eat. I'm ravenous."

Chapter Twenty-One

Innocent tragedy

"You're not on call, are you?" Robert nudged Maggie sleepily. He was sitting up in bed, holding the phone.

"No, I'm not," she mumbled. "Leave me alone."

"Sorry, darling. Whoever this is sounds pretty upset," he said, nudging her again. "She says she must speak to you." Maggie pulled herself up and peered at the clock. It was half past three in the morning. "Who is it?"

"I don't know. One of your mums, I guess. I can't make her name out 'cos she's crying so much. It doesn't sound good."

Maggie grabbed the phone and could hear the muffled sobs.

"Hello, it's Maggie, who's this?"

"It's baby, Maggie. I think she's gone. Honey's gone." Alice Peters's distraught voice sent shivers down Maggie's spine as she threw the covers back. "How d'you mean, Alice? Where is she? Are you alone?" Maggie urged her to explain as she hurriedly stripped off her nightdress without thinking, reaching for her clothes in the dark. "Where's she gone?"

"Honey's not breathing." She was wailing now. "I think it was Bobby."

Maggie's heart pounded. She was shaking and dressing clumsily in her haste to leave. Why was Bobby with her in the middle of the night when she normally only cared for him in the daytime? She could hear him yelling in the background. What had he done?

Somehow, she must instruct Alice to help her baby, but the girl was too distraught to explain what was going on, or take anything in. On call or not, Maggie realised she had to get to the baby quickly.

"Alice, listen to me," she said, pulling on jeans and grabbing a cardigan. "I'm on my way. Keep baby warm, d'you understand?"

She didn't wait for an answer, instructing Robert to dial 999 and pass on the little they knew, as she fled the house.

"Get hold of Susan too, darling," she shouted as she wrenched open the front door. "She won't mind; she's on call."

Maggie dreaded what she was going to find as she drove as quickly as she could to Alice's house, instructing herself to remain calm when the journey seemed to take twice as long as it normally did. As she parked and jumped out of the car she stopped to take some deep breaths, telling herself that, whatever was in the house, her training equipped her to deal with it. She felt instantly calmer as she jogged up the path, pushed open the door and ran up the stairs towards Bobby's cries.

Scanning the room, she saw the baby. Honey, inert and still, looked like a doll on the bed. Alice was sitting on the floor, clinging onto Bobby, who screamed as she rushed in.

"Take him downstairs, Alice. Give him an ice lolly, anything, I'll see what I can do," she said, opening her nursing bag.

As she picked up the lifeless, ice-cold baby, she pushed away the thought that she was too late, kneeling down on the rug by the bed, placing the baby gently by her, fitting the mask and bag over the baby's nose and mouth, pumping in air, trying mouth-to-nose breathing, blowing small volumes of air from her puffed-out cheeks into the tiny mouth.

There was no response. Frantic, she was about to apply a little pressure to the baby's tiny chest when she heard vehicles stopping outside. Minutes later the ambulance men rushed into the room, followed by Susan, in time to observe Maggie's last desperate effort to revive Honey. She got to her feet and silently passed Honey to one of the ambulance men, who placed her with great tenderness on the bed. Maggie could also hear Ethel downstairs now, trying to comfort Bobby, and then Alice reappeared, shaking uncontrollably, falling into her arms, clinging tightly, as Maggie told the men the exact steps she'd taken to try and revive the baby. They watched anxiously as one of them repeated what she'd done; there was no response. Moments later the two men exchanged the saddest look Maggie had ever seen, while one of them gathered the baby up and cradled her gently. Honey looked so tiny in his arms and Maggie could feel the lump building in her throat.

"This little angel's gone," he said softly to Alice, shaking his head. "P'raps you could give her a cuddle, love?"

Maggie would never forget the look of horror on Alice's face, as she turned and ran from the room, as if she could escape death itself. Susan put her arm round Maggie as she sank onto the bed. One of the men placed the tiny baby in her arms, stepping back in silence as the tears streamed from her face and onto the child. "You did all you could, Maggie," murmured his companion. "We couldn't have saved her either."

It was seven o'clock when Maggie arrived back home just in time to give Charlie his breakfast. "I'll tell you what happened later, Rob," she said, shaking her head quickly before he could ask. "You're late. You've got a meeting at eight, haven't you? You'd better get going, darling."

"Daddy said we'd feed the chickens," said Charlie.

"You and I can do them now, can't we? Go and clean your teeth, poppet, and then we'll give all the animals their breakfast." She sounded as if she was on auto pilot, she knew she did, but it was the only way to keep going.

"Biscuit and Crumble too?"

"Yes, they can have some carrots and you can choose them. Off you go." Charlie skipped away, lost in a happy world that baby Honey would never know.

"He'd prefer a donkey diet," she said, tearfully wrapping her arms round Robert as he was leaving. "We lost the baby," she said. "I can't talk about it now. I was too late. It's just so awful."

"Oh no." Robert looked shocked. "What happened?"

"Please, not now."

"I'm so sorry; that's terrible," he said, drawing her closer, aware she was shaking. "You're exhausted, darling. Can you get some sleep? Surely you're not expected to work today?"

"Susan's doing my visits and the clinic. Off you go. I'll be okay."

Doctor Southgate examined Honey for the formal confirmation of her death and, although the coroner would decide, Maggie hoped a post mortem wouldn't be necessary. Alice, calmed by the mild sedative he'd given her in the early hours of the morning, tried explaining to them all, and the police, how Bobby had unwittingly caused the baby's death.

Bobby had been staying for the night so that Alice's sister could go to a party, and Alice, worn out with his "naughtiness" during the day, running away from her twice, and having to be fished out of the pond on the green after chasing the ducks, had finally managed to settle him down in the spare bed in Honey's room, and had propped two chairs at the side of the bed to keep him tucked in. Having given Honey a late-night feed she placed her in the carry cot in the nursery and, with both little ones settled, she'd fallen asleep, exhausted, in the armchair in the sitting room. She didn't hear Bobby wake up or topple the chairs over. Honey, fast asleep on her tummy in the room, must have attracted him and he'd piled up all the soft toys on top of her, including a very large teddy bear they'd won at the fete. The weight of toys was sufficient to suffocate her. Bobby had woken Alice by going downstairs and demanding a drink and wanting to play and it was an hour or more before she managed to get him back upstairs. It was only then that she discovered her baby hidden beneath the pile of toys and blankets, not breathing. Lifeless.

Maggie slept fitfully and when Robert appeared after lunch she broke down. He'd been worrying about her, desperate to get away from the office early, he told her, as she sobbed in his arms. She was going over and over the baby's death, the anxiety that she could have done more, could have got there sooner, gnawing away at her mind.

"Could I have saved her? I really did try," she sobbed. "She was such a beautiful little girl."

"I know you, darling. I also know that you would have done everything possible," he said, holding her close. "It was not to be because it was too late for any of you to save her," he said, caressing her like a child. "Even the ambulance chap said so. It sounds as if she'd stopped breathing long before you got there anyway and there was absolutely nothing else that anyone could have done."

"Poor, poor Alice," gulped Maggie, mopping her tears with Robert's now-sodden handkerchief. "She's got to live with this and she'll probably never forgive herself. And her sister, too: she's bound to blame herself for leaving Bobby with Alice for the night."

"How have the old folk taken it? You said they cared for her a lot?"

"They're heartbroken, devastated; they'll probably never get over it."

"It's so sad," he said, kissing her damp cheeks. "Come on, you really mustn't blame yourself. Stay in bed now, while I go and put the kettle on."

Maggie nodded. There was nothing more to say.

CHAPTER TWENTY-TWO

IN MOURNING

The baby's death and the tragedy that surrounded it were picked over, discussed, investigated, reviewed and reported on to such an extent that Maggie, on the advice of her supervisor, took leave of absence for a week.

She understood the importance of why so many people had to go over the baby's death and this added to her concern, not just for herself but for Alice. She could cope with all the questions but the young mother was not coping well. Her family, who had given her little support in pregnancy, were proving even less help to her now. Her mother had helped in the first week of Honey's life but was no longer visiting. Bobby was being looked after by a friend of her sister. Alice was isolated, except for her elderly neighbours, who knew her family were saying that the baby's death was all her fault, almost accusing her of letting it happen. And, since she had blamed Bobby, her sister was no longer speaking to her. Once more, Ethel and George were her only refuge from the distressed state she found herself in, adding to their own despair. Maggie felt so concerned for Alice that she called by daily until the tragedy of the baby's death began to take its toll on her and she felt she was losing control.

"Are you sure you can manage, Rob? I'll be away for three whole days and Mum is going somewhere with Frank at the weekend. I'll be back on Saturday."

"Do stop fussing, darling. I'm more than sorry that we haven't made it to Cornwall 'cos I know you could do with a proper break. We'll go in the spring. That's a promise."

"I know I'm being silly. It's just that I can't stop going over and over the moments I was trying to resuscitate Honey. I've coped before when babies have died; remember last month when Susan had to tell a first-time mum that she couldn't hear her baby's heartbeat? A terrible tragedy for them as they'd been trying for a baby for such a long time. It was perfect too, and they couldn't bear to let him go, but somehow we coped and moved on even though I'd helped to deliver their beautiful little boy. It was desperately sad for them and for us. It is just so awful the way Honey died. It should never have happened – Bobby was too young to know what he was doing when he piled those toys on the baby. He was playing, and Alice will regret falling asleep for the rest of her life." Maggie's voice broke as Robert put his arms round her.

"I know, darling, I know," he said, gently sitting her down on the sofa and kissing her tear-stained cheek. "But you've a train to catch in an hour. Have you packed all you need?"

"Yes." She blew her nose noisily. "Yes, now Angela and Tom are back they'll help with Charlie if you need it. James loves doing the animals; he'll muck out the donkeys for a little pocket money. Promise me you'll call them?"

"Of course. But I'm sure I won't need to. Charlie seemed quite happy for you to go, didn't he? Not at all clingy, was he? When I dropped him off at Dawn's he asked me to tell Mummy to bring back some of the special mint cakes they make where Granny lives."

Maggie dabbed her eyes, sniffed and smiled. "That's so sweet; he's so precious, Rob. He gave me such a big cuddle."

"Yes, we're very lucky. Come on or you'll miss the train."

A few days being mothered was just what Maggie needed. Elizabeth allowed her daughter time and patience, finding it hard work to begin with. All Maggie wanted to do was stay in bed and sleep, but gradually she'd persuaded her to talk about the baby's death and the tragic events that led up to it. They walked and shopped and relished the closeness they'd enjoyed in her early years. It was Elizabeth who had helped Maggie cope with the despair of miscarrying so many times before Charlie's arrival, and her patience and understanding helped her again this time. When Maggie brought up the subject of her house move and her close relationship with Frank, she skirted over it in her determination to see her daughter surface from the gripping misery she had arrived with. It worked well and Maggie returned home feeling stronger, ready to resume her duties, able to cope with Honey's funeral.

George and Ethel had insisted on covering the funeral costs and were determined that baby Honey would not be buried in an unmarked common grave. Edna, helped by Jennifer and Dawn, filled the church with flowers and arranged tea in the village hall.

Maggie was glad to see that Alice's mother and sister had made the effort to support her for this distressing moment. The tiny white wooden coffin was visible beneath a teddy bear of white chrysanthemums as the slow cortege made its way to the church. Several villagers stood in and outside the church raising the roof to sing "All Things Bright and Beautiful" as tears streamed down their faces. The church porch was piled high with small posies and soft toys and the vicar was visibly overcome when the tiny coffin was carried to the grave and finally lowered into the small vacant plot.

For Maggie it was an end and a beginning, spiritually helpful and a focal point from which she could build from the rock bottom she'd found herself at.

Alice was broken, pale and silent, dry-eyed, clinging not to her mother but to Ethel instead. She seemed to go through the whole funeral as if she was functioning mechanically, almost coldly, unable to give expression to her grief. Maggie half hoped she would give vent to her feelings at the funeral but despite the tears of those surrounding her she remained virtually speechless after finally scattering a few grains of earth on the coffin.

Afterwards Maggie sat with Ethel and Annie in the village hall. Alice had left with her mother, unable to face the community once the service was over. When Maggie asked where George was, Ethel told her how worried she was. He hadn't been able to face the funeral service and she'd never known him so withdrawn.

"He's hardly touched his food and he's even neglecting his bees. My George was never one to cry. He's an old soldier but losing little Honey like this has broken his heart. Mine too, love," she said, wiping her eyes. "I know we must try and be strong for Alice."

"It's caused a total breakdown in the family," Maggie said to Robert later that day. "Not that they cared much for Alice anyway. Now they're completely adrift."

"Families," he muttered. "That's tough for her."

"Funny you should say that," said Maggie. "I was thinking of our family and how lucky I've been with my mother and sister. D'you wish you saw more of your brothers?"

"Well, yes, darling, it would be nice but Ben's a bit far away in South Africa and Chris is womanising all over Europe, from what I can gather," he said, laughing. "He phoned last week actually and may finally find a place in Edinburgh to live and settle down a bit. Too many girlfriends."

"When did he last get in touch?" Maggie asked.

"Christmas."

"How's his business doing?"

"Very well, from what I can gather. Buying and selling property over there seems to be quite lucrative. He takes after Dad. Same sort of business brain."

"You too. You're that way inclined," said Maggie approvingly.

"Not as good as our father was, though."

"Don't be modest. Frank thinks you're brilliant."

"I know. Funny that. He's always encouraged me, hasn't he?" said Robert.

"No, it isn't – he knows talent when he sees it. Wise man. But, changing the subject, you know someone I'd really like to have got to know a bit more? Your aunt Jenny."

"Haven't heard from her since our wedding. She's a bit of a recluse; just lives for her animals, I think."

"That's why I think I'd like to have got to know her," said Maggie. "We could talk animals."

"Right, and next thing you'd be bringing more home. By the way, Danny duck is going to get caught by a fox if we're not careful. He keeps wandering off and messing about in the pond in the front; it took me hours to get him in last night."

"He's really grown. Have the hens been laying well?"

"Not really. A few of them are good layers but most of them seem to natter on their perches all day."

"They're Charlie Watt's old birds. I guess they think they've retired from egg laying."

"Why are we feeding them, then?"

"I'm not putting them down, Rob. That really would upset our little boy all over again."

"What can I do with you, Maggie? We're spending a fortune on cats, a dog, rabbits, guinea pigs, chickens, ducks and donkeys and none of them earn their keep. We're like an animal care home, for heaven's sake!"

"A happy retirement home," she said. "Just think how we could expand if I spread out into Angela's field. We could have those little pygmy goats; they're really cute." She nudged him off the settee. "Are you making that pot of tea?"

"Hopeless, quite hopeless," he muttered, bending to kiss her. "Goats? Don't even tease; they'd be a nightmare. No goats, thanks. I'm playing darts later with the lads, by the way."

"Good; you need a break too," she laughed. "Your brain's on the wane. You forgot to feed Ebb and Flo, and the other fish."

Chapter Twenty-Three

Missing

Doctor Southgate looked grave as Maggie joined him in his consulting room after the antenatal clinic.

"Maggie, this is nothing to do with your work, my dear. I've called you in because I know you've had quite a bit to do with two elderly patients of mine, George and Ethel Jones?"

"Yes," she said, noting the concern in his voice. "D'you remember I encouraged Ethel to keep an eye on Alice Peters? Is something wrong?"

"I'm afraid so, my dear."

Maggie had never seen him look so serious. His kindly,

benign features and smile that lifted all his patients were now replaced with concern and a furrowed brow.

"Has something happened?"

"I'm afraid so. George appears to have had a heart attack. Ethel found him collapsed by the beehives just after she'd attended my morning surgery," he said, gesturing towards a chair for her.

"Oh, my goodness." Maggie sat down heavily. "That's awful. Is Ethel alright? It'll have been a terrible shock for her."

"It was, my dear, and I'm particularly worried about her because I've another piece of bad news."

Alarmed now, Maggie wondered whatever was coming next.

"You see, Ethel came to see me for some advice this morning to do with George, and, more worryingly, to tell me that Alice Peters has disappeared. No sign of her anywhere, it seems, and she has not apparently taken anything with her: clothes, belongings, nothing. Ethel told me that Alice, who as we know is in a fragile state, has been inconsolable since her sister turned up and accused her of lying and making up the story about her little boy, Bobby. They had a row, shouting and so on, which only ended when Alice ran into Ethel's house screaming that her sister had hit her. That was two days ago and George was very upset by it. He is still very depressed about the baby's death and Ethel wanted me to call on him and talk things over with him, which I'd planned to do. But Alice Peters has not been seen since yesterday."

Maggie grasped the arm of the chair. Alice's disappearance was significant. She'd spoken to Susan and the health visitors, expressing concern about Alice's state of mind since the baby's death, and what she feared she might do.

"I've been worried something like this might happen, to Alice, I mean, but poor George? Where is he now? In hospital?"

"Yes. The ambulance arrived quickly and he's survived the journey. His condition is apparently stable."

"D'you want me to go and see Ethel?"

"No, I'm about to visit her again once I've seen my last patient. I know she'd appreciate it though, Maggie, if you could find someone to take her to visit George this evening. D'you know anyone in the village who could take her?"

Maggie nodded.

"I've spoken to our health visitor and asked her to contact the social worker whose been dealing with Alice and think she should call on Alice's family as soon as possible. We'll have to inform the police if she and they think it necessary," he went on, getting up to open the door. "It seems unlikely but the mother might know her whereabouts. Thank you, my dear. I'll keep you informed."

Maggie drove home, shocked at the turn of events in such a short space of time. Honey's death was a tragedy the whole village suffered together. Now the impact on Ethel and George added to her personal despair. She felt a responsibility towards them. It had been her idea to get them involved initially and her own regret at not being able to revive the baby would remain with her for ever, but for the old man to be so affected and so distressed was intensely upsetting. Now, dear kind Ethel was alone and had nearly lost her husband. They had cared for Alice and the baby as if she were their own daughter. Maggie wanted to go straight to Ethel but hurried home as Charlie would be having his tea, and Robert needed to eat before a darts match at the Dog and Duck, between the home team and the Waldersby lads.

Preoccupied by these thoughts and overwhelmed by sadness, she swerved too late, swearing loudly as she tried to avoid a large herd of fallow deer dashing across the road, plunging her car into the hedge.

Robert fed Charlie his tea and left him settled in the sitting room in front of his favourite television programme, *Blue Peter*. He'd been joined by Angela and they were sitting in the kitchen, catching up on the delights of her family's holiday in Cornwall and the holiday cottage they'd rented, which sounded to Robert as if it would be ideal for a spring break for them. Maggie was unusually late and he kept anxiously peering up the lane. He was beginning to worry about her and had been telling Angela that he'd wished he'd persuaded her to take more time off before resuming her duties as she'd been so traumatised by the baby's death. It was getting late and if Maggie didn't arrive back home soon he was going to miss the match.

"Look, I can stay here if you like. Tom will look after James and Rosie. He got a lot of practice on holiday."

"Thankfully, you won't have to. That's her car now," Robert said, jumping up. "Oh no, what on earth's she done? Hit something, by the look of it."

Out of the window he saw Maggie driving slowly towards them closely followed by Trevor the vet in his Land Rover. There was a huge dent in the car's bonnet and the bumper was hanging off.

Robert rushed straight out of the door as the two vehicles stopped on the drive.

"I wanted to make sure Maggie got home okay," Trevor said, leaning out. "I was coming up behind her when the deer crossed; she didn't have any alternative but to swerve, unfortunately."

"Last time it was a pheasant. Are you alright, darling?" Robert asked, wrenching open the car door.

"I'll live," she said, as he helped her out and gave her a hug. "I counted fifty deer plus. They just appeared from nowhere and I ended up in the hedge."

"We need some road signs up for the deer," Angela said, clutching her arm. "You okay? They're far too many. Tom nearly hit one the other day," she said, grabbing Woody by the collar. "Calm down. Down, Woody, down, she's okay."

"I suppose it's that time of year. They're getting all excited," Robert said, turning back to Trevor, who'd started to reverse out of the drive.

"The rut, you mean? Yes. They'll need culling badly next year."

"Thanks for escorting her back, Trevor, good of you."

"That's okay; she was a bit shaken up. As anyone would be."

"Thank you so much, Trevor. I hope I haven't held you up too much?" Maggie called over her shoulder as he waved to her before driving off.

"I'll catch up," he called back. "Give my regards to the donkeys."

"Will do. Any tea in the pot, you two?" Maggie said, hurrying inside with Angela and sinking into the chair by the Aga. "Was I glad to see him behind me! Thank goodness I made it back with the bumper dragging like that; it was making an awful noise."

They listened with concern as Maggie told them how distracted she'd been, worrying about George, and Alice's sudden disappearance.

"It's my own fault. I wasn't concentrating properly, I suppose. Anyway, how are you? Everything okay? You always look so well when you're pregnant."

"Yes, I'm fine. I don't like the sound of that young mother leaving like that, though," said Angela. "A bit ominous, isn't it, after all she's been through, poor girl? Don't worry about Ethel, though. I can easily take her to the hospital; Tom will take care of the children."

"Thanks, Angela. That's good of you. It certainly is worrying. I've been imagining all sorts. Doctor Southgate said he'd let me know what the social worker has found out, if anything. She's not our responsibility but he knows how involved and concerned I am, and have been."

Angela got up to leave but not before thinking how unwell Maggie looked: her normally happy attitude to her work and the joy of her home and family had taken a severe knock with each tragic event and these seemed to be mounting daily. She looked tired and drawn as she sat clutching the mug of tea while Robert was on the phone to the garage.

"I'll be alright," she sniffed as Angela bent down to give her a hug. "I'm dying to hear about your holiday too, the children and this little one," she said, patting her neat bump.

"We'll chat tomorrow. I'm due for a check-up with Doctor Southgate. This has been my best pregnancy. I'll go now and let Ethel know I can take her later and I'll ring you in the morning. Get an early night if you can. You look like you need more sleep."

"Will do, thanks. We need to catch up properly," Maggie said, waving her off as Robert returned.

"I can get your car seen to in the morning, darling. They've been very helpful," he said. "Now, will you be okay if I go to the pub? I feel a bit mean leaving you but I'll be too late if I don't go now."

"Yes, I'm fine, silly. Charlie's watching telly, isn't he?"

"Yes. He's had his tea and thankfully he didn't hear you come back so he's blissfully unaware anything's happened."

"I'll watch it with him and see what John Noakes is up to this week. What about Woody?"

"I'll take Woody for a run when I get back. Perhaps you can get an early night?"

"What about your supper?"

"I'll eat with the lads later as it's a match. Are you sure you feel okay? I can easily tell them I can't make it," he said, kneeling down and giving her a hug.

"Don't be daft. I'm fine. I might make myself an omelette later. I'm really not that hungry."

"Thanks." He kissed her. "If you're sure. Charlie knows I'm going."

"I'd be more upset if you missed the match. You can let them know about George too. Might get some chauffeurs."

Maggie lay in bed, unable to sleep, her mind drifting as she tried to read. Charlie had fallen asleep during story time and she'd relished a long soak in the bath instead of bothering to eat after settling all the animals, but that had proved no inducement to sleep either. Her mind was full of dark thoughts. What if Alice had run away and been hurt? What if she harmed herself? What if George died? What would happen to Ethel, who loved him so and was devastated by the loss of Honey, and cared so much for Alice? The worrying thoughts and memories played over and over in her head. She got up and phoned her mother. Elizabeth listened attentively, aware that her daughter was finding it difficult to cope, letting her go over and over the death of baby Honey again, and these latest unsettling events. She'd hoped the time they'd spent together would enable Maggie to recover, but now she'd been knocked backwards once more, and this time she wasn't there for her.

It was late when Angela phoned to say that George was not at all well, and that Ethel was going to stay at the hospital.

"Poor dear. She won't let go of his hand. The nurses are very good with her and she has a comfortable armchair by his bed. I've collected her little dog, Sammy. He seems quite happy. He's in his basket in the kitchen and has eaten his supper so hopefully she doesn't have to worry about him at least. Dawn has offered to collect him tomorrow and she'll also go and see what Ethel needs."

"Thanks, Angela. I'd completely forgotten about Sammy. D'you think George's bees will be okay?"

"Well, I'm not going to look after them, that's for sure," she said, relieved to hear Maggie chuckle.

Chapter Twenty-Four

Too many trotters

Maggie set off on her rounds, driving her car with care along a rutted farm track, her vision hindered by the early-morning sun. Robert had had the damages checked at the local garage the evening before but the large dent was still visible in the bonnet: a repair that would have to wait. Despite its injuries Maggie was fond of her car. It had never let her down and it was roomy enough to carry Charlie, shopping and food for the animals, with straw and hay wedged in the boot. However, it was not coping well with the uneven track and she was uneasy about the ominous crunching sound as it lurched slowly over the hard ground.

Robert had also been checking out some second-hand cars while waiting at the garage and unbeknown to Maggie he'd found a little red Mini in good condition. He'd done the deal, arranging for its delivery the following Friday. He hoped it would give her something else to concentrate on, helping to take her mind off the sad and difficult situations that had arisen.

Maggie was looking forward to being off duty the following weekend. Sensitive to her need for some distraction, Robert suggested they have a family fun day, starting with a trip to Cambridge, where he could school Charlie in the joys of punting on the river. Dawn Creasey offered to "babysit" for an evening outing to the Arts Theatre. As she neared the farm she reflected on the toll the last few weeks had had on her ability to be, in her mind, a proper mother. Working long and unpredictable hours, she was not always there for Charlie.

She was lucky to have such an understanding husband and a child that was unfazed by being passed from one person to another when her midwifery duties intervened.

At last the familiar sight of the old farmhouse isolated in the valley and backing onto a wood came into view, one she never tired of. Cows and sheep dotted the surrounding fields. The house, almost shrouded in ivy, was set neatly in the middle of a large lawn. Swings and a slide had recently been erected where there once there had been a herbaceous border. Her car was greeted by three dogs, two sheep dogs and a golden retriever, whose tail waved majestically. The younger dogs circled her, clambering at the car windows, scratching the dented bonnet.

"Down, down boys," boomed a voice from the front door. "Come here." The sheepdogs slunk away to stand meekly by the man's side but the retriever ignored the commands and was now dribbling saliva onto Maggie's shoes as she stroked his handsome head. Collecting her nursing bag, wiping her shoe on the long grass, Maggie headed for the entrance, looking forward to the visit, the joy of this new baby's arrival and the large slice of fruit cake or freshly made scones that she knew would follow.

Maggie had first visited Jeremy and Amanda when they had had undiagnosed twin girls just after she started on the district two years before. Now it was a baby boy who had arrived just inside the hospital entrance as Jeremy had parked the Land Rover twenty-four hours earlier.

The twins, Lily and Lottie, seemed equally excited to see her, having got to know her in the clinic for the routine check-ups when Maggie helped them listen into their mummy's baby. They were entranced by their baby brother and Maggie, having agreed with Amanda that he would enjoy a bath, let them help undress him. The bath was awash with bubbles, rubber ducks and bobbing toys. The twins squealed with delight when the baby cried as she gently lifted him out of the warm water. Maggie let them help pat him dry, giggling helplessly when he pooed in his clean nappy and had to have his bottom washed again. Both helpless with laughter when he peed in the air and then splattered the floor. Both covered in cream misapplied to his tiny bottom, their small fingers smearing too much in every crease. By the time the baby was dressed and ready for his feed Amanda and Maggie were laughing so much that Amanda needed to lie down.

"I've only got two stitches but I don't want them to burst," she said, clutching herself tightly.

George, unfazed by all the attention, was soon guzzling away at her breast. The twins watched, fascinated.

"Look midknife, our baby eats our mummy," said Lily, looking concerned.

"Why does he bite you, Mummy?" asked Lottie, also looking worried.

Maggie, enjoying her new title, had an idea. "Amanda, shall we squeeze a little out into a cup and then Lily and Lottie can see it's milk and baby's drinking not eating you? Your milk's already come in, by the look of it."

"Okay. Didn't think of that," Amanda said. "You're a bit upset when I'm feeding George, aren't you," she said, patting Lottie reassuringly. "I suppose it does look as if he's munching; he's such a strong sucker. Thankfully I'm finding it easy this time."

"That's good," said Maggie. "You were successful with them, I remember, but goodness me you suffered, didn't you, at the beginning?"

"Don't remind me. I can still remember plastering Friar's Balsam on my poor bleeding nipples. Ugh! That smell," she shuddered. "I thought they were going to drop off."

"I've got some rather nice cream we can use if you do get sore; remember, it helps to smear some breast milk on your nipples, air them a bit."

"Jeremy won't mind that," she laughed.

Reassured that their baby was drinking milk and not eating their mummy, the twins went off to play just as

Jeremy arrived with a tray of tea and two large slices of lemon sponge.

"Tuck in, you two. I need to check the sows, love, so call me if you need me. Are we seeing you tomorrow, Maggie?"

"Thank you. Yes, probably late morning, all being well," Maggie said. "Who made this? It's delicious?"

"I do all the cooking and I made this one for the WI sale," said Amanda. "Can't let Jeremy loose in the kitchen. The farm's keeping him busy enough at the minute. That's why he's glad to have a son."

"Girls make good farmers, don't they?"

"Maybe. We'll see as they grow older. Jeremy will certainly encourage them and Lottie loves the piglets."

"Oh, so do I," said Maggie. "Can I see them before I go?"

"Sure. Just give him a shout on the way out."

Ten minutes later Maggie was gazing in awe at the large Gloucester Old Spot sow lying down with a dozen tiny piglets eagerly tugging at her teats. "They're adorable, aren't they?"

"Couple of runts there," said Jeremy.

"Really?"

"Those scrawny little buggers'll never make anything. I'll give them a day or two just to see if they'll pick up."

"And if they don't?"

"Shoot 'em."

Maggie was shocked. "No. You don't mean that, Jeremy? Surely you won't shoot them?"

"Yep, that or drown them. Have to. Quick and simple."

"That's terrible." Maggie felt tears pricking her eyes. "I'd never make a farmer if I had to do things like that; they're so cute. That's so sad."

"You've got a few animals already haven't you? Tell you what, you can have those two tiddlers there. They'll be okay for a family. You'll get a few good meals off them if you fatten them up."

"You're joking. We'd never be able to have them killed," she said, gathering up her bag. "Nice of you to offer, though, thanks, Jeremy. See you tomorrow. By the way, I'm now a midknife; my colleague was called a middle wife."

"Great kids, aren't they." He laughed. "Midknife suits, very apt. Take care."

Maggie had four more visits to make before lunch and was eager to see two new mothers. All the visits were spread out and with a journey between each she would probably not have time for a sandwich and a catch up with her colleague Susan before her parentcraft class in the afternoon. Fortified with Amanda's cake, she drove off, pursued for a short distance by the two collie dogs. The visit had lifted her spirits and made her realise once more how privileged she was to have her job. The piglets' fate niggled and invaded her thoughts between her visits, however. After all, there was the old sheep pen in the corner of the meadow.

Eight young mothers were waiting for her when she arrived late, and apologetic. But the wait had been beneficial as the group were already chatting and eagerly exchanging information.

Lying down on mats and pillows, they breathed and puffed their way through imaginary early labour. During the tea break Maggie was delighted to see how well they got on. Not all first-time mothers gelled so quickly. She felt thankful once more that yet another group would be helpful to each other in their early weeks of new motherhood, complimenting the support she and the health visitors gave and retaining their friendships for years.

She left them alone for five minutes to make some phone calls before returning to lie them down for a period of relaxation. Checking they were comfortable, she played a gentle, soothing melody and quietly talked them through the exercise, finding it tempting to nod off herself. With the two-hour session over Maggie was waving them off and saying goodbye when she felt an overwhelming sadness, as memories of Alice enjoying her first days with baby Honey came flooding back.

She busied herself tidying the room and filling in notes and was about to leave the hospital when one of the desk clerks called her to answer an urgent message.

"Doctor Southgate here, Maggie. Alice Peters is now officially a missing person. The police are organising a search, starting in the village. I'm sure you'll want to be involved, dear. Let's pray they find her alive."

Chapter Twenty-Five

Community care

It was scary for the villagers to see the green awash with what appeared to be the entire population of Little Fordham, armed to the hilt with rakes, walking sticks and even golf clubs, any implement that could be used to search in the undergrowth. Old and young, with an army of assorted family dogs champing at the bit, anxious to get going, directed by policemen with two-way radios and specialist sniffer dogs. Alice Peters's disappearance so soon after the tragic loss of her baby, Honey, touched the close-knit community's heart. They were determined to find her. Major Gibson and PC O'Sheridan called an emergency meeting. Edna Newbold distributed reprinted maps of the area, in her element issuing instructions. The police were delighted at the response from villagers, young and old.

It was Maggie's weekend off, but the family punting trip would have to wait. Angela got Tom to take Charlie and James to the pictures to keep them out of the way.

The police searched Alice's home twice, making house-to-house enquiries in Little Fordham and surrounding hamlets. Waldersby Hospital was alerted, and the local press, eager for news, mingled with the waiting villagers on the green. Reporters interviewed her family when they appeared, pushing and shoving each other to get "a story". The family wisely kept their recent arguments close to their chest.

"I'm glad you haven't got to go down into the gravel pit and get scratched to bits," Angela said, joining Maggie and reading the instructions the police had issued after the police divided the villagers into groups. "Remember the state Jacky Richards was in when she found Woody? I'll just come with you to the woods and around the badger sett, and then if necessary Tom can relieve me when he gets back. Rosie's quite a handful at the minute."

"That's okay. Robert's got plans for them later. He'll see they're fed after the cinema, if Tom's not already filled them with popcorn," said Maggie. "You know what our men are like with them: anything for a quiet life. You've no need to come."

Angela shuddered. "I felt I had to. I can't believe this is really happening, can you?"

"I'm just praying that we don't find Alice and that she's holed up in some safe sheltered place, not in a field or the woods, cold and wet, frightened and depressed. We were concerned about her mental state before the baby's death; God knows what state she's in now."

"It's unimaginable, poor girl. Even when we find her she still has to face life without her baby," said Angela, gently patting her bump. "We've been so lucky."

"You know, it's awful to say this, but I'll quite understand it if she's taken her own life. She's probably wondering what she has to live for," said Maggie with unusual bitterness.

"We mustn't think like that, Maggie. She's young. She's got her whole life ahead of her."

"She can't see that, though, can she?"

"No, but with the right help she'll get through this."

"I wish I could be that certain. Doctor Southgate's equally pessimistic. Postnatal depression is serious enough without losing your baby too."

"How are the old folk taking it? I hear George came back home yesterday."

"Yes. That's really good news. Ethel was heartbroken about Alice and the baby. If George hadn't pulled through I think she might have passed away."

The villagers were moved in different directions with their maps and instructions as Maggie and Angela stopped to speak briefly to Edna, who wanted to pet Woody before they went. "Now, you find that young woman for us, Woody," she said, handing Maggie a packet of his favourite treats. "These'll encourage him."

"Thanks, Edna. I'll see you later," said Maggie. "I've left another batch of scones at the village hall."

"Good. Dawn's got the over-sixties ladies organised. Teas, coffees and soft drinks will be available all day, and every day if needs be. Waldersby WI ladies are offering their help too."

Maggie and Angela scoured their marked area with three young lads Maggie recognised from the darts team, accompanied by one of the police officers. It was damp and muddy in the wood around the badger sett and they worked in silence, intent on missing nothing. It seemed that even the birds were holding their breath as the stillness surrounding them in the woods felt eerie in the silence. This was Robert and Maggie's favourite walk. They always felt at peace here. But today the atmosphere was different, the grim task chilling. Even Woody seemed to sense it.

The day ended in the village hall at five o'clock with a report that, sadly, there wasn't a trace of Alice. Disheartened and weary, the villagers decided to continue to search until dusk, and if necessary they'd meet again at dawn.

After breakfast the next morning, helping Maggie to collect up the donkey droppings in the field, Charlie announced, "I'm on a poo hunt," proudly wheeling his own small wheelbarrow round the meadow. Distracted, as his barrow became a racing car, he left Maggie to cart the load to the manure heap in the corner. She treasured these moments with him and was glad he'd developed the same love of animals as she had, even though it meant he'd refused a bath the evening before, insisting that two enormous spiders lurking there be left undisturbed. He had no fear of any bugs and was particularly entranced by ants, ladybirds and snails.

"It's called animal magic," she explained to Robert, who was complaining that he'd found evidence of the guinea pigs, Midge and Mungo, in Charlie's bed again. "Great if he ends up as a vet or naturalist like that Attenborough chap they had on *Blue Peter*," she retorted.

"It's just a small matter of hygiene," Robert muttered.

"You're quite wrong, darling. Bugs and dirt are supposed to be good in small doses; helps build up their immunity."

"Okay, you win," he sighed, knowing some arguments were lost before they began.

Charlie stopped racing round the meadow and decided to join Crumble and Biscuit, who'd now retreated to the stable. They particularly disliked the squealy noise and loud "brrrm brrrrm" emanating from the boy.

A small partitioned section at the back of the stable housed bedding and the box of treats, favourite polo mints for the donkeys, plus a few apples and carrots. Charlie, now busy hugging Biscuit, didn't notice the small figure sitting on the bale of straw in the gloomy interior, until a voice spoke.

"Hello." The woman moved towards him, her outstretched hand trembling.

Charlie screeched and fled from the stable, followed by two frightened donkeys, spooked by his high-pitched scream.

"Mummy, Mummy."

Maggie, alert to the fear in his voice and thinking he'd been hurt, dumped her barrow and raced across the meadow to gather him up in her arms.

"Darling, what happened?"

The two donkeys halted, trembling by the field gate, looking back anxiously, curious at his dramatic reaction.

"Mummy, there's a lady."

"A lady, darling? Where's a lady? What d'you mean?" she asked, holding his trembling body tight, aware of her own heart's missed beats. Her thoughts immediately turned to Alice. She felt sick, dreading that it might be her and that she could be lying dead in their stable. Worse still, Charlie had seen something, and her heart was now racing.

Putting Charlie down gently, she took his hand and said, "Oh, I expect she wants to talk to the donkeys. Run and talk to them while I speak to the lady."

"She said hello to me," said Charlie, now reassured.

"She spoke to you?"

"Yes. The lady said hello."

Maggie thought her legs were going to give way. Thank goodness whoever it was wasn't dead.

On reflection, Maggie thought it was the most obvious place for Alice to hide, but not one that she or anyone else had considered. Charlie, having discovered her, had to face questioning the next morning.

"Well, Charlie. Can you tell me again how you found the young lady?" PC O'Sheridan and another policeman were in the sitting room in Nut Tree Cottage, clutching mugs of tea while Charlie perched on Robert's lap and examined one of their helmets. "You're a very clever little boy and if Mum can bring you to the station we've got a nice surprise for you. How about that?"

Maggie looked on, eyes glistening with unshed tears, relieved, proud and thankful for one happy ending.

"Do you have a big train?"

"No, young man. We don't have trains. It's called a station but p'raps Mum and Dad can explain why we have no trains."

"D'you have a truncheon?"

"Er, yes. I might manage to show you that," he said. "D'you think your mum and dad might like to see one too?"

Charlie's eyes lit up. "Can we go in a police car with a siren?"

"I might manage that too."

Maggie prompted him. "What d'you say?"

"Please, Mr Policeman?"

The ambulance had made its way down the lane and carefully collected Alice from the stable, weak and hungry but bodily warmed by Biscuit and Crumble, whom it appeared she'd clung to in her distressed state at night, nourished only by the odd apple. They took her to hospital in Waldersby as the villagers, relieved by the outcome, ended up in the Dog and Duck.

"'Away in a Manger' just about sums it up," muttered the ambulance driver to his colleague, slamming the door and driving off at speed.

The pub was a hubbub of noise and chatter as villagers swapped stories of their own searches, even displaying unusual finds but mainly reporting rubbish and disgust at human disregard for the countryside. The relief that Alice was alive was palpable. It helped the beer to flow and soon they were all in party mood, singing at the top of their voices.

"There'll always be an England…" could be heard in Waldersby.

George and Ethel, clung together, thankful to know that Alice was unharmed. Ethel grasped his hand tightly.

"Thank the Lord we've still got each other, and Alice can stay here with us, George. Till she gets herself sorted out dear," she said, tearfully.

"If you say so, Ethel."

Chapter Twenty-Six

Away in a Manger

Maggie would never forget the tragic sight of Alice that day, tear-stained, trembling, her face haunted as she appeared through the gloom of the stable. She'd held the young girl's frail body tightly to her as Alice sobbed.

"My sister's so angry. She thinks I made it up about Bobby." Tears coursed down her cheeks as she rubbed at her face with her sleeve. "I want my baby. I want my baby back."

"Hush now, Alice," Maggie said as Charlie, frightened by what he couldn't understand, pulled at her, shouting and crying now too.

"I want Daddy. I want to go home."

So do I, thought Maggie, leaving Alice tucked up in a rug and hurrying back across the field, with Charlie running beside her as fast as his young legs would go.

"Don't move, Alice. I'm going to get help; don't move from here."

"Why on earth was she in that draughty stable, darling?"

"She panicked, Mum. She thought her sister wanted to hurt her and she thought my stable was the best place to hide."

"Poor girl. How on earth can you help in this situation now? She must be feeling so desperate."

"It's absolutely heartbreaking. Doctor Southgate's been wonderful, visiting her practically every day, and the old people who're so distressed by everything too. Alice is seeing a special bereavement counsellor."

"It won't bring her baby back," Elizabeth sighed. "How's she ever going to survive this?"

"Ethel and George are looking after her for now. She has a room in their house as she can't bear to go home, even though it's just next door. I think she'll leave the village soon. Ethel's cousin has a flat in London, in Lewisham. She's offered to have Alice there when she feels up to it. She'll need to start looking for a job and earn some money."

"What sort of job?"

"I don't know but she wants to get away. She could do her hairdressing up there. At her age there's nothing here for her really and although the family have been back in touch it's still a prickly situation. She only talks to her mother occasionally."

"I'm sure you're doing all you can for her darling. And what about you and our Charlie? I'm looking forward to seeing you all next week. I'll be there Tuesday now."

"Good. Can't wait. He's fine. Robert told him that Alice had come to visit the donkeys and made up some story about one of them standing on her foot and making her cry. He was much more excited by his trip to the police station. He's been in the garden with Danny the duck. D'you want a quick word? He's just come in?"

"That would be lovely."

Charlie, excited at being offered the telephone, shouted, "Hello, Nana."

"Hello, darling. Mummy tells me you've been to the police station."

"I had a ride in the police car."

"Did you, dear? That's nice."

"Mummy came too. He's got a truncheon. Bye, Nana. Mummy wants a piggy," he said, giggling and dropping the phone as Danny waddled through the door.

"That's all she needs," Elizabeth muttered.

"Right, Mum. Got to go. See you next week, bye." Maggie hung up, hastily shooing Danny towards the garden.

Maggie drove slowly down the lane, her new Mini finding this farm track even more bouncy and difficult than her old car. She zigzagged round the potholes, conscious of the increasing snuffles and snorts coming from the large cardboard box on the passenger seat.

She was at the bottom of the hill when the lid burst open and two tiny piglets fell into the well of the car, squealing with surprise.

Maggie pulled onto the verge, chuckling as she gathered them up, forcing them gently back into the box, before speeding up the hill and down the lane, parking by the field gate.

How she was going to explain this new development to Robert was difficult but the way he was behaving towards her after everything that had happened over the past weeks might prove helpful, she hoped.

Unbeknown to Robert the piglets' home was ready and waiting, a square of straw bales where the sheep pen had been with a few sheets of corrugated iron made a cosy pig pen, thanks to the obliging Major Gibson, and Tom and Angela's help. Jeremy, the farmer, had given her enough food for a fortnight and strict instructions on their care, although she preferred to forget his ruling that he was going to check on their weight in a few months' time.

"So. You thought I wouldn't mind? What are you going to do when they have to be made into pork pies after all your weeks of devotion?"

"Well, you see, Rob, they either live for a week or we just have them a bit longer and give the poor little things a reason for being born. I couldn't bear the thought of Jeremy shooting them. They're so sweet."

"Well, don't ever ask me to eat them. Come on, Woody. Let's go before I say something I'll regret," he said, picking up the dog's lead.

"They've already got names, darling. James told Charlie to call them Crackling and Streaky."

"Oh, for heaven's sake. You're incorrigible," he said, slamming the door.

It was Elizabeth who commented a few days later that she noticed Robert took more care with the piglets than the other pets.

"I know," said Maggie. "He's fallen for their charms so goodness knows how we'll handle it later. They're adorable now but what happens when their time's up. I shudder to think."

"Well, you will do these things so you'll have to manage. You're far too impetuous. By the way, Eleanor rang to say she can't come after all this week."

"That's a shame. Nice that Frank's taking us all out to dinner tomorrow though."

"Yes. He's booked a table at the Dog and Duck as they do a very good steak."

"Yummy. Whatever you do don't order a pork chop."

It was late afternoon the next day. Maggie was reflecting on the fathers' evening she'd held the night before as she drove home. The group had been learning to bath a baby. Two young fathers found bathing a doll nerve-racking enough; the prospect of doing the real thing terrified them. Maggie smiled to herself: it was amazing how quickly people caught on and she looked forward to seeing the two dads again in the coming months.

Turning into the lane, she was surprised to see Robert and Charlie outside Angela's cottage in earnest conversation with Tom. She'd hoped Charlie would be ready for bed, ready for Edna Newbold's niece, Jennifer, who'd be looking after him while they went to the pub.

Winding down the car window, she also realised that it was no casual conversation.

They all looked rather agitated.

"Is everything okay? I thought Charlie would be in bed by now."

"Well, you're unlucky there. I simply haven't had time to get Charlie sorted out as I've been otherwise engaged!"

His sarcastic tone stung. It was unlike Robert, but before she could say anything Angela came hurrying down the path.

"Oh dear, Maggie. Your piglets have done a runner."

"No! Where are they?"

Running towards the field gate, she saw the straw bales were tipped over and the donkeys happily munching their way through the piglets' house.

"What happened?"

"They've escaped. We've tracked them down. They're in the wood but we can't catch the little beggars."

"Woods are a big attraction for pigs," said Tom sagely.

"Surely not. They're hardly Iron Age pigs. How long since they got out?"

"A couple of hours. Tom and I tracked them down but every time we get near they scuttle off. They ran into the big badger sett at one point!"

James and Charlie started to giggle, running up and down snorting and squealing like piglets.

"Sheepdogs: that's what we need," Maggie said, jumping back in the car.

"Where on earth are you going to find sheepdogs?" they chorused as she called to Charlie to join her.

"Rob, can you and Tom redo the pen and put a strip of that electric fence round so the donkeys don't touch it? Charlie, you come with me."

"Oh, great idea," Angela said. "Dawn's husband is looking after the neighbours' two sheepdogs and they round things up all the time, even keep rounding up their chickens and the two cats – they'll be perfect," Angela explained as Maggie drove off.

"I'll have another gin and tonic, if you don't mind," Maggie said as they waited for their table in the Dog and Duck two hours later.

"Well, glad to see pork on the menu," said Robert. "I'm quite looking forward to the day—"

"Stop it, Rob. Streaky and Crackling are going to be with us for weeks yet."

"There's always suckling pig," said Frank, raising his glass.

"You know," said Maggie, "I've always fancied a sheep dog and Woody would love a doggy companion."

"Then I really will leave," said Robert. "She's your daughter, Elizabeth. Can you take her back up north or better still pop her over the side when you're on that cruise?"

Chapter Twenty-Seven

Visiting time

"I'm a bit worried," Susan said.

"Why? What's the problem?" Maggie asked.

They were grabbing a rushed lunch at the clinic so Susan could hand over her caseload to Maggie before going on holiday.

"I know it's only for ten days but the two home births I've booked both want water births."

"Well, I'm sure I can manage those – unless of course they go into labour in unison, then I might have a problem swimming from one house to the next."

"I wish we had more experience with these water births at home."

"I think I did rather well with the mother I had last month, jumping over the side when she shouted "It's coming" and almost drowning Doctor Southgate." They were both giggling now. "Poor man. He was absolutely soaked," Maggie chortled.

"You never told me you jumped right into the pool, Maggie."

"No. He and I thought we'd better keep that one a secret. It was a bit crowded as the dad to be was also in it, looking all helpless in his yellow Y-fronts."

"No!"

"Yes!"

Now the pair were laughing so loudly that the receptionist put her head round the door. "Bit noisy, you two."

"Sorry, Andrea. We've nearly finished."

Maggie drove slowly down single-track lanes to the remote cottage. She was feeling emotional, singing in tune with the radio as Elvis Presley crooned "Love me tender", The programme commemorating his life for a world still shocked months after the singer's heart attack. Even her colleague, Susan, had almost been persuaded to use precious annual leave to take her mother and auntie, devoted Elvis fans, to visit Graceland, the singer's legendary home.

With her commitments and the animals Maggie realised that she'd jeopardised the idea of a family holiday for another year. They'd also missed that punting weekend that Robert had been looking forward to, so she was glad

Elizabeth was spending a few days with them. She was off duty this coming weekend, so maybe they could go on a punting trip or drive to Norfolk and find a sandy beach where Robert could build sandcastles with Charlie. It only remained for Elizabeth and Frank to agree to manage the menagerie while they were away.

The dilapidated cottage with its moss-strewn thatched roof set in an overgrown wilderness appeared as she rounded the bend. It was undergoing restoration and her way was barred by a cement mixer.

"Hi, Maggie. You'll be alright. Leave it there," called a high voice from behind the hedge.

Cindy Russell appeared, her attractive face and currently rather bedraggled copper-coloured hair showed signs that she was in the throes of painting. Her full-length pinafore was spattered with yellow paint and whitewash. She waved a hand, clutching a large brush. "Walk across the plank. It's quite safe," she called, noticing Maggie's timid approach. "You missed Doctor Southgate. He came about an hour ago. Such a dear, isn't he?"

"We certainly think so. I'm afraid baby Jasper's not going to like me today, though," said Maggie.

"I know. You've got to do that blood test, prick his heel, haven't you?" Cindy said, shoving the brush into a bottle of turpentine. "I'll be glad to stop; I'm dreading it too."

"Where is he?"

"Under the apple tree. I'll get him."

"I can do that. You really shouldn't be doing anything but resting, you know. It's far too soon to be painting and decorating. I bet Doctor Southgate told you off."

"Yes, but I'm afraid I've been languishing around long enough."

"I'm afraid my wife won't listen, Maggie," said her husband, Clive, joining them. "Even if it means splitting her stitches."

"Don't nag, darling. I'm being very careful."

Maggie could only advise and as Doctor Southgate had only just been and given her a gentle lecture she didn't persist.

Maggie disliked pricking any baby's heel for this routine test and always felt dreadful making a happy, sleeping baby cry.

Jasper was the couple's first baby and Cindy had a similar obstetric history to Maggie's own. She had had three miscarriages and they'd been planning to adopt a baby when she'd suddenly become pregnant. It had been a troublesome pregnancy, forcing an occasional stay in hospital for lengthy bouts of morning sickness, followed by persistently raised blood pressure, then her waters had ruptured too early. Cindy ended up having Jasper by caesarean section two weeks before his due date. Her wish to have natural childbirth thwarted. She was now courageously determined to breastfeed, despite red-raw nipples making her cry with pain when Jasper fed.

"Lactating like a Jersey cow, aren't you, my love?" Clive said, gathering up Jasper and rocking him.

Maggie knew Cindy would be brokenhearted if she had to give up breastfeeding. The remoteness of her home allowed her to walk round, exposing her body to the air, on Maggie's advice. When Jasper's sucking became too much to bear she spooned it in. The freezer was rapidly filling with bags of expressed milk, which delighted them both.

"We've contacted the premature baby unit at the hospital, like you said. They'd be grateful for any spare so we'll do that later."

Despite their problems the couple were a joy to visit and Maggie spent time with them over a cup of tea after checking Cindy and "top and tailing'" Jasper for them, relieved he hadn't been too upset.

Cindy and her husband, Clive, were opera singers and Maggie had heard them in full voice singing together as she'd approached the cottage on more than one occasion: one of their reasons for choosing to live somewhere remote. The two were also keen to develop the smallholding. Chickens clucked around the yard and they were excitedly waiting for the arrival of two goats, convinced goats' milk would be better for them and Jasper later on. They loved hearing Maggie's stories about the donkeys and other animals but were disapproving of her plans to fatten up the piglets, even if they were runts and condemned to a short life. "You'll find it so hard to; you'll rue the day," they intoned.

Her notes filled in and visit complete, Maggie drove back towards Waldersby and a small hamlet near the town, slipping in a tape of *Madame Butterfly* that Cindy had insisted she have to enjoy on her round. So much singing was making her hoarse so she switched back to her car radio. The next visit was to one of the mothers planning a water birth.

When she arrived the first thing she saw was the birthing pool. It filled the small sitting room. Frances and her husband, John, were excited and anxious for labour to begin but as the baby wasn't due for another week Maggie suspected their enthusiasm might wane, especially as they had two other little ones to look after.

Maggie knew the family well, having helped Susan deliver their last child, and she hoped Frances wouldn't go over her dates. Unfortunately, she noticed that Frances had a tendency to do just that, delivering rapidly once her labour began.

"Why the pool this time?" Maggie asked, after checking her and the unborn baby.

"Oh, hubby and I just think it's such a wonderful way for them to come into the world. So peaceful."

"It takes a while to fill it, John, so I suggest you start the moment Frances has a twinge, just in case."

Unsure whether the couple had chosen the wisest way, and at quite a cost to themselves, she stayed to talk them through the process again, finishing another mug of tea before carrying on her round.

One of Maggie's great pleasures was bathing babies and it was much needed when she called at the next house, on the outskirts of Waldersby.

The week-old baby boy, Sammy, was lying contentedly, sucking his fist, in a carrycot, but his young mother, Charlotte, was in tears.

"I don't know how to pick him up. It's everywhere, Maggie," she sniffed. "He's not stopped feeding all night and most of this morning but he hasn't been for three days. Mum says he's overfed and I'm giving him the gripes."

"If it's any consolation, Charlotte, you can't overfeed a breastfed baby and they can actually go days without a poo. I'll bath him and then he might settle."

"Oh, thank you."

"Is Mum staying with you?"

"No. She just popped in. Danny's gone to the shops."

"We used to be much stricter in your mum's day. Babies were timed, you know: only so long on each breast, then off. Ideas are changing."

Maggie surveyed the baby lying in a sea of runny mustard poo and gingerly undressed him. It had seeped into every crevice and after lowering him into the bath she realised that Sammy would need two baths to remove the cloying goo. Thankfully he seemed quite content and, powdered and creamed, he was placed back in his new clean crib. Moments later there was a deep rumbling noise from his tummy and he released another torrent, filling his nappy. By the time Maggie finished her visit little Samuel had enjoyed three baths and four nappy changes and was latched onto Charlotte, sucking eagerly.

Maggie had two more visits ahead of her and was getting behind but the importance of leaving the new parents comforted and reassured was what made her job so satisfying. They never complained, however late her visit. They knew that she would turn up and that they would be left feeling more confident as the days went by, particularly if it was a first baby; that's what mattered.

Passing through the green in the village she decided to call on Annie. Annie hadn't been seeing so much of Ethel now that George and Alice filled the old lady's days and she wanted to put her mind at rest by asking her if she was feeling lonely.

Socks, the cat, was sunning himself in the porch as she knocked.

"Well. Fancy seeing you. New car?"

"Yes, like it?"

"It's pretty. Heard the kettle whistling, did you?" Annie teased, ushering Maggie into her sitting room.

"Just popped in for a moment, Annie. Wondered how you were."

"Nothing that can't be cured," she said, pouring the tea in two cups.

"Have you seen Ethel this week?"

"No, and not likely to. She's got far too much on her plate, if you ask me."

"She's been so good to Alice, even though she's had to cope with George as well."

"Ought to put that young woman in a home."

"What?"

"There are perfectly good mother and baby homes. Why can't they put her in one?"

"She hasn't got a baby, though, has she?"

"I know that and I'm as sorry as the rest, the way she lost it, but Ethel's got too much to cope with."

It was apparent that Annie was feeling lonely and a bit neglected, missing her old friend's visits. Maggie enjoyed a piece of Annie's gingerbread and yet another cup of tea before explaining that she had to get back to feed Charlie and the rest of her family.

Annie cut a forlorn figure waving her off. She only had Socks, her old cat, for company. Maggie resolved to return soon.

Chapter Twenty-Eight

Water baby

As was often the case, the call came in the early hours of the morning. Maggie dressed swiftly, anxious not to wake Robert, or Charlie. They had enjoyed the weekend and with all the excitement of punting, and too many goes at the funfair on Midsummer Common in Cambridge, it was unlikely either would stir. Only Woody lifted his head as she closed the front door.

She drove slowly down the lane, avoiding gravel and potholes. Angela was a light sleeper. Maggie was not surprised that she seemed to know precisely when she left and returned from her night visits.

"Does she get any sleep, Tom?" she'd queried, passing him in the lane on her return from a visit the week before.

"Not a lot. She seems to know exactly when you come and go."

"Pregnant women are tuned in to me," she laughed.

The moon was so bright that she could have driven without headlights. She'd noticed Biscuit and Crumble grazing contentedly as she passed the meadow. She was on her way to the other side of Waldersby, and to a mother Susan had booked for a water birth. It was their first baby and the husband had sounded calm and unflustered when he'd rung, assuring Maggie that all was going as planned. They'd discussed the pool and she was glad he'd already started to fill it aware of the water temperature needed. Maggie smiled to herself. She was looking forward to meeting them. An interesting couple to be so in control the first time round. Susan had told her they were a bit "new age", whatever that meant.

The house stood at the end of a small cul-de-sac and it appeared to have candles flickering in every room as she approached. She knocked quietly, conscious that a loud doorbell or knock could wake the neighbours.

She heard footsteps racing down the stairs and then the door burst open, revealing a young man, stark naked with fair long, tousled hair.

"Hi. You must be Maggie," he said, panting breathlessly before her, picking up her bag. "I just needed a pee. Gabby's in the front room."

Maggie followed his neat bare bottom to the room and

was now confronted by a naked Gabby on all fours on the floor, rocking back and forth reciting a mantra to herself.

Maggie was encircled by candles and the heavy aroma of oils. The pool, filled to the brim, stood silently waiting in the corner. She had been well trained early in her career to be surprised by nothing she might see or hear, and not to react or offend. Her only reaction now was to suggest to the young man that perhaps they should reduce the water level in the pool. Filled near to overflowing, she could visualise the water cascading over the top again.

Gabby and Lee had enjoyed preparing themselves for this birth and their contained excitement was contagious as Maggie got down on her knees to greet the young mother. A background tape of gentle harp music created calm, as the pair breathed together through her contractions, declining offers of pain relief and resisting the urge to get into the pool too soon. They sang together, allowing only the briefest interference from Maggie as she checked on their baby's heartbeat.

As dawn broke Maggie assured Gabby that it was the right time for her to enter the pool as she was well advanced in labour.

Lee, naked, carefully listened to her advice and clambered in too, tenderly supporting Gabby from behind when she indicated she was ready to push. The birth was one that would stay with Maggie. The pair continued breathing and singing together even as their baby emerged. Lee calmly took hold of her, bringing her to the surface of the pool and placing her gently on

Gabby's chest. No anguished cries followed. The baby, eyes wide open, showing no signs of distress, inched towards a nipple and within a few minutes was sucking vigorously. It was such a beautiful and private moment that only then did the impact of the baby's arrival affect them as they physically dissolved, crying with happiness tinged with relief. Maggie, tears streaming, was just overseeing the rest of the delivery as Doctor Southgate arrived.

Leaving the young family tucked up in a bed an hour later, notes filled in and ceremonial tea drunk, Maggie drove home very slowly, moved by the enchanting and strangely spiritual experience.

Baby Eve's birth affected Maggie deeply. She knew that, whatever the outcome, she herself had to get pregnant again. She knew that for her the possibility of another miscarriage was always a risk. But it was a risk she was wanted to take. How wonderful it would be if she could produce a baby brother or sister for Charlie.

"I've been trying to point this out to you for ages, darling," Robert said as they walked back from the Dog and Duck the following night as Maggie explained how Eve's birth had affected her and how important it was for Charlie to have a sibling.

"You've been filling the place with animals when all the time what we really should have is more kids."

"I know, I know. But what if I miscarry again? That's what's stopped me. It's so upsetting for both of us."

WATER BABY

"Well, it's not going to stop us making love, is it?" he said, stopping in the lane, pulling her close. "In fact, that's exactly what we'll do – as soon as I get you home."

"Mum will still be up."

"I'll send her packing," he said, hurrying towards the cottage.

They stopped at the gate. "Come here, wife," he said, chuckling, cupping her face in his hands. "We can try every night and if it doesn't work out we'll have had a hell of a lot of fun."

"Glad you're back," Elizabeth said, opening the door at the sound of their laughter and sending Woody racing round the garden. "I'm dying for my bed. Frank took me for far too long a walk round the village this afternoon. Charlie's been angelic, although I'm hoarse from reading."

"Thanks so much, Mum. Don't let us hold you up," grinned Maggie. "We'll be up in a minute."

"You bet," muttered Robert. "G'night Elizabeth. Fancy a nightcap first, darling?" he said, propelling Maggie towards the sitting room, shooing Woody into the kitchen.

"Good boy, no whining, we're busy now," he said. "I've work to do."

Maggie was rather sorry when Susan returned to take over baby Eve's postnatal care. She'd formed a strong bond with the little family. Gabby and Lee spent most of their time in bed with their baby, who appeared to be permanently attached to her mother, suckling contentedly and gaining weight rapidly. Lee took to the

219

role of new father eagerly, and having been shown by Maggie how to bath her decided that he and Eve would bath together daily, with some comical results resulting from her very full tummy. An extraordinarily intense love exuded from them both. Maggie was aware that Eve had never cried for more than a moment before being cuddled; wrapped, carried and caressed between feeds, she was never isolated in a separate crib. Gabby and Lee showered Maggie in kisses when she left, promising to call on them when she was in the area. She felt she owed them a debt of gratitude for making her realise her need to get pregnant once more. If she were lucky she and Rob would know in a few weeks; getting pregnant had not been her problem and she'd not had to worry about it before: it was the anxiety and not carrying the babies to term that caused them both distress. She and Robert had enjoyed almost constant sex since her admission that she wanted get pregnant until he had declined her advances the night before, claiming to be too tired. A point she'd reminded him of when he'd tried to rouse her in the early hours of the morning.

Her sadness over baby Honey's death and her fears for Alice faded gradually. If they'd conceived and if she managed to go the full term she'd decided their baby would be welcomed to the world just as little Eve had been. She chuckled to herself as she drove between visits, amused at the thought of a naked Robert romping around in his Y-fronts in the birthing pool. Arriving at the clinic she felt happier than she'd felt for weeks.

"You look as if the cat has swallowed the cream, or is it a private joke?" Doctor Southgate teased, patting her on the back. "We've got a lot of mothers to see this afternoon."

Smiling, she joined him in his room. "I'm trying to get pregnant again, Doctor."

"Excellent," he said. "What fun you'll have, 'trying.'"

Chapter Twenty-Nine

End of an era

"George Jones – dead in his bed yesterday morning. Thought you'd want to know." Maggie gritted her teeth. Early morning and Edna at her worst.

"Oh no! Poor Ethel; when did you hear, Edna? Have you spoken to her?"

"Not yet; one of their neighbours came in for a loaf first thing."

"I'll call on her at lunchtime. I've got a lot of visits this morning. Does Annie know? Was it another heart attack?"

"Don't know. One of Annie Watson's neighbours came

in the shop early on. I told her so you can be sure the whole village knows by now."

"He was such a dear. She'll be heartbroken. They've had so many upsets."

"'Artful old bugger. Never gave nothing away."

"Edna, how can you say such a thing?"

"I've known him all my life, girl. I can tell you a thing or two, right old card sharp he was in his younger days."

"Don't speak ill of the dead, Edna. Isn't that what they say?"

"She's alright, though. Doted on him for years 'fore he married her."

"I must go, Edna. Thanks for letting me know. I'll see you later. I was going to call in for some ham and cheese anyway," Maggie said, resisting the urge to slam down the phone.

Robert was in the small room next to the kitchen he used as his office.

"I heard some of that, darling. Edna on form, was she? Who died?"

"George Jones. Found dead in bed yesterday," said Maggie with a sigh, perching on the side of his chair. "Poor Ethel. They'd been together almost sixty years, I think. I can't say I was too surprised to hear the news after all they've gone through. I don't suppose you heard Edna's comment? She can be so awful, even when an old mate of hers dies."

"He was pretty ancient, wasn't he? Was he the old boy that kept bees at the top of the gravel pit?"

"Yes. Remember Alice, the girl we found in the stable? Well, they named Alice's baby Honey because of his bees. I'm sure I told you how much he adored that baby, how the old couple treated her like their daughter."

"Yes, all very sad. A lot of that generation have died since we moved here, haven't they?"

"It's natural but I was thinking the other day that when each one dies the history of the village dies with them, doesn't it? Lost forever. Charlie Watt used to fascinate us with tales of his youth."

"Maybe someone in the village should start recording the history of the place. Waldersby has a very active local historian. I read an interesting piece in the local paper about their market square recently. Perhaps the Major could be approached?"

Maggie hugged him and stood up.

"Ask him. Must go or I'll never get round. Don't forget to pick Charlie up and that we're meeting in town at four o'clock. I'll try and see Ethel at lunch time. Everyone's fed and watered."

"Elizabeth's still in bed. I'll take Woody when I've finished sorting these figures out."

"Leave Mum. She never normally gets up till nine anyway. I've left her a cup of tea."

"Okay. Bye. Cold tea?"

Maggie had a busy morning bathing four babies, removing stitches, and tending to breastfeeding problems, staying as long as possible with one young mother who was not coping. She was depressed and tearful, more than the usual "baby blues". Maggie was concerned enough to call at the clinic and consult Doctor Southgate, who agreed to visit her that afternoon.

Lunchtime found Maggie parking by the gravel pit and hurrying past cars to Ethel's house, where several villagers had gathered and were chatting over teacups in her front room. Maggie recognised some of them, saying a quick hello before finding Ethel alone in the kitchen. She started to weep as soon as she saw Maggie.

"I've lost my George, and we lost our Alice and the baby," she sobbed, clinging to her. "He was a good man but he never got over the baby's death, you know. I believe that's what really killed him at the finish."

"I know, I know," Maggie soothed, mopping her own face with a tissue.

Ethel slumped into a chair. "I wish this lot would go, mind; they don't seem to understand like you do."

"They mean well, Ethel; they're all wanting to support you."

"It was peaceful, mind. George wanted a bit of cake with his tea and then he had a lie down. When I went back to fill his cup he'd gone. I tried to rouse him but I could see it was no use so I rang the doctor."

"A wonderful way to go but a shock for you, of course."

"Could you ask them to leave?"

"I'll say you want to have a little lie down, shall I?"

The women were so busy talking they seemed to have forgotten where they were and hurried away after offering help and promising to be at the funeral. Maggie rang Susan to explain she'd been delayed.

"Thank you, Maggie. Stay a bit, won't you? Annie might come by later but that's enough visitors for now. The vicar came early on and those nice men from the funeral parlour are coming this evening to go over the funeral hymns and such like. They took George's best suit and shirt and promised to put two pairs of woolly socks on him 'cos he hates the cold."

"That's kind."

"I'd like young Alice to come but she seems settled in Lewisham now with my cousin; they're getting on really well. Alice has had visits from a lady who works for a charity – something to do with babies that die in their cots. We know what happened to Honey but some little mites die for no reason; terrible for the parents. Anyway, she helps her talk about Honey. She's also going to have a little holiday in Norfolk before looking for a job again. I know it would be too upsetting for her to come you know to George's send off, remembering Honey's funeral in our church. She's promised to come and stay sometime. She'll be upset about George, won't she?"

It was too much for Ethel again. Maggie held her as she sobbed quietly before leading her into her front room and settling her in an armchair.

"She was the daughter we never had, you know. We both loved her and I've never known George to be like he was with little Honey. You saw how we took to her and that baby gave us such a lift, then she died and now my George has died too."

Maggie sat silently, holding her hand, waiting patiently for Ethel to calm down, before collecting up the teacups and making a fresh pot of tea.

"I'm going to have to get on my way, Ethel. I'll be back tomorrow. You must, if you can, try and have a sleep," she said, settling her little dog, Sammy, who'd shadowed their every move, on her lap."

"I'm not sure I can cope with this too," Maggie thought, parking hurriedly in the main car park in Waldersby, rushing towards the market square, where Elizabeth, Robert and Charlie were waiting outside a gentleman's outfitters.

"Mummy," he called. "Daddy, Mummy's here."

Maggie felt tearful and found herself getting shaky as they made their way to the end of the shop.

"Well, laddie. Let's see how smart we can make you for your mum and dad," said the young man, fielding his tape measure and jotting measurements down in his notebook. "Smaller than average," he muttered. "Long legs. Right, laddie, come with me."

It was too much for Maggie. She got and made for the exit. Elizabeth stopped her and put her arms round her, "Come on, darling. You're over-tired; don't upset yourself. Charlie's excited, look."

Robert grasped her hand as Charlie stood proudly kitted out in his new school uniform.

"I've got a tie like you, Daddy," he said. "And a badge."

Maggie could not concentrate as she sniffed and snivelled her way through the evening routines. She spent longer than usual feeding the pigs and brushing the donkeys, anything to stop her picturing their little boy, who had in an instant jumped from being her baby to a schoolboy, increasingly independent of them. She knew she was being quite irrational and her emotional state was fragile after trying to comfort Ethel in her loss on the same day as attending to such an important moment in Charlie's life. She was glad her mother had taken charge, understanding how their firstborn starting school was a defining moment in their lives. Elizabeth often mentioned how she'd felt seeing her girls do just that.

"It affects us all, darling, but don't let Charlie see you upset. It's exciting for him and his mother crying will only puzzle him," she said, serving up the evening meal. "He's gone to sleep with his new tie and school blazer on big teddy."

"Don't set me off either," said Robert. "I felt the same. D'you remember saying to me, 'treasure each day; they're only on loan', when he was born, Elizabeth? We'll just have to produce some more," he chuckled, pouring her wine.

"Hey, what about me?"

"I think you'd better stick to water, just in case." He smiled.

"Not tonight, Rob, I need it."

Elizabeth glanced at them. "Is there anything I should know?" she said.

"No," said Maggie, grabbing the bottle and pouring herself a glass. "Nothing, Mum."

Annie stood at Ethel's side in the front pew as the coffin was carefully balanced on the trestles. She could feel Ethel trembling and neither found a voice to sing the first hymn.

The church was half full with locals and a few family, not that Ethel could remember all their names. The vicar spoke warmly of George before Dawn's husband read the eulogy and recalled his working life on the Major's estate. The service ended with Bing Crosby crooning, "Every time we say goodbye", just as at Jack Newgate's funeral, as tearfully they filed out into the churchyard, making their way to the graveside.

It was comforting for Ethel to see George buried next to Charlie Watt as they'd been schoolfriends but she was needlessly upset by Edna who was heard to announce that the "partners in crime" would get up to their old tricks again, once "dead and buried".

"You know, darling, there are times when I could slap her," Maggie said as they walked back down the lane. "She doesn't think at all. She comes out with such hurtful comments."

"I'm sure they're used to her. They'd probably be more shocked if she said something nice."

They stopped, seeing Angela was waving from the window. "I'll see what she wants, Rob, because you'll need to collect Charlie soon."

Angela looked uncomfortable as she walked down the path. "Thanks for stopping. How was the funeral?"

"Sad, of course. I wondered what had happened to you. I thought you were coming. You missed the nice tea the old folk put on."

"I'm itching. It's driving me nuts. I've made an appointment to see Doctor Southgate tomorrow as I've scratched my stomach to bits."

"When did this start? You didn't tell me." Maggie was alert now; pregnant women often complained of being itchy but Angela looked bothered. It could be a complication that she needed checked.

"Last few days but it got really bad last night. I can't sleep. Tom bought me some calamine lotion but it isn't helping much."

Back in the cottage a glance at Angela's inflamed skin confirmed Maggie's initial thoughts. "I'll get you seen this evening," she said.

Chapter Thirty

A furry encounter

"Darling, it's all done and dusted. We've exchanged contracts!"

Maggie felt slightly irritated. She should be enthusiastic about Elizabeth's house purchase, but instead she felt sad at the thought of losing the home she'd grown up in, where memories of life with her father and sister were strongest.

"That's great, Mum. Well done. So what happens next?"

"The couple who've bought our house don't want to move in till next spring. He's relocating from South Africa. My little cottage is empty so I can move in when I like and

Frank thinks we should arrange that as soon as possible, so that I'm settled in before the winter months."

"Sounds as if he's moving in too…"

"No, darling. We've an agreement, remember? I must ring Eleanor so I'll speak to you later. Are you at home this evening?"

"Yes, we're both in."

"Okay. I'm so relieved everything's gone smoothly. Lots of love, catch you later. Bye, darling."

It was lunchtime and John, the farrier, was coming to trim the donkey's hooves. She checked on Danny the duck and the chickens, picking up a tin of cat food to take up to the stables. The cats were becoming quite feral and needed only a small amount of food from her now; they dined out nightly on mice and rats. Edna was kindly keeping Woody for the afternoon and Robert had business meetings in Manchester all week.

She hurried down the lane. Crumble and Biscuit were generally placid donkeys and stood calmly as she put their halters on but their demeanour instantly changed and they became agitated when John parked by the gate, heading towards them. Maggie managed to control them as he helped her tie them up, all the while talking quietly and gently stroking them. It wasn't John's first visit and gradually his calming manner helped.

"I've been studying horse whispering," he said. "It's a brilliant idea and it really works. These two probably had it a bit rough in the past."

"They're getting used to you, aren't they? I love the tone you use. Bit different to the chap I bought them off."

"Well. He was only after your money and I don't suppose he'd dare get fond of any of them knowing they were for slaughter."

"No, that's right. He was nice enough but it was just a job to him. He rang the other day and asked me if I'd take another pair."

"Really? What did you say?"

Maggie looked across to the pigs, who were busily rooting a corner of the field, and laughed. "I think my husband would kill me if I brought more donkeys home."

"I sympathise," John said. "You're as bad as my wife, only her weakness is sheep. We had an orphan lamb and now we've got a flock of twenty ewes, let alone three kids to look after too."

"I'll tell Robert. I hadn't thought of sheep," she said, laughing, untying Biscuit. "That was quick."

"Well, her hooves are a lot better than when I first saw them. Keep doing whatever you're doing 'cos it's working a treat."

Crumble shied away as John pulled the rope gently towards him. "This one was the worst, if I remember rightly."

Ten minutes later, both donkeys, hooves neatly trimmed, were enjoying mints and a carrot. John waved goodbye after arranging his next visit and Maggie left them to check on the pigs, who were getting fatter by the day, leaving the cats' food in the stable before hurrying back to the cottage to wash and change.

She had arranged to meet Susan and attend a lecture and was just closing the cottage door when she heard the phone ringing. It was Jennifer, Edna Newbold's niece, sounding agitated.

"Maggie, can you come, please? There's been an accident." She was crying as she spoke. "It's Woody."

Maggie froze. "Where is he?" Her voice was high-pitched, her legs shaking as she made to sit down.

"He's not here. Please can you come?" Jennifer sounded as if she was finding it difficult to speak. "Can you come?"

"I'm coming. Is he…?" Jennifer had put the phone down.

Maggie grabbed her car keys and reversed out of the drive so fast that she almost backed into the pond in front of the cottage. Her heart pounded in her chest as she muttered, "Please, God, don't let him be hurt."

She found a small crowd gathered outside the shop, milling onto the green. She could see an ambulance stationed near the Dog and Duck. A small blue car was embedded in the hedge, and Maggie could just make out the figure of a woman being stretchered towards the ambulance as she parked and rushed into the shop.

Edna Newbold sat rigid in a chair by the door, speechless now, making no cutting comments or thoughtless remarks, watching the ambulance crew transfer the woman.

"Where's the dog, Edna?" asked Trevor the vet, who'd also been called by Jennifer and arrived ahead of Maggie.

Edna jerked her head. "Over there," she said, pointing.

"They took Woody into the pub," Jennifer said, appearing from the back of the shop. "We don't know if he's alright, but they carried him in after the car hit him."

Maggie gasped. "Oh no. Woody's been hit by a car?"

"Yes. He was in his basket in here and this lady came in, never seen her before, wanting to know if the pub had rooms to let."

"So. What happened?" asked Trevor.

Maggie turned to the door. "Can we get him, please, Trevor?"

"It was the woman's cat. It followed her in and Woody shot out of his basket, chased it and that other car was just coming round the bend. The cat ran straight under it. It swerved, hit Woody, and..."

"I'll kill her if he's dead," muttered Edna. "I'll kill her and her bloody cat."

Maggie didn't wait to hear any more, racing with Trevor across the green.

A few people were having lunch as they rushed into the bar, but Mick, the publican, grabbed Trevor. "Thank God you've come, mate. I've tried to save him. He's in here."

He led them into an office behind the bar, where Woody was lying on a blood-spattered blanket on the floor, a heavily bloodied towel wrapped around one of his back legs. A young barmaid was sitting on the floor next to him gently stroking his head and Maggie, shaking, trying hard to remain in control, knelt beside Trevor to comfort her dog.

"Is he...?" she whispered. "Is he dead, Trevor?"

"There's still a pulse," he said. "Hold this."

Gently, Trevor removed the towel to reveal the leg, which they saw had been almost severed.

"I need to get him back. He's lost a lot of blood but he might make it."

"Tell me what to do," said Maggie. Suddenly Woody opened his eyes, whining pitifully on hearing her voice. "You're safe now, Woody. You're going to be alright," she sobbed, gently stroking him.

Trevor lifted Woody, while one of the bar staff was sent across the green to fetch his car. The dog, sedated now, was carefully carried outside. Trevor sped away as Maggie made her way back to the shop to contact Miss Thomas, the tutor, who was unusually understanding and assured Maggie that she could catch up on the lecture another day. "I'd like you to see me next week," she'd said, commiserating. "I have a little dog at home."

Maggie was relieved when Edna told her that the driver involved in the accident had escaped with only minor injuries despite burying the car in a hedge. The cat had been reunited with the mystery woman, who'd wanted a place to stay, and she'd callously driven off without leaving her name. Edna was distressed and agitated as Maggie left her to collect Charlie from Dawn.

"Edna, no-one's blaming you. It's Woody's own fault, I'm afraid. He can't resist chasing other people's cats."

"She'd no right bringing a cat in here."

"It wasn't intentional, was it? Some people travel everywhere with their pets."

"Should've been in a bloody cat basket."

"Well, we can't tell people what they should and shouldn't do. I'll phone you later and let you know what's what with Woody."

Trevor had rushed Woody to the animal hospital near Cambridge and was just leaving theatre when Maggie arrived.

"He'll make it, Maggie, but he'll only have three legs, I'm afraid," he told her. "He won't be the only dog on three legs and they do well. He's a strong little chap but it will take him a while to get over the shock, of course. He'll have to learn new tricks, balance and so on. But in a few months he'll be able to go for walks and lead as normal a life as possible. He's a very lucky little dog after losing so much blood but he'll pull through. Don't you worry."

Robert was upset when Maggie phoned him. He offered to rush home but Maggie assured him they were all coping and that Dawn was giving her a hand. "Mum got back okay, by the way. I'll tell you what she said later. Oh, Rob, the sweetest thing was when they allowed Charlie to hold Woody even though he was drugged up to the eyeballs. He held him so gently and the vet had to stop him from kissing him too much. I'm a bit concerned for Edna, who's taken it very badly, though. She's feeling responsible and thinking it was all her fault."

"That's understandable."

"He's doing well. They considered a blood transfusion at first but decided against it. He'll have to learn to cope with three legs but they've assured me he'll manage and I've already spoken to another dog owner there whose dog lost its leg in a car accident too. Apparently it's running around as if nothing's happened."

"That's amazing."

Leaving the veterinary hospital Maggie and Charlie went back to the village shop to reassure Edna that Woody was going to survive. Jennifer was by the till and had just finished serving a customer as they walked in, pointing Maggie in the direction of the back room.

"Can I have an ice cream?" Charlie asked as soon as they entered.

"Of course, you deserve one. Let Jennifer help you," Maggie said. "I'm just going to see Edna."

Edna was sitting in the gloom and looked like she'd been crying for some time. She broke down again as Maggie bent to hug her, a gesture that she'd rarely made before but she instinctively felt a surge of sympathy for her. Edna had such an extraordinarily loving bond with Woody and she listened intently as Maggie told her about the operation and the consequence of the dog being left with only three legs.

The description upset her even more and it was Charlie who came to Maggie's rescue as he ran in clutching his ice cream.

"I'll never let that dog off a lead again," Edna said. "Never."

"You can have a lick too," Charlie said, thrusting the cone into Edna's hand. "Two licks if you like."

Edna often tried Maggie's patience, but knowing how much she cared for Woody was far more important and Charlie had inadvertently lightened the atmosphere. Her son had been surprisingly unaffected by the initial sight of Woody, even mentioning how Woody could be Jake the Peg, like the funny man on the television.

Seeing Woody wag his tale at him in the hospital she had realised that her little boy was made of sterner stuff than herself. It was Charlie who was supporting her now and if he could cope then so must she.

Chapter Thirty-One

The waiting room

Maggie surveyed the occupants in the waiting room. She and Charlie were at the vet's surgery to collect Woody, assured he was ready to go home. Charlie, enchanted by pets in arms, baskets and cages, befriended a little girl learning how to weigh a reluctant puppy.

A family group, mother and three teenage sons, sat huddled in the corner, anxiously peering into the gloomy interior of a cat basket, where Maggie thought she could just see the tabby fur of their cat. An older woman sat nearby, nervously clutching a paper bag. Maggie, intrigued, smiled at her reassuringly. "Have you a pet here too?" she asked.

"Oh, yes, dearie," she sniffed. "It's little Alfie here," she said, patting the bag. "Found him upside down this morning."

Maggie was even more intrigued as the woman, summoned by the intercom, hurried off down the corridor, just as a nurse came to tell her that Woody was almost ready but was having his dressings replaced. Moments later the little lady reappeared, still clutching the paper bag.

"Natural causes, love," Maggie overheard her say to the receptionist. "The vet says fish do that, just die sometimes. Shame, 'cos he's been with me four years. I'll make him a nice little grave when I get him home."

The young receptionist showed not a glimmer of surprise, and appeared genuinely concerned. Maggie was impressed as they shared a conspiratorial look when the clinic door closed behind Alfie.

Charlie's attention was drawn to a young woman clutching a shoebox. She allowed him and his little friend to peep at her guinea pig, which had been clawed by a neighbour's cat, just as the tabby cat family were ushered into a side room. Maggie noticed their sad faces glistening with tears and felt quite overcome herself when they reappeared moments later clutching their empty basket. Suddenly the waiting room door burst open and a large man was dragged in by his dribbling Labrador, who peed straight up his leg as he waited to be booked in. A Jack Russell attracted by the smell almost followed suit as its embarrassed owner hurriedly shortened its lead and looked the other way.

Maggie was glad to be called as Charlie and his friend had a fit of giggles when the waiting room erupted with a mixture of barks, yapping and miaows.

"Now I can see how James Herriot had so many tales to tell," Maggie said, as she and Charlie were shown into a side room.

"There's never one day the same," the nurse said as Trevor appeared carrying a subdued and sleepy Woody.

Charlie wanted to cuddle him and sat on the floor, covering the little dog with kisses.

"He's going to be fine. He's been very brave and I promise you he'll get used to being three-legged in no time. I've arranged for him to have a fairly new treatment, hydrotherapy, twice a week for the next six weeks. It does wonders for equines so we'll give it a go. Can you can manage to bring him in?"

"Of course, we'll sort it out. That's wonderful. I'm sure it'll help," she said, nudging Charlie. "Woody will be in the swimming pool, darling."

"Can I swim with him?"

"No, just other dogs for their exercises," she laughed, preparing to go. "Thanks, Trevor. Thank you again for saving him."

Maggie picked up Trevor's written instructions before she and Charlie carried Woody carefully out to the car. Passing through the waiting room once more she overheard the large man mutter to his dog, "Look at that poor little bugger, mate. I'll chop your leg off if you cock it up again."

They stopped at the village shop to show Woody to Edna, who had been waiting for their news, glad to give her some comfort and reassurance as Edna had not stopped blaming herself since his accident. Woody perked up enough to wag his tail when he heard her voice, and despite her normal stern exterior she managed a smile.

"It's good to see you," she said, stroking the dog gently as she handed Charlie a fistful of doggy treats. "One at a time, lad, mustn't spoil him, must we?"

Charlie held Woody tightly on his lap as they made their way down the bumpy track to the cottage, the dog whining, obviously scenting home. Placing Woody gently in the cage she'd prepared for his recuperation in the kitchen, Maggie explained to Charlie that it would be a couple of weeks at least before they could let him run around or play chase again, a lesson that Woody was going to find very difficult to understand.

Preparations for Charlie's first day at primary school were almost complete. He was excited starting big school with his friends from playgroup. An end-of-term party gathered in the village hall, where Maggie and some of the other mothers commiserated with each other as they bade farewell to the playgroup staff. The children gobbled their way through sausage rolls and sandwiches in a hurry to get to the ice cream and jellies before being let loose to run around.

"I'm dreading it, aren't you? Our babies now proper schoolboys," Maggie said as the small group sat watching their offspring.

"The first day's the worst," someone muttered knowingly.

The first day, when it came, certainly felt the worst. Maggie drove to the school in Great Fordham rather than put him on the school bus; that would have to wait. She watched as Charlie, so smart in his new uniform, ran into the playground, giving her barely a second glance despite her tears plastering his little cheeks.

Driving home, choked with emotion, she rang Robert at the office to tell him all about it.

"Well, that's good, isn't it, darling? We want him to be happy, don't we? You'd have been gutted if he'd gone in crying, wouldn't you? Remember how awful you felt when he cried that first week in playgroup."

It was true, and she realised how irrational she was being. Far rather their little boy enjoy his schooling, among friends he'd known all his life.

Maggie put the kettle on and sat down to tell Woody all about Charlie's first day at big school. The dog, ear cocked, listened as if he understood, before whining to leave his cage.

"Come on, time for your swim," she said, tipping the remains of the tea down the sink. "And tomorrow we're going for a walk. Well, I'll walk. You can hop."

The evenings were drawing in. Autumn was approaching, with leaves showing a glint of gold before the fall and the fun of scuttling through heaps of russet leaves. There was a good harvest of blackberries, sloes, hips, haws and damsons, while squirrels scampered busily round the garden, digging fresh hiding places for nuts they'd gathered. Their frantic activity amused

Maggie as every year they buried them but then seemed to forget where. Numerous saplings would appear in odd places in the spring. If left, trees would have enveloped the cottage so Robert offered to dig them up later to help edge Tom's new field. Following Maggie's tip Robert made regular trips to the gravel pit to gather the harvest of berries and sloes for his elderflower wine and sloe gin.

Maggie and Charlie were busy brushing the donkeys and picking up the poo when she remembered that Charlie Watt's old apple press was stored at the back of the stable. Robert was delighted, already having persuaded fellow members of the darts team to help him organise an apple pressing event on the green to use up the season's abundance of apples. It seemed a crime to let so much fruit go to waste, though wasps had benefited from the glut. Maggie persuaded the over-sixties ladies to provide teas and light refreshments. Edna advertised the event and had Jennifer delivering flyers to every house.

Apple press day came and Maggie who'd offered to help with teas and supervise some of the games for the children as she was off duty, found herself answering an urgent phone call as she served up breakfast.

"Maggie, can you come, please? Angela's gone into labour and she doesn't think we'll make it to the hospital."

"Oh no, she's not due yet. What's she up to, Tom? Have you rung the hospital, ambulance?"

"I'll do that. Her waters have gone. She says the pains are really bad. She'd like you to come if you can."

Maggie called Robert to take over and hastily loaded her bags and gas cylinders into the car, which was facing down the lane. The idea of having a home birth and a birthing pool again had altered when Angela had developed high blood pressure in the last weeks of pregnancy. A spell of itching had led to her having special blood tests. The itching subsided but her blood pressure had risen and her ankles were puffy. A hospital birth had been rebooked, but now it seemed the baby had decided to alter all the arrangements. Tom was trying to stop their little daughter, Rosie, crying as Maggie hurried into the cottage.

"I've rung everyone like you said. We'll never get her to hospital now; will she be alright?" he asked, agitated.

"Yes, of course. Upstairs?"

"They said they're sending another midwife," he called after her.

Maggie was running up the stairs when there was a shout from the bathroom.

"It's coming. Baby's coming, Maggieeeee!"

She was too late; the baby lay sprawled in the soggy surroundings of a pile of bath towels, protesting loudly. Angela, propped against the radiator, was shivering uncontrollably as Maggie gave her a quick hug and prepared to separate mother from baby. Grabbing more warm towels from the airing cupboard, she wrapped the baby up and cocooned her in the empty bath. Maggie was unfazed. She'd seen her fair share of impromptu births since the start of her career, but this was her best friend and a premature baby at risk, which heightened her emotion.

"It's another gorgeous little girl. Clever mum," Maggie said. "Just a prick," she said as Angela winced. "It'll help to stop this bleed."

"Will she be alright, Maggie?" Angela clutched at her tearfully. "She's so small."

"She's going to be fine. We'll get her into an incubator as soon as the Squad arrive." Maggie quickly grabbed pillows from the bedroom to make Angela more comfortable, taking frequent glances at the baby tucked up in the empty bath. "You can hold her as soon as we can stop this."

Her concern mounted as Angela continued to bleed heavily despite her endeavours to control it. She heard Tom calling to James in the garden and shouted down the stairs, urging him to leave Rosie with James and join her upstairs.

A car screeched into the lane. Hurried footsteps paced to the front door and the next moment the nervous face of a substitute doctor appeared at the bottom of the stairs.

"Up here, quickly," she called out. Maggie had forgotten Doctor Southgate was on holiday. He would have leapt into action straight away. She had no idea who this doctor was. He appeared to be very young and alarmed as she explained the emergency, instructing him to hurry the Flying Squad. "Phone again: we need them here now."

"Try not to look so worried," she murmured, unaware it was the first home birth he had attended alone.

Tom appeared, standing anxiously in the doorway. "Is everything alright? Anything I can do to help?"

Maggie thrust the baby into his arms. "Congratulations. Another gorgeous little girl. Just hold her tight, Tom. Keep her warm while we sort Angela out. I'll call you back in a minute," she said, quickly guiding him out before turning back and working to control the bleeding.

"What a mess. I'm so sorry," Angela whispered, clinging to Maggie's arm. "I'm sorry to spoil your day off."

"Don't be silly. I'd have been really upset if you hadn't called me." Maggie tried to look cheerful as she listened out for the Flying Squad while instructing the young doctor, who seemed paralysed with fear. Moments later they arrived. The team sprinting up the stairs, taking immediate control as Maggie told them what had happened, disguising her relief from Angela.

"Thank goodness you were home," Susan said, some time later, as the pair sat in Nut Tree Cottage discussing the birth.

"It was all bit worrying before you all got here," Maggie confided. "I know Angela can be stubborn and she really didn't want to go into hospital, but she didn't plan for this to happen, poor love. I think she might need a transfusion. At least they got the little one into the unit quickly and she's doing well."

"She'll be worried about her other two."

"Tom'll manage. They have plenty of helpers. Gordon will have James and I expect she'll be back with Abigail before we know it, and you'll be back too, won't you?"

"Yes. That's a pretty name."

"She'd decided it would be Abigail or Thomas weeks ago."

"Abi's nice too. Now you get back to Rob and Charlie and your apple pressers and I'll see to the rest. I'll see you Monday and we'll catch up then."

"Okay. I'll keep back a couple of bottles."

"We might need something stronger than apple juice," Susan laughed.

Chapter Thirty-Two

This little piggy

Jeremy surveyed the pigs. "You've made a bloody good job of fattening this lot up, Maggie. Well done. Not so sure I should've parted with them after all," he said, with a laugh. "They're a good weight. Ready to go."

Maggie's heart sank. This was the moment she'd been dreading, and Robert had said she would rue the day the piglets would be ready for slaughter. She tried to conceal her feelings as she thanked him for checking them, aware he was in a hurry to get back to the weekly market in Waldesbury.

"I might see you there next week," he said. "Now

you've proved you can fatten this little lot you might fancy a couple of calves."

"Robert would have me put down if that ever happened," she said. "Thanks for coming though, Jeremy. We've really loved having them. Give my love to Amanda, won't you, and the twins. How's George getting on?"

"Spoilt to bits; the twins never leave him. Idolised and plump as a pudding," he said as they reached the gate. "Nice donkeys," he nodded in the direction of Biscuit and Crumble, grazing on the far side. "I might get one for the twins later. They make good pets, don't they?"

"Yes; you'd need two, though."

"Someone else told me that," he said, clambering into his Land Rover. "Right. I'll be off. Good to see you. Let me know what the pigs taste like. Make sure the butcher doesn't snaffle the loins. That's the best bit."

Maggie cringed. The thought of her poor pigs being chopped up was making her shudder. Her biggest worry was how she was going to explain what had to happen to Charlie. Robert wouldn't be happy either. He'd become very fond of them, and she knew he'd leave all the explaining to her.

"You got us into this, darling. You can get us out of it," he said with an "I told you so", mocking look. "I suppose you think I'm going to enjoy carting them off?"

Charlie was in the bath, covering himself in bubbles, when Maggie told him that the pigs were leaving them. To her surprise and relief he was so anxious to tell her all about his friends, and how much he loved his teacher, that she sensed her little boy was far more interested in his new life now. The destiny of their pigs was far more upsetting to her than to her son and she guessed Charlie's previous dramatic reaction to the death of Doris the chicken was not going to be repeated. Knowing this made it easier to prepare for their last day, a day she spent weeping, unable to look either pig in the eye, promising herself that she would never again have animals that had to be dispatched. Some of the old hens were still enjoying life, despite no longer laying eggs, and as far as Maggie was concerned that was how it would be for all her animals in future. She had made a big mistake but it was too late to back out now. She had to cope with it somehow finding consolation in the knowledge that at least she'd given them a life they might never have had.

Dawn's husband came to her rescue in the end, offering to load the pigs into his trailer and help Robert, while Maggie looked on. The pigs eagerly followed a line of pellets up the ramp, which made it sadder somehow. Charlie had gone off to school, saying his "goodbyes" quite cheerily that morning as Maggie pondered whether he really understood what was about to happen. Well, he'd soon know – when they were returned, packaged, labelled and in bits. Robert, reluctant as he was, allowed her to stay behind, sensing how much she regretted ever having got the piglets, cheerily waving with a "gung-ho" pretence that he was not in the least affected.

As they moved off the pigs turned and Crackling looked straight at her, trustingly, as he always did. Maggie dissolved, sobbing, back to the cottage and slammed the front door. It was the worst moment she had experienced with her animals since moving to Little Fordham, and Crackling's look made her feel wicked; she had betrayed them. Never again.

Dismayed to see the butchers van arriving so early the next day, Maggie and Robert surveyed the pile of neatly packaged and labelled pig.

"Would you like a pork chop tonight?" Robert said, giving her a comforting hug.

"Would you? Edna said she could put them in the shop freezer for us and sell them if we wanted. Funny, to think she anticipated how we'd feel."

"Well, she's right and that's a good idea. I'm afraid I couldn't touch any part of them," Robert said, pouring two large glasses of wine. "It's a bit early but here's to Crackling and Streaky."

Maggie couldn't bear to look at the packages and pushed the glass away. "You have it," she said, bending down to stroke Woody, trying not to dwell on the pigs' remains. "Woody was running well on our walk. He doesn't hop unless he's really tired, does he?"

Robert looked at Woody fondly. "Bet you'd like a chop, wouldn't you?" he said, ruffling the dog's ears. "We could get a bit sozzled, darling. We've a good enough excuse. Promise me you'll not get any more animals without talking to me first."

"I promise."

"So, drink up," he said, pushing the glass back across the kitchen table.

"I'd better not. I've already got an upset stomach."

"Well, I must say, I think you're being rather silly, darling," Elizabeth said, sounding curt on the phone. "After all, that's what you had them for, isn't it?"

"I know, Mum. It was so upsetting sending them off and then getting them back in plastic bags. I felt dreadful. We both did. I've sworn we'll never have animals again that have to be slaughtered."

"I really find you difficult to understand. D'you remember you and your sister going through a phase of wanting to be a vegetarian when you left school? Your father used to get so cross with the pair of you, rejecting half the meals he prepared – you remember how he loved to cook, darling. That phase only lasted six months and you've been tucking into burgers ever since."

"Okay, Mum. I know, at least Charlie didn't seem bothered."

"Sensible lad. I'm so pleased he's loving school. I'd much rather hear about that than this silly nonsense. Has he made lots of new friends?"

Maggie, reprimanded, felt like a naughty child. Her mother's tone of voice changed the moment they discussed Charlie.

"He's made lots of new friends, and he loves his teacher."

"Good. That'll help him settle in. Is he tired? It's a long day for little ones to have to concentrate. Such a change."

"No, on the contrary. He's full of energy when he gets home. Dawn's being marvellous, of course, collecting him from the bus for me when I can't make it."

"She really is a dear. And how's Edna getting on?"

Maggie was miffed that her mother had dismissed her feelings about the pigs. Like a child, she felt no-one understood. She was in tears again as she said goodbye and picked Woody up for a cuddle. At least he seemed to understand.

It was some months later that one of the men in the darts team, who also worked at the abattoir, revealed that when Robert had arrived with the pigs for slaughter there were tears streaming down his face. Maggie found some consolation in that, at least.

Chapter Thirty-Three

The Rogue Element

Maggie, accompanied by Woody beside her, now coping so well on his three legs, paused by the gravel pit on her way to a late morning invitation for tea, with Ethel and Annie. She'd seen a flash of movement in the undergrowth, rust-covered, the tail of a fox. She remained motionless, fervently hoping the fox would reappear. Woody, sensing her tension, tugged at the lead just as two small fox cubs appeared in the open and started playing tag in the sunshine. Entranced, hardly daring to breathe, she watched silently as they raced around the bramble bushes, grabbing at each other's tails, bouncing, giving chase and then submitting. Their mother reappeared, allowing them to clamber all over her. Suddenly Woody barked, whining and straining at the leash almost pulling her over. The strong smell of fox had reached him. In a flash they were gone, the cubs pursuing their mother as she dived for cover.

"D'you see many foxes round here?" Maggie asked, as Ethel poured her a cup of tea and steadied a plate on her lap with a slice of gingerbread. "Tuck into that, love; Annie made it this morning, didn't you?"

"Yes. Made a good batch. Edna likes my cakes for the shop. What's this about foxes, then?"

Maggie was pleased that Annie was visiting Ethel. She had been concerned about the two old ladies, especially Ethel after George's death, and Annie had seemed terribly lonely when she'd last called.

She explained how she'd watched young foxes play while out walking, not mentioning that they were just yards from Ethel's front door.

"Vermin. They'll not be around much longer. The hunt will be meeting on the green soon. That'll catch 'em all."

"What a shame. I thought they looked wonderful," Maggie said.

Annie raised her eyebrows. "You wouldn't say that if they got into your chicken run, my girl, leaving the poor things to die, ripped apart, heads off."

"I know it can be devastating and I remember Charlie Watt losing nearly all his one night. They have to eat, though, to feed their young."

"They've got rabbits for that, plenty of those little buggers in my allotment too."

Maggie was enjoying her second cup when they heard a car draw up.

"That'll be PC O'Sheridan," Ethel said, seeing the police car outside her window. "He's come about your tomatoes."

"I'll leave now and come back another day," said Maggie, anxious not to leave Woody too long.

"You stay," said Ethel. "You might hear something worthwhile," she said, hurrying to open the back door. "Your little dog's okay, curled up with mine."

PC O'Sheridan acknowledged them all as he tucked in. "Good to see you, ladies, specially glad I've got you together."

Maggie stood up. "I'd better be off. I expect you want to talk to Annie and Ethel?"

"Yes. It's nothing that concerns you but a well-known problem and one you could p'raps help us with, you being out and about so much," he said.

Maggie hesitated. "Okay, if it's not too private then," she said, sitting down.

"We've got a few lads causing trouble up on the large estate in Waldersby. Seems they've recently taken to joyriding round the villages, targeting allotments."

"Threw my tomatoes all over the place," said Annie.

"Oh dear. I'd heard nothing of this. How upsetting for you, Annie," Maggie said.

"I know the ringleaders but it means catching them at it and that's where you and your colleagues could help, Maggie. If you spot them you just give us a shout." PC

O'Sheridan brushed the crumbs from his uniform. "I just came to assure you that I'm on the case."

Annie sniggered. "It'll be the first crime you've solved if you catch the little varmints at it."

"We do our best, ladies. I just need to know if they've done any more damage since your report of the tomatoes."

The Creaseys' cucumbers had been ripped up too.

"Yes, that was reported."

"Hours of our hard work, tending all them plants," said Annie. "If I catch them blighters at it, it won't be you I'll be ringing. I'll be wringing their bloody necks."

"You mustn't take the law into your own hands, Annie," Maggie said, alarmed at the thought of the old lady getting hurt.

"Quite right," said PC O'Sheridan, getting up. "You must let us deal with them. I'll be off, then. Thanks for the tea and cake. Most welcome. Better than the wife's but I'll not be telling her that. I'll report back if we have any more trouble out this way."

Reassured they waved him off. Maggie lingered as she craved news of Alice and knew that Ethel was preparing for a stay with her in Lewisham.

"She's got herself a little part-time job. Hairdressing, of course. She's still seeing a counsellor regularly and my cousin thinks she's doing really well. She's made a few friends that way too, and even told them about little Honey," Ethel confided, wiping away a tear. "What's really surprising is that she's talking of training to be a nanny or a nursery nurse."

"Really? That's brave."

"She was good with Bobby, remember?"

"That's very true." Maggie was relieved to hear that Alice appeared to be coping. She couldn't resist giving Ethel a hug as she made to leave. "It's all down to you, you know. You've been like a mother to her."

Annie nodded in agreement. "She's right there, Ethel. I reckon you saved that girl."

Ethel, tears threatening to spill onto her cheeks, returned Maggie's hug. "And this one's saved me after losing my hubby."

Maggie slowed to peer after the foxes as she and Woody passed the gravel pit but there was no sign of them. She felt the little dog tiring as they made their way up the hill and into the village. He was stronger but it would be a few months before the loss of his leg could be completely ignored. She stopped and sat on the bench they'd installed at the top of the hill to let him rest for a couple of minutes, rubbing clean the small tarnished brass plaque in memory of Charlie Watt, before turning down the lane to collect the car. Biscuit and Crumble were by the gate, twitching their tails and occasionally stamping their hooves. She and Woody fussed them as she made a mental note to get them more spray and fringes to ward off the relentless flies. This was dubbed an Indian summer and it really was very warm. The curtains were drawn in Angela's bedroom as she passed. She'd call on her later but was now hurrying as she had a lunchtime hairdressing appointment in Waldersby, and never allowed herself to be late to collect Charlie.

Conscious of Annie's certainty that her chickens were at risk of foxes, she checked on them and the rest of the menagerie. Danny the duck was sunning himself in the porch.

"Well, you're a sitting duck," she said, promising herself that she'd check all the fencing later as she settled Woody in the kitchen.

She parked with ease in the town and was soon enjoying the luxury of being pampered in the hair salon by the young man Angela had recommended. It had been a while since she'd had a trim; she usually did her own hair but was giving herself the added treat of a shampoo and set. It was an opportunity to study her own face and ponder her mother's frequent comments whenever she visited. Elizabeth always said she was getting thin in the face and looked tired. As she looked keenly in the mirror she found she had to agree; they really could have done with a holiday this year.

The children were just lining up in the playground when she got to school and some parents were already collecting their little ones. Maggie was concerned: there was no sign of Charlie. She hurried to the reception area to ask one of the teachers where he was.

"Oh, I'm so glad you've come. We've been trying to get hold of you," the teacher said, looking agitated.

Maggie's heart missed a beat. "Why? Where's my little boy?"

"I'm afraid Charlie's been taken to the hospital. There's been an accident. I'll let our headmistress explain."

Maggie was trembling from head to toe. "What? What are you saying? Is he hurt? What happened. Tell me!"

The headmistress joined them. "Come, Mrs Groves. I'll explain," she said, ushering her towards the office.

Maggie had to sit down; the strength in her legs had drained away as a terrifying fear gripped her.

Mrs Jennings, the headmistress, laid a hand on her arm, "I'm so sorry. I'm sure he's going to be alright. They were having their cycling proficiency lesson in the cul-de-sac where we always take the little ones. Some lad on a scooter apparently raced up the road; he was showing off and then realised his mistake, so trying to be clever he turned his bike round and roared past our children, catching the bicycle that Charlie was on. It knocked Charlie over and he banged his head, I'm afraid."

"How bad did he bang it?" Maggie's voice cracked.

"The ambulance came straight away and he's been taken straight to the hospital in Cambridge." She patted Maggie's arm again. "I'm so sorry, Mrs Groves. I'll take you there now; my car's ready. We must go."

Chapter Thirty-Four

Love hurts

Robert stood in the hotel lobby, waiting for the taxi to take him to the station, regretting the train journey he'd taken rather than driving to Manchester this time. Maggie had rung him just as he'd finished his meeting with the northern group of company reps, and luckily he'd been able to leave at once. To his relief a fast train would leave within the hour. Maggie had sounded oddly calm and composed when she explained that Charlie was in the head injury unit in Cambridge, he thought, almost choking on the coffee he was trying to swallow. His head thudded with anxiety as his trembling hand spilled the hot liquid down his jacket. Dear God, please let him pull through, he whispered, as the taxi pulled up.

Maggie sat immobile, watching the clock on the ward, hypnotised by the blinking and beeping of individual machines in the unit. Four other children, ranging in age, lay still, as trained staff worked tirelessly, checking, recording, monitoring as they moved from bed to bed.

The doctors and nurses handled her, and the other parents, with meticulous care. Upbeat conversations, though brief, were all they needed to keep their sanity, Maggie thought, as the desire to scream was her first reaction on seeing Charlie lying there, silent and still, his head swathed in bandages, his small hand lifeless in hers as she willed him to open his eyes and come back.

"Tell me again, what were they doing. Who was supposed to be looking after them, for heaven's sake?"

Robert and Maggie clung to each other outside the confines of the ward as she went through Charlie's accident in detail, repeating what the headteacher had said.

"It was no-one's fault, darling. Mind you, I'd like to get hold of that lad on the scooter."

"Why the hell didn't they catch him?"

"I told you why, Rob. Come on. We need to get back to Charlie."

"I think your idea of taking turns sounds best. D'you want a coffee or tea?"

"Look, you go home, sort Woody and everything out, then come back and meet the ward sister."

"Okay. What about food? Shall I get something at the shop? Not that I feel I could eat anything right now."

"Dawn's seen to all that. She's put meals in our fridge. Go on, darling, please."

"I really don't want to leave you, Maggie. You look exhausted."

"*Go*. I'm alright, darling. We must be strong for Charlie," she said, eyes sparkling with unshed tears as she pushed open the swing door. "Give Woody a hug."

Conducting an early-morning round, brash Mr Baines, the brain consultant, announced, "No harm done. Massive bump but fortunately no fracture seen on X-ray," as if their Charlie were nothing but a specimen for students to learn from. The cowed students gathered at the end of Charlie's bed seemed even less concerned about Maggie and Robert's son – terrified by the consultant's barrage of questions. Robert and Maggie were waiting nervously, anxious not to miss their discussion.

"We've sutured the small scalp wound and initially treated him for concussion, sedating him with bromide and chloral." He paused, turning abruptly to a female student. "Tell us the signs of a fractured skull, and what are the dangerous complications?"

The student paled and visibly took a deep breath before answering.

"Quite right." Mr Baines paused before facing the other students. "Glad to know some of you are paying attention," he said brusquely, turning to move on to the next ward.

Robert and Maggie, thanks to the ward sister, managed to stop him striding off.

"When d'you think he'll be able to go home?" Maggie asked. "It's such a relief to hear you say there's no fracture, doctor."

"He's a fortunate little boy," he said, his tone of voice gentler now. "He's sleepy. It's the drugs, of course, so we'll keep him another day in here, and then he may be fit to leave. I'll decide and see you beforehand," he said, heading off down the corridor after his students.

"Thank you," they chorused.

"What a relief. Charlie's certainly been lucky," Robert said, turning to the ward sister.

"Yes, we're being extra careful with him. I know Mr Baines won't let him go till he's certain he's fit enough. I'm sure he'll be back at school in no time after a few days' rest and quiet at home and he'll soon be back to normal."

The afternoon visit was very different as Robert entered the ward to be greeted by Charlie sitting up in bed, waving. "Daddy. Look what the nurse gave me."

One of the nurses winked at him. "We've a stock of donated toys. Charlie's chosen some and I said he could keep those soft toys, a chicken and a pig."

"That's no surprise, is it, Charlie?" Robert laughed, hugging him. "You'll soon be home to look after the animals again. Mummy's missed having your help."

It was three days before Charlie was finally allowed home. Mr Baines wanted a closer eye kept on him before letting him go. The wound healed. Charlie proudly showed off the stitches visible above his forehead.

The staff made a fuss of him as he left clutching not only his toys but a full box of chocolates his favourite nurse, Julie, had given him.

"I think you'd rather stay in hospital, darling." Maggie laughed, settling him in the car. "You've made a lot of friends, haven't you? Julie said you've been a star patient."

"Yes, and the doctor let me listen to his heart with his stefiscoop. He said I could be a doctor one day."

"That's a good idea. Then you can look after me and Daddy when we're poorly."

Charlie giggled. "Yes, and Nana and my teacher," he said, excited to be going home. "Can we get Woody now, Mummy?"

"I'm stopping at the shop to collect him. He's been missing you too, and then it's straight home. Daddy's gone into Waldersby for fish and chips."

"Woody likes chips. I'll show him my stitches too. They're bigger than his were."

Woody was so excited to see them that Maggie decided Robert would have to pick him up later rather than have him tumble all over Charlie in the back of the car. Edna, sorry as always to let the little dog go, had already packaged up extra treats for him. She waved to Charlie as she tucked a box of choc ices into Maggie's basket.

"Everyone's been coming into the shop to ask about Charlie. Worried sick, we all was."

"It's been a bit of a nightmare, I must say, Edna, but thankfully he's going to be fine. He just needs a few days' peace and quiet at home and then he can go back to school."

"Reckon you should sue them," she said, sniffing indignantly.

"Sue? Who?"

"The school?"

"Why?"

"Well, I call it neglect."

"No-one's to be blamed at the school," Maggie said, trying hard to sound calm.

"Shouldn't be in the streets riding bikes at his age."

"I'll tell you all about it another day, Edna. I just need to get him home now," Maggie called, hurrying back to the car. "Thank you for the ice creams."

"Thank goodness he's not too badly hurt, darling. I can't imagine how worried you must've been. Are the doctors absolutely sure he's going to be alright?" Elizabeth asked. It was her third phone call the following day. "I'm coming down tomorrow so you can tell me all about it and at least I'll be able to look after him for you. Poor little darling. I can't wait to see him. Poor Robert too. I keep thinking of the shock he had being up in Manchester and then both of you seeing Charlie all sedated. Oh dear..."

"Slow down, Mummy, please. Charlie's absolutely fine now. In fact, you'd hardly know anything had happened apart from the stitches. The district nurse is coming to take them out tomorrow; they won't let me do it." Maggie said, holding the phone at arm's length as her mother's voice got shriller and more agitated. "I've got to go now. I'm just serving up so looking forward to seeing you. I take it Frank's bringing you here. Robert will be here as

I'm having to do a clinic as Susan's off. Sorry, must go. Charlie's absolutely fine, I promise. In fact, he's shouting out for more spaghetti hoops."

"Alright, darling. Give him a cuddle from me. See you tomorrow, then."

"Bye, Mum."

Maggie hurried back to the kitchen to empty the contents of the saucepan onto Charlie's outstretched plate. "Another sausage?"

Charlie nodded, his mouth too full to speak as Maggie piled another sausage on top, "Nothing wrong with your appetite, darling, I'm glad to say."

Maggie's relief at knowing Charlie was fully recovered overwhelmed her, and the knowledge that she was now pregnant remained their secret. She'd been frightened that she would miscarry following the shock, and had had a scary moment the day after Charlie's accident. She was prepared to lose the baby as long as their child survived and the griping twinges and slight loss she experienced were no surprise. It proved more of a surprise and a relief to hear Doctor Southgate reassure her that all was well.

Cuddling up to Charlie in the sitting room as he watched his favourite television programme after scoffing one of Edna's choc ices, she was overcome with the love she felt for him. To have lost the baby would have been a sacrifice; to have lost Charlie would have destroyed them.

Chapter Thirty-Five

Moving day

Elizabeth stepped through the front door of Nut Tree Cottage, waving a cheery farewell to Frank Sutton reversing his car, before he headed back down the lane.

"I've been so worried about you, darling," Elizabeth confessed, removing her coat and wrapping her arms around Maggie. "You were quite short with me yesterday on the phone."

"Was I? Sorry, Mum, didn't mean to be. How was your journey?" Maggie asked, returning the hug and breathing in her mother's familiar perfume. "Missed you."

"Have you? I'm glad to be here now. Frank's not stopping – he's exhausted and he has to go and pick up the keys for the cottage. But I've been so worried," she said, flopping down heavily into an armchair in the sitting room and pulling off her silk scarf. "Goodness me, that wood burner pumps out the heat. I hope it's the same for the stove in my cottage."

"Hi, Elizabeth," Robert called, opening his office door. "With you in a minute. I'm just on the phone."

"The kettle's on. I've got to get to the clinic, though, but I'll try and be back early," Maggie said. "Tea or coffee? Did you have lunch on the way down?"

"Oh, tea, I'll make it. Yes, we stopped at a very nice hotel," Elizabeth said. "Now where's my grandson, darling? I'm dying to see him. You keep telling me he's alright but I can't seem to stop worrying."

"Dawn's bringing him back in a minute so I'll get going, if that's okay. She took him and Woody for a walk, bless her. Look, I'm sorry I was a bit 'short', Mum. We're just trying to get back to normal and Robert's had so much work on this week. I'm making sure I'm with Charlie as much as possible, not that we need to be worrying about him anymore because he's completely recovered and I'm sure he'll want to show you his scar. He's shown it to everyone, even the postman."

Elizabeth found it difficult to hold back her tears when Charlie returned. Her grandson perched on her lap proudly showing her his scar, and sitting meekly beside them a three-legged Woody wagging his tail.

"Woody can run faster than me and he jumped over a big log," Charlie announced. "I think he likes having just three legs, Nana. I'll show you where his leg came off," he said, jumping down and gently lifting up the dog's back leg. "Look, he's got a stumpy bit."

"So I see, darling. I'm sorry you've both been in the wars, though." She blinked, dabbing at her eyes. "Mummy says you've kept your stitches to show me?"

"Yes, come on," he said, guiding her back towards the kitchen.

Elizabeth peered into the glass jam jar to examine the contents. "Goodness me, there are a lot," she said, amused now at the serious tone of voice Charlie adopted as he counted each one.

"Nine, Nana, but Woody had more than me."

"You haven't kept his too, have you?"

"No, they're at the hospital."

"The vet kept them, didn't he?" Robert said, joining them and winking at Elizabeth. "Pop the stitches back. Your tea's ready now, Charlie. Mummy'll be back soon."

After supper Maggie and Elizabeth settled down in the cosy sitting room, while they waited for Frank and Robert to come back from the Dog and Duck, where they'd gone to enjoy a darts match. Charlie's bath time had left both mother and daughter exhausted. Elizabeth had allowed far too much bubble bath and both Nana and grandson had had hysterics as bubbles reached the ceiling. It had taken Maggie quite a time to settle him down afterwards, but two chapters of *Wind in the Willows* had done the trick.

"He wants to get back to school next week," Maggie admitted. "The consultant at the hospital has discharged him and says he won't need to see him again."

"I must say, he doesn't seem bothered at all and he's very proud of his stitches. It must have been such a trying time for you both."

"I've never been more frightened. At one point we thought we were going to lose him, which was beyond awful, but they were wonderful in the hospital. The worst time was when they'd sedated him and there was talk of a possible brain injury."

"Oh, darling." Elizabeth gently squeezed her arm. "Thank goodness you can put it all behind you now. You've had far too many worries to deal with these last few months. I'm so thankful I'm moving down here. I can't get over Woody either. He doesn't seem a bit bothered about the loss of a leg. Remarkable."

"He's such a brave little dog. Charlie and he are quite inseparable. And I have some brilliant news," Maggie said, topping up her mother's glass of wine. "Despite everything, Mum, I'm pregnant."

Elizabeth almost spilt her drink. "No! Really, darling? Now, that is good news. How long have you known?"

"Not long. In a few weeks I'll be more confident of keeping this little one."

"I'm surprised after the terrible shock and with your history that you've managed to hold onto it. You are clever," said Elizabeth, her voice breaking.

"Doctor Southgate has convinced me this baby will be

alright. And I feel different, I really do. I feel much further on. My tummy's huge, probably no muscle tone."

"I just thought you'd put on weight, darling, you know, comfort eating."

Maggie laughed. "That too. I wasn't going to tell you yet. No-one else knows."

"I won't tell, or can I tell Frank?"

"No, not yet. You've a lot to think and worry about too, moving house, leaving your friends. Leaving Daddy!"

"Now, don't upset me. I tidied his grave last week and as you and Eleanor said I can always visit. I've promised to go and stay with some of our oldest friends. You remember the Wyndhams, the Scotts, the Richards? They've all said I can stay. The house was difficult to leave but it's lovely moving nearer to you and my grandchild – grandchildren – soon," she said, laughing. "Hopefully your sister will move this way too. That's all I want. My family around me."

With Frank Sutton in charge, the house move had gone without a hitch and now Elizabeth was proudly showing both her daughters round her new home. Eleanor had arrived earlier that morning, determined to be her mother's first house guest.

"D'you see the church spire, darlings, from my bedroom? Such a pretty view over the rooftops. I love this old part of town, don't you?"

"It's lovely, Mummy," Eleanor agreed. "I had no idea the garden was so big. A little greenhouse too. You'll be growing tomatoes like Daddy always did. I love the brick and flint wall. It affords you a bit of privacy."

"There're some well-established shrubs, and look at these roses," Maggie enthused, as the three of them investigated every corner of the garden. "Two apple trees, golly."

"No, that one's a Victoria plum. My favourite," Elizabeth said with a shiver. "Come back inside; we'll have a coffee."

Inside the cottage felt warm and cosy, Frank having lit the old-fashioned stove earlier. Elizabeth and her daughters moved from room to room, planning, rearranging and reminiscing as old familiar objects appeared.

"Daddy would have loved it, Mum," Maggie said. "I think you've done the right thing. So glad you can stay a couple of days too, sis," she said, giving them both a hug.

"So am I," said Eleanor. "I've got three days' holiday so I can browse the estate agents tomorrow."

Elizabeth sighed happily. "I'm so lucky to have you both here now. Pour the coffee, one of you. Can you stay, Maggie?"

"I've got half an hour before l need to leave to get Charlie. It's his first day back at school and I'm determined to be there to collect him."

Maggie's heart started thumping when she arrived at the school and saw Charlie running towards her in tears.

"That big boy pushed me over, Mummy," he sobbed, pointing across the playground. "He was pinching my friend Simon." He stopped to draw breath. "He pushed me," he said, tears squeezing through his tight fists.

Maggie hugged him to her as some of the other mothers drew close, murmuring their sympathy.

"I know the lad," said one. "Always a bit of a bully at playschool." There were several nods of agreement from the others as Maggie looked round for the offending child, who had disappeared from view.

Simon's mother came over. "I've spoken to his dad. I don't think he'll do it again," she said, grimacing. "He's got in a bit of a lather telling his son what was what. I almost feel sorry for the boy."

"No wonder the child's a bloody bully," said one sagely.

Charlie brightened up after waving goodbye to Simon, and the promise to stop at the village shop and choose one of Edna's ice creams.

Maggie tried to sound bright and cheerful in front of Charlie, but was seething inside. After all the trauma and injury her child had been through, knowing how he had been looking forward to getting back to school, wanting to play with his little friends. Instead he'd come up against the school's bully. Hiding her own tears, she decided to see the headmistress next day. Bullying needed to be rooted out as early as possible.

"You always get one in a school," Edna said. "Your young lad will have to learn to look after himself. Best tell his teacher, then she can keep an eye on things."

Maggie bristled, gathering up the few groceries Edna had put aside for her. "No-one should ever have to teach such a thing. I have to protect him after everything he's been through. We can't afford any more knocks."

"He'll get over it. Look: he's happy now he's back with Woody."

"Yes. Thanks for having Woody," Maggie said, wanting to change the subject before Edna could give her any more child psychology advice. "Did he behave?"

"I've never known him not to," Edna said waspishly. "Always good with me."

"Come on, darling, say thank you to Edna," Maggie called. "Thank you, Edna, I'll see you Friday. Mum's settled into her cottage in Waldersby, by the way."

"Thought she was going to be living with that chap, Frank Whatsisname."

"They may decide to do that but not at the moment," Maggie said, moving away quickly before Edna launched into one of her lectures on living in sin.

In the lane Maggie waved to Angela, standing by her kitchen window, and mouthed, "See you later," as they stopped at the field gate for another ritual. The donkeys seemed to sense exactly when Charlie would be coming home, and were standing waiting. Woody licked their eyes and ears as they bent their heads against the bars of the gate, affection they both seemed to relish. Maggie smiled as Charlie told the donkeys how the big boy at school had pushed him. In return they nudged him through the bars, looking sadder than usual, as they chomped on the peppermints he offered.

"They know what I'm saying, Mummy," he said with a little grin.

"They do, Charlie, they do," said Maggie.

CHAPTER THIRTY-SIX

DOUBLE TROUBLE

A week later a shivering group of parents, mainly mothers, stood huddled together at the school gates waving goodbye, as their children ran off towards their classrooms. It was bitterly cold and all the talk among the children was of what they'd do later.

"Daddy's making me a sledge if it snows," Charlie announced.

"Mine is too," shrieked Simon. "We can whiz down the hill."

"Mummy says we can pinch my donkeys' carrots for a snowman's nose," giggled Charlie.

Maggie and Robert had attended the parents' evening and were relieved to hear how confident Charlie was becoming. He had quickly got over being pushed by the bigger boy. Their child had learnt a lesson they'd hoped he'd never have to face. The teacher explained how she'd teamed the same boy up with Charlie and Simon and their other friend Alex for some of the games in the playground. The headmistress had addressed Maggie's concerns about bullying and the incident was now forgotten.

Preparations for Christmas and the end-of-term school nativity play were on everyone's minds. Charlie and Simon were to be cast as shepherds. Alex was one of the kings and the bigger boy, Nicholas, was to be Joseph, a surprising nomination which amazed all the parents, including the boy's own father.

"He's no bloody angel," he told anyone prepared to listen at the school gates. "Mind you, his teacher might transform the little blighter for us – here's hoping."

The shorter days and dark evenings of winter meant the animals needed more attention. Shuffling through autumn leaves provided more fun in the lane on the way to stable up the donkeys and give them their hay but snowfalls were brief, much to Charlie's disappointment. Maggie was surprised how thick the donkeys' coats were becoming when she brushed them – she wanted to buy rugs or winter coats for them, but Trevor, the vet, dissuaded her.

"Stabling them up is all these chaps need," he said, making one of his routine visits. "I hear they're booked up for the school nativity?"

"Yes," Maggie said. "The vicar's also asked if they can star in the crib service at the church."

"Both of them? You could be Mary. Ride in on Biscuit. That would cause a stir."

"No, Trevor, I won't be doing that," Maggie laughed. "I can't separate them, though; they go everywhere together. The vicar doesn't seem to mind, and the headmistress is delighted."

"Jesus is well catered for then," he said, amused at the thought. "I'll be in church for that service so I can help if they decide to do a runner."

"Goodness, don't even think it."

"If you want my advice, Maggie, it would be a good idea to have a practice first, just so they don't take fright."

"Thanks. Robert also suggested that so we're going to give it a go at the weekend –say your prayers!"

Maggie sighed sleepily, relaxing after supper that evening. Robert was idly flipping through the travel section of the *Waldersby Gazette*. "I've always fancied skiing."

"You fancy skiing and I'd rather go to a safari park but as we haven't managed a trip to anywhere this year we'll both have to wait," Maggie retorted. "Anyway, this has put paid to any such ideas," she said, gently patting her stomach. "I hope you're coming with me next Thursday."

"Of course."

"Dawn's happy to look after Charlie for us and if I sort out the animals can you give Woody a run before we go? Mum offered but we should be back by four. I've been feeling so sick this week. I don't want to drive if I can help it."

"When are you going to let them know? D'you have ideas for a leaving date?"

"Miss Thomas knows. She's arranging extra cover."

"What did Doctor Southgate say?"

"He's delighted that I'm hanging in there this time round. The scan will reveal all and confirm his suspicions, or not."

"Is having a scan a good idea? I thought they were a cause for concern."

"I'm sure one won't hurt."

"When shall we tell Charlie?"

"Not yet. I don't trust myself. The thought of losing two – if it is two – makes me even sadder."

"Come on, Maggie," Robert said, hugging her close. "Don't let's think of the sad times. I think it's amazing and *if* it's twins – well, I really don't know what to think really. It's incredible, isn't it?"

"I don't think there're any in our family but I haven't asked Mum yet. It's probably your fault," she said, dissolving into laughter. "We don't know anything about your lot."

"Want a cuddle?" Angela said, passing Maggie her sleeping baby. The two women were enjoying lunch in Angela's warm, newly decorated kitchen. All the work on Watt's Cottage was finished and Maggie had been admiring Angela's flair for brightening up the darkest corners in every room. "Another cup? You always said we should have the third baby first. She's an angel. Feeds like a dream."

"It's right, though, isn't it? You learn on the first, get confident with the second and ignore the third 'cos you're so busy, and they're as contented as can be. I've noticed it with all my mums."

"James adores her. Rosie loves helping me top and tail or bath her. No sign of jealousy there, I'm glad to say. We thought there might be."

"How's Tom coping with you all?" Maggie asked, hugging the baby close. "He was a bit harassed when I bumped into him last night in the lane."

"A bit fraught. No, he's fine really. He's been promoted and his department is busy so he's quite tired when he gets home."

"Good thing you kept the nanny on."

"Yes, and now your secret's out you'll have to get in some help if it's twins. You'll never manage Charlie, two babies and all those animals as well."

"Oh, we'll be fine. Mum can't wait to help out and now she knows she's beside herself."

"She's settled in well, hasn't she? D'you think Frank will join her here? Maybe they'll eventually move in together."

"I'm not sure. Mum quite enjoys her independence and their current arrangement seems to suit her. She's already joined the WI as well as the history group and is hoping to start art classes. I guess the cruise they're going on after Christmas will be their defining moment."

"I meant to tell you that Gordon called yesterday. Sends you his love and says he's playing golf with Robert next weekend."

"Yes, I know. I'm glad you're still civil to each other. Rob's only managed four golf lessons with the golf pro so far. I have a feeling golf might take over from darts. He's enjoying it."

"Gordon's okay with Tom too, you know. They've found sharing James easy, not that Gordon has him to stay that often of course."

"What's Gordon's new girlfriend like?"

"Tom tells me she's very young and a bit brassy."

"That won't last, then."

"No." Angela laughed. "He's too choosy."

"You were his best choice."

"Kind of you but we really weren't suited. Tom's the perfect partner for me. You and Robert are a perfect match too, I always think."

"We've had our moments but Charlie's the cement in any cracks and if I manage to hang onto this pregnancy our lives will certainly be enriched. Here, she's wriggling; d'you want me to change her before she wakes?"

"No, I'll feed her and she can have another nap before the children come back. Rosie's sure to waken her, little menace. James always insists on having a long cuddle too."

The baby stirred, stretched, yawned, opened her eyes and gazed unwaveringly at Angela as she took her from Maggie, before latching on and feeding eagerly.

"So, have you finally agreed on Millicent for her name?"

"Yes, we all like it. Millie for short. I'll have to fix a date with the vicar for the christening. Late spring, we think."

"I love the name. I'll be huge by then, a giant godmother," Maggie laughed as she got up and stretched. "That was a nice cuddle. I'm just going to pop up to the shop. D'you need anything?"

"No, thanks. Now take care." Angela raised her face as Maggie bent to kiss her and tenderly stroke the baby's head.

"Enjoy these precious moments," Maggie murmured.

"Will do."

"Love to Tom. Bye, Millie."

Maggie held Robert's hand tightly as the minutes ticked past.

"Nervous, darling?"

"Yes. Silly, isn't it?"

"No. I am too."

"Deep breaths; that's what I always tell my mums."

"I thought that was just for the birth."

"It's calming," Maggie whispered, giggling nervously, glancing round the clinic, trying to cross her legs. "I'm going to burst if we don't go through soon." Right on cue, a stern voice called, "Maggie Groves?"

Maggie hardly dared breathe and flinched as the cold gel was smeared over her stomach. The radiographer peered intently at the screen as she probed. Robert was now holding his breath too, watching her, scrutinising the complex images, trying to make sense of what he could see. Suddenly the radiographer stopped probing. Smiling broadly, she turned to face them.

"Look." She pointed to the screen. "Congratulations. It's definitely twins."

Maggie burst into tears. Robert gripped her hand tightly.

"Are you sure?" he said, his voice cracking.

Chapter Thirty-Seven

Two for the price of one

"What on earth did they use before striped tea cloths?"

"They were around in your day too, darling," Elizabeth said, chatting with Maggie on their way to the school for the afternoon performance of the nativity play. "The essential headgear for all budding shepherds."

"So I gather. Robert's hoping to get back in time, by the way. He'll go straight there to help Tom unload Biscuit and Crumble. Thank goodness they offered to look after them."

"You couldn't have managed, darling. Angela has her hands full with her little ones, doesn't she, so she can't help you as much these days."

"Yes. Tom's busy too but he's such a nice chap, always offering to help where he can. He and Robert have become good friends. Rob will be tired after three days' business and a stopover at his Auntie Jenny's, which I'm dying to hear all about."

"He hasn't seen her for months, has he? I'm sure he wouldn't want to miss this, though, and he's definitely needed for the donkeys."

"No, he'll love it. Charlie was so excited this morning. I hope he remembers his lines."

"Does he have many to say?"

Maggie laughed. "No. Just three words – 'Follow that star.'"

"Ha. I remember you and Eleanor dressed up as angels. Daddy and I were so proud of you. It was upsetting for our friends' little boy though. I don't expect you remember the incident. You were too little."

"What incident? Sounds ominous."

"I remember the child's name now. Percy. Poor little lad. He was so nervous playing one of the kings that when it was his turn to offer his gift of frankincense he burst into tears, and a very large puddle formed at his feet."

"Oh poor thing. What did we do?" asked Maggie.

"I'm afraid you all got the giggles."

"His parents must have been mortified."

"They were."

"I don't think Charlie will have an accident but he may well get the giggles, especially if Biscuit or Crumble disgrace themselves in any way."

"Might they?"

"Who knows? Hope not but I wouldn't be at all surprised if Biscuit decided to do a giant poo."

"Goodness, that would cause an upset. A ghastly smell, apart from anything else. Ugh, quite horrid."

"Don't shudder, Mum. It's all perfectly natural."

"Yes. In their stable, darling, maybe."

"Well, he'll be in a stable, won't he?" Maggie said, almost swerving off the road, overcome by laughter.

"Careful, darling. This car could so easily be crushed; it makes me quite nervous. I don't find it at all comfortable and I'm not pregnant. You'll never be able to get into this in a few months' time will you?"

"Rob's been checking out a family-size car for us. I'll be sad to lose this little Mini, though. I love it." Maggie was still smiling at the image of poor Percy and his puddle as she parked. "Oh good, Rob's made it. He's parked over there next to the horsebox."

Seated, Elizabeth and Maggie beamed at the sight of Charlie and the children gathered on the stage, each waving excitedly to their own mummies, daddies and grandparents. Teachers hidden behind straw bales tried to subdue them to no avail before a hush fell. The headmistress made a short speech and the lights dimmed for the performance. All was going well until Mary unfortunately dropped baby Jesus as she appeared on the stage. He was grabbed by one of the sheep and placed upside down in the crib as the first loud "hee-haws" heralded the entrance of Biscuit. Crumble, now separated from his companion and being held by Robert backstage, kept up a mournful braying, which drowned out everything the children said.

Tom, dressed in a long cloak, hung onto Biscuit, who was tucking in, hungrily, to the straw lining the manger. A brief moment of silence was broken by the sound of Crumble passing wind and the familiar aroma of dung. Elizabeth looked shocked. Maggie, gripped by a wave of hysterical laughter, rushed out of the room, thinking that she could quieten Crumble, who had started braying again. The headmistress jumped onto the stage, flapping her arms in an attempt to control the giggling children.

"I hope you don't think we should still take them to the crib service," Robert said, relaxing in the sitting room after supper with a double gin.

"I can't let the vicar down, can I?"

"Of course you can, darling. I'm sure he doesn't want a similar pantomime."

"It'll be different in the church if we keep them together, won't it? Crumble just can't bear losing sight of Biscuit. That was the trouble. They were beautifully behaved when you rehearsed them."

"Maggie, you're being quite irrational. I don't know what happens to the minds of pregnant women."

"What's that supposed to mean?"

"Exactly what I said. There was nothing to distract them when I took them there the other evening. It could be very different when the church is full of people and giggling kids. It's a religious service of great meaning to many people and our donkeys cavorting up and down the aisle might – just might – cause a little offence to some."

Maggie flopped down beside him on the settee as laughter and tears took hold.

"I'll say this for our babies; they must be hanging onto their umbilical cords because I haven't laughed so much for ages."

"I must say you had me worried, laughing so hard. I'm not sure the headmistress was that amused."

"Did you hear the caretaker? He'd already cleared up the dung and put it on his flower bed by the time we left. I told him he's more than welcome to collect as much as he'd like anytime he's passing here," Maggie said, making a mock dive for his glass. "I could really do with a drink."

"Well that's out of the question."

"Rotter. Frank's taken Mum out to dinner. She'll probably drink far too much. She was so mortified and kept apologising to the headmistress for our 'naughty donkeys'. What a hoot."

"Here, darling," Robert got up and poured her a tonic. "Imagine the gin. Lemon? I haven't had a chance to tell you about my visit to Auntie Jenny. Can't wait to fill you in."

"Oh, Rob. I almost forgot. Tell me, how was she? Does she still have a lot of animals?"

"Not anymore. She's quite frail and only has her two old dogs and a few chickens. She said she'd love to see you one day but I explained that we'd probably leave that until after the babies arrive."

"We should have made an effort to visit her, you know."

"I wouldn't worry. She's quite reclusive and not keen on visitors."

"Did you ask her about twins in your family?"

"Well, that was interesting. She thinks she was a twin and that she was told the other baby died before they were born. She was a bit vague about it. D'you think that's possible?"

"Yes. Perfectly possible. It's called the vanishing twin syndrome."

"It sounds awful."

"We get scanned now so it's picked up more easily."

"How upsetting."

"Fairly unusual for twins down the male line but not unknown so you are possibly to blame after all."

"We'll probably never know. One day, when I've got more time, I'd like to do a bit of digging into our backgrounds."

"Great idea, especially if we discover we're descended from royalty."

"Infidels and bank robbers, more like. Come on, let's get to bed. I'm bushed."

"Carry me up."

"What? Three of you? No way," Robert said, giving her a hand to get off the settee. "Steady now," he said, hugging her. "After you."

Chapter Thirty-Eight

Another Beached Whale

Maggie slumped heavily onto the settee, knowing exactly which cushion to stuff into which gap for comfort, raising her legs so she could actually see her feet again. Sipping her mug of tea, balanced on the ample shelf developing beneath her breasts, she gazed out of the sitting room window. The spring sunshine and display of daffodils beneath the glory of the magnolia tree in front of the cottage lifted her spirits as she contemplated what the future held for her and her family. Robert had returned to his office in Waldersby after accompanying her to the clinic for a check-up. Maggie had amused the staff she knew well sailing into the clinic, her bump before her and the rest of her seeming to follow five minutes later. She did indeed feel like the proverbial beached whale as Susan and Doctor Southgate checked her over and declared the babies to be "growing nicely". She had been off duty for a few weeks, having said her farewells to the mothers in her care earlier than she had hoped. Doctor Southgate was insisting that she rest more to ease some of the aches and pains she had developed in her back and beneath her bump. Robert also fretted about her puffy ankles and awesome size, but all was well.

She watched Danny the duck busily shovelling his beak beneath every plant, searching out juicy worms, accompanied by a visiting male mallard. Two squirrels raced each other up the trunk of the tree, and a pair of blackbirds fought over territory as a medley of blue tits, sparrows, two robins and a woodpecker sped back and forth between the peanuts and bird seed that she'd put out early that morning. A wild rabbit appeared through a gap in the hedge and a small muntjac deer hopped brazenly over the garden gate. Maggie was astonished and delighted by the amount of activity in the garden. She and Rob had been so busy that there had been little chance to watch the wildlife coming and going. Robert had almost given up trying to grow vegetables since Charlie Watt had died. Neither was a keen gardener; it was hardly surprising that everything looked a little chewed.

The old apple tree was coming into leaf and she mentally planned just where the pram would go. The thought gave her a jolt, knowing the demands of one baby was tiring enough. She hoped she would be able to cope easily with twins and the double demands they would make. She patted her bump, delighted as one of the babies moved inside her, causing small mounds to appear, which she gently pressed. She had felt babies move many times and enjoyed the pleasure her mothers experienced in her professional capacity. Feeling her own babies move inside her now was a special thrill. Contented and comfortable, she dozed, a precious moment to enjoy before Charlie crashed through the back door and demanded a cuddle.

Charlie had reacted well when he'd been told about the twins in his mummy's tummy and they had involved him as much as possible. He accompanied Maggie to most of her visits to see Doctor Southgate and loved being allowed to hold the doctor's "little trumpet" to his ear and hear their heartbeats. He went on a special shopping trip with Elizabeth to choose the twin pram and baby clothes and helped Robert prepare and paint the spare bedroom for their nursery. He was putting together his own collection of toys for them and a small pile of well-used teddies was deposited in the cot.

Woody also sensed the changes and had taken to sleeping outside the nursery door during the day.

Startled by the phone ringing, Maggie groaned as she eased herself off the settee and waddled to the phone. She'd always disliked the term used in connection with pregnant women, but it's definitely what she did. The caller was just about to ring off as she picked up the receiver.

It was not easy to hear who it was as there was loud music playing in the background, so she shouted, "Hello, hello. Can you hear me?"

"Maggie, it's me." A voice in the distance was barely audible.

"I'm sorry. Can you turn the music down?" She was yelling now.

It stopped instantly and an apologetic voice said, "Maggie, it's me, Jacky. I'm ringing from Spain. How are you?"

Maggie smiled, recognising her voice now. "I'm fine. It's good of you to ring; we haven't spoken for ages. Are you still with your son, Martin? D'you still have that boyfriend, Colin?"

"Yeah. Your memory's good. We're still an item."

Maggie listened as Jacky told her about her life in Spain, so different to the traumatised woman that had once lived in the village next to Ethel in Alice's council house and been beaten up by her violent husband, Len. Following the death of their son in a tragic road accident in the village, Maggie had befriended her. Len had been imprisoned after committing further crimes, including an assault on Edna in the village shop. Jacky had fled to Spain to join her son, Martin. Maggie enjoyed telling her about Charlie and the expected twins. There was so much to catch up on that it was nearly thirty minutes before Jacky rang off with a promise to visit if she returned to England. Maggie patted her bump – another classic and protective move, she mused – before following Woody and wandering into the kitchen to make a pot of tea. She was in a reflective mood, awakened by Jacky's phone call, thinking back over the years they had spent in the village, the people they had met and the friends they had made in the community. She felt comforted and safe and despite the dreadful memory of losing baby Honey she knew that this place was where she and her little family were rooted.

The phone rang again and Maggie knew it would be Elizabeth. Her mother had taken to phoning her daily.

"Darling, Eleanor's just arrived so we're popping over to see you. Is that okay?"

"Of course. I didn't know she was coming."

"Sudden decision. She's seen a couple of houses they'd like to view."

"Really? I didn't think they were planning to move until next year."

"You know your sister. Impetuous."

Maggie sipped her tea and wandered back to the sitting room as the phone rang again. A quiet restful gap in the day was becoming busier by the minute.

"Maggie, I do hope you don't mind me ringing but I just fell over and, although I don't think I fell on my bump, more my hip and grazed my knee a bit, I wondered if you thought I'd have hurt the baby at all?"

Maggie recognised the voice immediately. It was Edna's niece, Jennifer, who'd whispered to her in the shop that she was five months pregnant and had been keeping it a secret. Her neat little bump had remained well hidden beneath the overalls she wore when serving customers. Maggie reassured her, checking that she'd rung Susan and was going to have a proper check-up at the clinic later.

Edna had been difficult as she disapproved of Jennifer's boyfriend and was shocked that they hadn't got married before she became pregnant. Maggie wandered back into the kitchen, feeling pleased that Jennifer had rung. She hadn't realised until now quite how much she was missing her work, her daily contact with her colleagues and the joy of sharing in the pregnancies of so many young couples and their early days as new parents.

The boisterous arrival of Charlie, escorted by Dawn, shattered Maggie's final five minutes of peace as he wrapped his arms round Woody and told her what he'd done in school, in between mouthfuls of chocolate biscuits.

"You can never fill them up at this age," Dawn said. "He's had a sandwich at my place already."

"Dawn, you're a star. Thank you. My mother's coming in a minute. My sister suddenly landed on her and wants to look at a couple of houses in the area."

"You're jolly lucky to have all the family nearby, specially with these two on the way. Lots of help for you."

"Could be too much," Maggie laughed as she jotted down the times she'd like Dawn to help out. "Say goodbye to Dawn, darling."

Charlie, wiping his face on his sleeve, hugged Dawn and smothered her in chocolatey kisses just as Elizabeth and Eleanor's car appeared at the top of the lane.

"I'll see you tomorrow, young man," she said, smiling and nodding at Elizabeth as she reversed her car out of the drive.

"Wonderful woman," said Elizabeth as the pair greeted Maggie and hugged Charlie.

"Down, Woody, down," Maggie ordered, opening the back door to let him out. "Well, this is a nice surprise. Tea or coffee?"

Settled in the kitchen, with Charlie and Woody engrossed in *Crackerjack*, the three women discussed their plans. Eleanor was anxious to move nearer and was excited to be house hunting in the area. She and Elizabeth planned a couple of viewings for the next day. Seeing how uncomfortable Maggie had now become they agreed to visit the houses without her.

"It's so good to have you together again, darlings." Elizabeth said, with a slightly coy expression.

"Uh, oh. What's coming, Mummy?" Maggie could see her mother was bottling something up.

"Let me guess: you're pregnant!" said Eleanor, collapsing into giggles.

"Don't be silly, darling. No. Frank and I are off on our cruise in two weeks' time, as you know."

"Yes, we know."

"Well, we hope you'll be happy for us if we decide to get married after all."

"We keep telling you we'll be happy if you're happy," they said, hugging her.

"And don't you dare to get married at sea without us," Maggie said. "That would be unforgiveable."

"I'd never do that to you. Thank you both," she said, returning their embrace. "We can never replace your father but I hope you'll grow to see how good Frank is for me. Now, let's have another cup of coffee."

Chapter Thirty-Nine

A problem in the parish

Major Gibson faced the angry residents gathering in the village hall, rallied by Annie Watson.

"Order, order. Mrs Watson, will you please sit down?"

"I'll sit down when you lot tell me that you're protecting my tomatoes and what you plan to do about the allotments and the vandalism that's been going on there for weeks."

"Mrs Watson. The Major was redder in the face than usual and preparing himself for the sharp tongue of Edna Newbold who was glaring at the row of councillors from her position in the centre of the front row. "Mrs Watson. I am fully prepared to discuss this troublesome issue with you and all the members here from the allotment society when I get to it on the agenda. Now if you'll please sit down, Madam, I'll allow you to speak once I've opened the meeting. I believe the clerk has distributed copies of our last minutes and tonight's agenda?" he said, glaring at the clerk who flustered by being pounced upon, nodded as she hastily handed out more copies to the crowd flooding through the door. The Major was visibly relieved to see the local policeman following on behind, gesturing to him to join him on the platform.

The parish council were proud of the number of allotments they provided for the village and always had a waiting list. The destruction of some of the planted areas, Annie's tomatoes and her small cloches, plus the distressing sight of two burnt out garden sheds and three overturned water butts had caused dreadful alarm. Wheelbarrows had been left littering the green. Garden forks had been chucked into the pond, having first, it was assumed been aimed at the ducks. Some of the men in the village had threatened to form their own vigilante group and it was that suggestion that had brought PC Sheridan to the meeting.

The Major raised his hand as the last few found their seats. "Welcome everyone, I wish to make a change to the proceedings." he gestured to the clerk to shut the door and introduced the policeman. "I'm sure PC O' Sheridan is familiar to you all. He's very kindly agreed to join us this evening and inform you of the measures being taken to combat the disagreeable behaviour and the destruction that has been reported to me on the allotment site. "

"Bloody criminal, mate," shouted a resident. "It's a bit more than disagreeable."

"Quite so," said the Major, looking increasingly flushed as tempers rose. "As I said before I'll call upon him to tell us what can be done, and what his men are doing or have done, on our behalf," he cleared his throat and waved airily at PC O'Sheridan. "Over to you. Please could you clarify the situation for us all, thank you."

"Perhaps the councillors would care to look at these photos," PC O'Sheridan suggested, passing them to the Major. "This shows you a trail of wanton destruction in Waldersby and other villages." The Major looked shocked as he passed them round. "You, in this village, are not alone I'm sorry to have to tell you, but we are on the case."

"You always say you're on the case, whatever that means. It's action we need, mate."

Major Gibson glared at the man shouting from the back of the hall. "Please refrain from interrupting. Carry on please."

PC O'Sheridan then outlined the actions that the local force was engaged in. Adding the surprising news that one of the gang members causing the trouble actually lived in Little Fordham. This news caused immediate consternation and startled looks passed from one to the other.

Edna rose. "You don't need to hide his identity. He's been pinching sweets from my shop and didn't like it when I caught him."

"Who is he? We'll sort him out. How d'you know if it's the same lad?"

The hall erupted as neighbour eyed neighbour as the names of possible trouble makers were bandied about.

Major Gibson now flushed and redder than a ripe tomato angrily banged the table.

"Order! Order! Can I have order. Please!"

PC O'Sheridan continued in an effort to calm and reassure them.

"Now, you're all assuming it was a lad and I'm afraid you're wrong. You see this little gang is a mixed bunch and this young lady has been caught red handed."

"A girl?" gasped Annie, "What's a girl doing damaging our allotments?"

"It seems she's got in with a bad lot, her boyfriend for one. She's very very sorry I can assure you and she's led us to all the others. So you can rest assured that you won't be seeing any more damage. All these youngsters have now got work to do. Our officers have the unenviable task of accompanying these kids, sorting out the damage and returning all your tools, and such like," he said, sitting down. A look of relief crossed his face as the Major thanked him for his time and the police effort.

"It's been a pleasure, Major. I'll be talking to Mrs Newbold in confidence about the youngster she referred to and I'm happy to answer any questions?"

Edna scowled, peeved that her local knowledge was not up to scratch. At least another cheeky youngster might get his 'comeuppance' when he got a visit from the local police and hopefully that would teach them all a lesson. With Jennifer pregnant and talking about leaving her she needed to keep her wits about her, particularly when the school children piled in to the shop on their way home.

The members of the allotment society had been stunned into silence by the disclosure. All their anger evaporated when the Major added that the parish council could allocate money from the precept to replace the garden sheds, and cover any other repairs needed. He hoped that would be agreed by councillors that very evening he said, resuming his position at the top of the table as the policeman left the hall, closely followed by a gaggle of residents eager to question him further.

"We'll buy you a pint, mate," were the last words the councillors heard as the hall door slammed shut.

"Now. The Major smiled, his face growing less florid. That was indeed excellent news, excellent. Right, let's move on. Can we go through the minutes of our last meeting?"

Maggie listened with interest as Annie and Ethel told her all about the meeting over a cup of tea in Annie's house the next day. "You should have been there, took the wind out of our sails I can tell you."

"Yes, but I'm too uncomfortable to perch on those hard chairs for long. Anyway I'm delighted for you, Annie. And new cloches to boot?"

"Major Gibson rang Edna this morning. She's put a notice in the window telling us all that the council have promised to reimburse the allotment society. Quite right too. We pay them rent, well not much I agree. Still the parish council own the allotments. It's only right that they should fork out."

"The Major called on us yesterday again before he went to the meeting." Maggie said. "He's determined to get Rob on the parish council, trying to persuade him to stand for election in a couple of weeks. Rob couldn't go last night though. He and Gordon were at a meeting in the golf club."

"He'd be good, I'd vote for him. Did the Major persuade him?"

"I think it might only be a walk on part. Apparently they have a bit of a job filling all the places, so an election rarely happens for the parish."

"Is he interested? Busy husband you've got, what with his business and everything and your little babies on the way any minute."

"That's my argument but the trouble with Rob is he hates feeling he's letting anyone down. The Major's been very good to us. It's not a huge commitment so I think he's probably going to say yes."

"My George used to be on the parish council," said Ethel, becoming watery eyed. "On it for many a year, liked to be 'in the know' he always said."

"He was Chairman for many years, wasn't he?" said Annie.

"Yes, he got a lot done you know. You wouldn't have half these footpaths marked out and looked after if it hadn't been for him badgering the county people."

"Oh dear, I must be off, tell me more about it next time I come. I'd love to hear all about it. Thank you for your lovely gingerbread, "Maggie said, heaving herself out of the chair and squeezing Ethel's hand. "I'll love you and leave you both. Thank you for the tea. "I need to pick up some shopping from the shop."

"Jennifer's pregnant "said Annie.

"I know," said Maggie.

"Thought you might," said Ethel, "but you never said."

" I don't think she wants us all talking about it yet, in case it upsets Edna."

"Why should it do that?"

"You know what she's like."

"We know, dear. She's a mean old bat really."

"She'll have been visited by our policeman today about that kid stealing."

"Surprised any kid thought they could get past Edna," Annie said, laughing now, "Eyes everywhere." Maggie bent down with difficulty to stroke Socks who was winding himself round her legs and blew them both a kiss, "Lovely to see you. I'll pop in next week if that's okay?"

"D'you think you'll be here next week?" said Annie. "You're quite a size aren't you love."

CHAPTER FORTY

FOR RICHER, FOR POORER

Charlie sat on the bench in the churchyard finishing his picnic, a last sausage and his favourite bag of crisps. Maggie plonked herself down, breathing heavily after tying Woody to an old tree stump. "Here, don't forget your juice. I think Charlie Watt and Doris will appreciate your posy, darling."

"What's a posy?"

"The little bunch of flowers you picked in our garden. I'm glad you reminded me to come today. I've been neglecting them both."

"I like coming here, Mummy."

"Do you darling? That's nice. I do too. It's good to remember our old friends," she said as her gaze took in the headstones of Jack Newgate and George Jones in the same row as Charlie Watt, both adorned with fresh flowers. She knew Annie and Ethel were regulars here.

"I like those funny faces up there," he said, pointing at the gargoyles above the church doors. "They're spooky. Can we give the baby a posy too? The one you made?"

"Yes, finish your crisps and we'll pop over to the other side where Honey's little grave is." She was feeling pleasantly drowsy sitting in the warm sun, listening to the low hum of bees busying themselves. A large bumble bee droned past and vanished into a small crevice under Charlie Watt's headstone. She smiled as another exited and thought how fitting it was for them to have made a nest in her old friend's grave. He'd have been pleased.

"Finished, Mummy. Woody can have this sausage," he said, jumping down and placing the half eaten sausage in front of the sleepy dog. "Can I have my orange juice?"

Maggie was feeling so relaxed and at peace in the quiet surroundings that she felt loathe to move as she clutched at her stomach and eased herself into a sitting position.

"Will your tummy burst like a balloon?" Charlie was becoming more interested in the pregnancy as the days passed and often laid a hand on her tummy when the twins moved.

"No, darling, I'm not a balloon," she chuckled at the thought despite the resemblance. "Remember Daddy explained to you how the babies come out of Mummy's tummy?"

"Can I see?"

"Not at the moment."

"What if they don't want to come out? A boy at school said they come out of your bottom." Charlie was giggling now. "I don't want a baby coming out of my bottom."

"Our babies haven't got much room now and I expect they'd like to stretch their arms and legs soon," Maggie said, resisting the urge to giggle with him. Charlie, like all children she'd met found the mention of poos, farts and bottoms excruciatingly funny.

"I'll show them how to play football 'cos the doctor said they were good kickers didn't he?"

"They might be little girls."

"Can we swap them? I don't think I want girls now."

"We have to have what we're given darling. No choice. I'm sure you'll love them whatever they are. You can start the first girls football team."

Can they come out of your tummy tonight?"

"No. They're not quite ready and Daddy's away isn't he. Perhaps in a week or two?" she said, hopefully. With a month still to go she quite relished the idea of them arriving earlier.

"My friend said you're cooking them. He said his Mummy said you had a bun in your oven."

"Well, if that were so they'll soon be wanting to come into the world and meet their big brother." Maggie rose awkwardly, bending to give him a kiss. "Love you. Come on, darling. Honey's posy's beginning to wilt.

Elizabeth and Frank Sutton were officially 'in love'. The couple returned from their cruise and made no bones about declaring their intention to marry and live together, a change from their original idea of continuing to live separately. Maggie and Eleanor, not unduly surprised by the announcement on their return, were preparing for the forthcoming wedding celebrations.

"We'll get used to him," Eleanor said, sitting in Maggie's kitchen and surveying the list of jobs that Maggie had offered to help with. "I shouldn't feel like this. Daddy's been gone several years now and Mum's infatuated. We've convinced ourselves that her happiness is all that matters haven't we?"

"I've got used to Frank. I see more of him than you do. He really does love her and, yes, as far as we're concerned, little is, that's all that matters. He's very generous. He's already forked out for the double pram and he and Mum keep turning up with baby stuff."

"Okay, big sis! I wasn't going to tell you but Frank's offered to help us financially too when we move this way in the autumn. Martin's delighted, of course."

"Really? Well, that's good of him. D'you know what he's offering?"

"No. He suggested to Martin that we might consider buying his house as he's proposing to move in with Mum. She was delighted as she prefers her cottage, doesn't she? She's just longing to have us all around her. Frank said he'd like to help with our mortgage."

"Gosh. That's amazing. D'you like his house?"

"It's more modern than we really want but can't look a gift horse…! So – if you don't mind us staying till Monday?

Martin's coming down tomorrow to discuss it with Frank and have a look."

"Of course not; that's fine. Now, with the wedding all organised for this weekend, I think you and I need to look at what we're wearing this afternoon. Rob and Charlie have been kitted out in the outfitters in the town and are going to look very smart. Frankly, I just want to be comfortable. We need to go to the farm in Great Fordham to pick up my hat."

"Farm?"

"Yes. One of my enterprising mums has converted an old stable into a milliner's. She's making hats. They're amazing and beautifully made. I've looked at a few but it would be nice to have your opinion. Coming?"

"You bet."

The Dog and Duck were delighted to be asked to play host to the wedding reception to be held in their little-used lounge overlooking the green. Conscious of Maggie's increasing discomfort, Elizabeth had made the decision and turned down all suggestions of using the village hall or a hotel.

"No, darling. We don't want a lot of fuss. We'll have a small ceremony in the Town Hall in Waldersby, then back to Little Fordham."

"Will you be going on another cruise for your honeymoon?" Eleanor asked when she was given the news.

"Certainly not. It was a lovely experience but one's enough for me. Frank's wife was a keen cruisegoer but he and I prefer our feet on the ground. We might take a little walking holiday in Ireland later in the year. Besides, it'll be all hands on deck – literally – for the new babies."

"I thought Maggie was going to get a nanny for the first few weeks."

"She won't need a nanny if I'm on hand, will she?" Elizabeth clucked.

Eleanor smiled to herself. She and Maggie loved their mother very much but she could take over, hence the nanny idea. Oh well; it was a matter of wait and see but Eleanor hoped it would not end with her mother taking offence if others offered Maggie help.

As wedding arrangements were finalised, Edna felt put out. She liked being in charge of "functions" in the village hall, and was shocked to learn that the reception was to be held in the pub instead. "We're not good enough for some," she muttered darkly and was even more offended when Dawn told her that she and her husband were helping out at the reception in the pub.

Dawn ignored her, delighted to have been asked. She'd also be on hand to help with Charlie if needed. Edna was finally asked to have Woody for the day, a role she enjoyed, and it stopped her complaining.

Chapter Forty-One

Stop pushing now, dear, just pant!

The plain and uninviting registry office was at the top of a flight of stairs. Elizabeth and Frank were dismayed to learn that the lift had broken down on the Thursday and would not be working in time for their wedding on Saturday.

"This is ridiculous," Elizabeth said, angrily remonstrating with the voice at the other end of the phone. "My daughter is heavily pregnant."

"I am very sorry but I'm afraid I can do nothing about it. Do you wish to cancel the wedding?"

"Certainly not," she said, slamming down the phone. "Really! It's quite disgraceful."

"Don't worry, Mummy. I'll manage and Robert will carry me up if necessary."

"And end up in hospital with a hernia, no doubt," Elizabeth snapped.

"Tom will help too, so stop fussing. There's nothing we can do about it." Maggie was in Elizabeth's sitting room for a brief dress rehearsal. "Don't get all upset, please. You look really lovely, so smart. You know you always look good in a suit. D'you like my hat?"

"Love it. That friend of yours is very clever. I'd already chosen this outfit or I would have paid her a visit too," she said. "Let's make another pot, darling; that woman's got me so riled. D'you want some of my fruitcake?"

"Yes, please. My hat's okay but I'm sorry to look so baggy otherwise. Nothing looks smart when your body is this shape," she said, gently caressing her bump.

"You must be very uncomfortable, darling."

"I am."

"Frank's been going through the guest list in case we've missed anyone out."

"Have you?"

"No. Most of his old office staff are coming; well, they work for Robert now, of course. He has a few golfing friends here, two couples we met on the cruise, and you know some of our dear neighbours are coming down from Kendal. Frank's arranged bed and breakfast for them in that lovely country house in Great Fordham as you suggested." Elizabeth poured the tea and passed a cup to Maggie. "Are you happy for me, darling?"

"Oh, you know I am." Maggie tried to hug her, tearfully. "I can't get near you," she said, laughing now at her attempt to embrace her mother. "So's Eleanor."

"Will your father forgive me?"

"Now you're being silly. Daddy would only want you to be happy and you know that, same as us."

Maggie felt mildly hysterical as Robert and Tom shoved her up the winding staircase. The problem she was trying to control was a desperate attempt to stop weeing with every jolt. It was becoming difficult to control her bladder but she was thankful that she was well padded and that she was the only one aware of the problem. At last they reached the room and she could settle into a comfortable chair. Charlie was looking sheepish, his hair slicked back and his neat grey suit with a yellow rose buttonhole adding adult years to him. The registrar was fast and efficient and Maggie found herself embracing old friends and family in no time, before being escorted down the stairs once more. The troubles going up lessened for her on the way down. The guests made their way back to Little Fordham and celebrations began in the happy atmosphere in the Dog and Duck.

Maggie was sipping illicit champagne when she felt an unmistakable dribble that she really was not able to control. The speeches were over and the guests had hungrily tucked into their meal. Laughter and the general hubbub of raised voices in a noisy restaurant prevailed. Robert was engaged in an animated conversation with Frank; Elizabeth was wandering among the guests, her voice louder than most as she thanked them, slurring the words, for coming. Eleanor and Martin were engaged with old friends on the Kendal table and Charlie had disappeared with James to the snooker room, their meal scoffed down as soon as they had been told to tuck in. Maggie was reassured by the babies moving but with almost a month still to go she needed to get to the safety of the hospital now her waters had broken. She waved her napkin at Robert, who waved back and continued his conversation with Frank. She felt the dribble increase to a leak. She was relieved when she spotted Dawn collecting dishes and gestured to her, mouthing, "Come here, quick." Dawn, just controlling a heavy tray of dishes, hurried over.

"Thank goodness you're here. My waters have gone and Robert won't stop talking."

"Oh, Maggie, love. You're not due yet, are you?"

"No. I'll be alright. Get Robert, please; he'll have to get me to Cambridge. Can you take care of Charlie?"

"Of course. Shall I call an ambulance?"

"No. Robert can phone the labour ward and organise things. I don't want to spoil Mum's day."

"Your babies aren't going to spoil her day, love. She's telling everyone in the room about them. I'll get him for you."

Premature they might have been but two babies weighing nearly six pounds each were sleeping soundly in the ward nursery. Maggie had just finished feeding them both together. Assisted by a colleague, she managed to attach them easily, relieved to discover that breastfeeding her twins was not going to be a problem for her or them. Her exit from the wedding reception twenty-four hours earlier had hardly been noticed by most of the guests, despite Elizabeth's tearful hugs as the ambulance whisked them away. The birth had been a less than private affair as colleagues and medical staff filled the delivery room to witness the novelty of a twins arrival. Maggie was relieved that she'd managed to deliver the babies normally without recourse to a caesarean section. She giggled her way through the birth, high on gas and air, and alarmed Robert by chorusing "Stop pushing now, dear, just pant" as the second twin emerged. It was a favourite mantra she'd said to many of her mothers as their babies were born. The twins arrived within five minutes of each other and delighted everyone present by crying loudly within seconds of entering the world. Neither baby needed extra attention. Robert, with tears cascading down his cheeks, held each of them, neatly swaddled, announcing he felt faint with emotion and intense pride.

"I'll go and fetch Charlie, darling," he said as Maggie was ready to be wheeled into the ward after the birth. "He'll want to know their names. Any thoughts?"

"No. Don't tell him what they are until he gets here. Thank goodness you remembered to buy the baby's presents for him."

Robert bent to kiss her. "I can't believe you look so well after giving birth with only the gas to help. I'm so proud of you."

"I've been lucky just practising what I preach. The breathing really worked well to start with. I got a bit too fond of the gas and air, didn't I? It's such lovely stuff. Of course, it helped that I had to deliver two little ones rather than one big baby."

"You're a star. The watching crowd were impressed too. Must say, I found it a bit off-putting to start with, having so many gawping at you."

"I knew that would happen, darling. It's the only way they can learn; it's good experience. I remember being excited when I watched twins being born for the first time."

The two babies were beginning to stir when Robert arrived back at the hospital with Charlie, who watched in delight as they sucked imaginary teats and giggled helplessly when one baby clung to his finger and wouldn't let go. Gently unwrapped by Robert, he was entranced by the size of their fingers and tiny toes, alarmed by the cord clamp on their tummies, wanting them quickly covered up. He studied their tiny ears and wanted to cry when one cried and the other sneezed, and was nervous of cuddling them.

"They've bought you some presents, darling," Maggie said, signalling to Robert. "Look under Mummy's bed."

Thrilled with a new football, books and a large bar of chocolate, Charlie was quite impressed with the new babies.

"Can we take them home now?"

"No, darling. Mummy's staying in hospital for a little while. You have one baby brother and one baby sister."

"Yeah!" Charlie was delighted. "He can play football with me, can't he?" he said, looking serious. "It's alright, Mummy. I told you I didn't really want girl babies, didn't I?"

"Girls can play football too, darling."

Charlie, keen to dribble his new football down the ward, was getting bored. "Are we going to get Woody, Daddy?"

"Yes, say goodnight to Mummy and your baby brother and sister. Sleep well, I hope, darling. See you all tomorrow," he said. "I'll miss you."

Chapter Forty-Two

A new beginning

Maggie was dozing in the warm early-summer sunshine. She had positioned the pram under the apple tree after settling the twins. Susan had called and between them they had bathed and weighed them. Arranging her pillows, Maggie fed them both but what had been easy to start with was beginning to change as the little boy was hungrier and waking more often. She thought about Charlie and how he was enjoying the babies too, helping to dress and top and tail them, fascinated as they guzzled at her breasts, and he'd become accomplished at "winding" them. He'd also helped push the pram up the lane to show them off to the donkeys. Maggie had just stopped him from popping the guinea pigs in their cot in his eagerness to introduce the other animals. He was back at school now and Dawn had stepped in to take him if Robert was unable to leave the office. Maggie was content and overwhelmed with love for her family but weak with tiredness. Her head jerked awkwardly as she woke to the sound of Robert's car on the drive.

"Sorry, darling. You were having a nice snooze there. How's the day been? Did your midwife friend call?"

"I was dreaming. I'm having really vivid dreams these days," she said, stretching up and yawning. "It's so nice sitting out here. Doctor Southgate called as well. He's so sweet and brought them both a little cardigan that his wife had knitted."

"Really? He's very fond of you, isn't he?"

"I like to think so. After all, he's been through a lot with me these last few years."

"Maggie, we really must make up our minds about the babies' names," Robert said, patting her on the head as he perched beside her. "Everyone in the office keeps asking me what they're called."

"Okay. Let's go in and put the kettle on and concentrate on the shortlist we drew up the other day."

"Good. I'm parched; we had two meetings this afternoon," he said, helping her up.

"It's difficult when Charlie insists on calling them Tiny baby and Small baby like the *Clangers* on the telly," she chuckled. "I'm beginning to call them that too."

"I've had so many names in my head."

"I was thinking it would be rather nice to call our little girl Jenny, after your auntie."

"Funny that, because I was thinking it would please your mother, and you and Eleanor, to have your father's name – Jonathan."

"Daddy was always called Jonny. I love that idea, Rob. Jonny and Jenny? Perfect."

"We're agreed. Well that was easy! Why on earth didn't we think like that before?"

"D'you think either of us have been rational lately? We're so tired. I don't know what I'm doing half the time, apart from feeding."

"I think we should see if we can find us a nanny or someone to help out for a few weeks, don't you?"

"That's just what I was going to suggest. We really can't expect Mum, Dawn and Edna to keep pitching in. Angela and Tom have their own little ones to look after, and James. Speaking of which, Angela's left us a cottage pie in the fridge for tonight. She brought it round yesterday, plus a rhubarb crumble. She's been an absolute godsend. I half hoped we could call on Edna's niece, Jennifer, to help but that was before she got pregnant."

"It's not just our children, darling, but the animals too."

"Mum's been up most days and she's been so good with Charlie, doting on the twins, but she's not keen on the animals, as you know. She and Frank are visiting Eleanor and Martin next weekend to discuss the idea of their moving into Frank's house, so we'll be on our own."

"Okay. I'll ask some of the lads in the darts team if they know of anyone in the village who could give us a few hours."

"Major Gibson rang to ask if he and his wife could visit Jenny and Jonny. We must call them by their names now."

"Really? Coming here? We are honoured."

"I suggested next week."

"Okay. He'll probably bring us a bottle of whisky. I don't think they're very baby-minded. Uh oh. I hear a bark. I think someone's stirring."

"Now, would it be Jenny or Johnny?" Maggie said. "I'll make a guess: it'll be Johnny. Woody sleeps by the pram all the time, on guard. He barks if they stir and gets agitated if they cry."

"I thought he'd be protective. Great choice of names: they really suit, don't they? I wonder how Charlie will like them."

"I think they'll still be Small baby and Tiny baby for a while. Be a dear and get him for me. I'll give him a top-up."

"When's the health visitor calling?"

"Monday. Susan will be coming back to fill me in on some of my mums hopefully. Apparently the male student is with her again this month and he's loving it. She said he's particularly good with first-time mothers and she'll bring him for coffee next week, if they have time. He's keen to see and hear about me having a normal birth."

"What else is she updating you on? You won't be back at work for months, if then."

"I asked her to keep me in the picture, especially with my mums. Can you take Woody for his walk while I'm feeding, Rob? I think he's feeling a bit left out."

"Will do."

Two days later Maggie was lying down, exhausted. It was midday and the twins had been feeding for what seemed like most of the previous twenty-four hours.

"It's a natural growth spurt, as you know," said the health visitor sympathetically. "Sleep when they sleep." Charlie, disturbed by their crying in the night, had also crawled into bed with her until Robert had taken him to sleep with him in the spare room. Now she was alone and feeling anxious and over-tired. Jonny was putting on more weight than Jenny and his demands were increasing. She was determined to feed them herself for as long as she could but his demands were such that she had a little extra milk to keep in reserve and reluctantly had used formula to pacify him this morning, and now felt full of remorse. It had been so easy for her to give advice to mothers but it was so different experiencing the same anxieties herself. She'd have told them not to feel guilty. The twins had just settled again under the tree with Woody beside them. She'd netted the pram to satisfy the health visitor, not that any cat would get anywhere near, and had assured her that they were safe with Woody on guard. Tired and tearful, she drank two glasses of water and made herself a sandwich. She dozed in the chair in the kitchen until jolted awake by Woody barking noisily and whining. The front doorbell rang and she hurried to open it. She didn't recognise the young woman smiling at her until she spoke.

"Hello, Maggie."

"Alice!"

"Hope you don't mind me calling."

Maggie hugged her. "It's so lovely to see you. Ethel said you might be staying with her soon."

"Yes. She and Annie told me all about your babies."

"Would you like to see them? Just don't wake them, though: they've been little tinkers and I'm shattered." Maggie felt awkward, unsure how Alice would react to a new baby. "Perhaps we'll leave them asleep. I'd rather you tell me what you've been up to," she said, directing her towards the sitting room.

"I've got a new boyfriend."

"That's good news. Is he with you?"

"No. He's coming down here at the weekend, though. Ethel's met him."

"What have you been doing in Lewisham? Are you still hairdressing?"

"Well, actually I've decided I'd like to be a nanny. I'm hoping to do some training. There's a college in Cambridge I can apply to."

"Won't you find that distressing, Alice? Working with babies after all you've been through?" Maggie asked, hoping her astonishment didn't show.

"I know it sounds strange after losing my little Honey and all that but working with kids makes me happy. My sister and I have made it up and you know I really loved having Bobby even though he was a bit much at times, and then we lost the baby but I thought, if it's possible, that I could do some proper training. Me and my boyfriend want to get married next year. He's a bit older than me and wants to set up his own business – gardening; he loves that – and he's already caring for George's beehives. Ethel thought it would give me good experience if I could come and help you with your babies." She was talking so fast that she had to catch her breath. "You were good to me and I wonder if I could have a job with you?"

Maggie's cheeks were damp. "Can you start tomorrow?" she asked, hugging her.

Three months later

The colourful bunting flip flapped gaily across the lane, filling the gap between Nut Tree Cottage and Watt's Cottage. Passers-by could have been forgiven for assuming there was a late village fete. Angela and Tom had mown their new meadow and with the help of the darts team had erected the Major's marquee in the middle, now also adorned with bunting and balloons.

In the kitchen of Nut Tree Cottage Maggie and Angela were discussing the final arrangements for the party. "The cake looks wonderful," Angela said, patting Maggie on the back. "Don't think we'll get all the candles on it, though, will we?"

"No, so I've opted for one big candle. Mum actually made the cake. I just did the icing."

"Thank goodness we've had no rain, it's so warm. We'd be okay in the marquee but I expect the kids will want to run around. Biscuit and Crumble are by the gate watching the activities. They look so smart in their new halters, bless them. Biscuit took fright when the bunting went up."

"Woody's got a new collar too. Robert bought himself a new blazer and Charlie's copied your James. He wanted the same T-shirt, so no expense spared for the occasion," Maggie laughed. "Just wait and see what Jenny and Jonny are wearing. Alice chose their outfits last week when we went into Cambridge."

"She's so good."

"She's been amazing. I don't know how I'd have managed without her."

"She's enjoying the training?"

"Loving it. She's about halfway through. You must see what her boyfriend's done with our garden, by the way, especially the vegetable patch at the back. Tom said you're hoping to employ him for a few hours?"

"Yes. You told me he'd made a lovely job of Ethel's garden and loves looking after George's bees now he's done the course with the bee society. We could do with some help. Tom's too busy. He seems such a nice chap. He's quite a bit older than her, isn't he? Just what Alice needed, d'you think? Steadier?"

"Yes. He thinks the world of her and knows how to support her when she feels low. He's asked me a lot about baby Honey's death, which has helped him understand her moods better, I think," said Maggie. "She still struggles at times, especially if our babies are fretful."

"She'll never get over it, will she, poor girl? Could anyone? I can't bear to think of it," Angela mused.

"Right." Maggie glanced at the clock. "We'd better get a move on. Don't let's get depressed. Can you take the cake with you? Dawn and Edna said they've got teas and sandwiches ready as the oldies are celebrating their club's fifth birthday too. Robert and Tom are sorting out tables. James and Charlie are helping, I hope, and not mucking about."

"The men will sort them out. Millie was fast asleep so I expect Tom's asked James to look after her if she wakes. Charlie's good with the babies, isn't he?"

"He adores them. He loves it when they get giggly. He and Alice have struck up a lovely friendship. You know, she's a knack with children and I'm glad she realised it herself. She'll sail through her training. I hope."

"Good. Right. I'll see you up there; sounds as if your little ones are awake."

Villagers were arriving in the meadow as Maggie wheeled the pram up the lane, trying to avoid the potholes from jolting the babies about so soon after their feed. Biscuit and Crumble watched her approach.

"You two look so smart," she said, holding each twin up to say hello. Jenny grabbed at Biscuit's ear and squealed with delight as the donkey tried to lick her tiny hand.

Robert and Charlie waved from the marquee. The table was laden with a variety of cakes and sandwiches and the special birthday cake looked inviting, towering over the rest.

"You shouldn't be having anything yet, Charlie," Maggie said, as the boys hovered. "Special guests first. Keep Woody on a tight lead, darling."

More families arrived in the lane, slowing to talk to the donkeys before making their way to the marquee.

Tom had rigged up the music playing gently in the background. Maggie spotted Doctor Southgate and his wife and tried to wheel the pram towards them. She made little progress as neighbours stopped to admire the twins, who were enchanting them with toothless smiles, looking so pretty in their new matching outfits and special bonnets. She just recognised PC O'Sheridan appearing extra smart out of his uniform when he caught her up.

"I expect they're full of mischief," he said. "Was this your idea?"

"Not just mine. Edna and Dawn wanted to do something for their club's anniversary, so we added on this special treat. The darts team also won against Waldersby last month, as you know, so everyone felt it was time to party."

"Good to see this community working together," he said. "Looks as if the star guests are arriving."

At a signal Tom changed the music as a car driven by Alice's boyfriend, Andy, appeared in the lane and bumped its way into the field.

Edna and Dawn, having rehearsed the arrival, sprang into action and opened the car doors to a bewildered-looking Ethel, followed by Annie.

"They don't look ninety years old, do they?" Elizabeth said as she and Frank watched Charlie tucking into another cake. "You'll be sick, darling, if you have any more."

"Mummy said I could," Charlie said, quietly dropping the remains of a ham sandwich and a sausage on the grass for Woody.

It was Ethel's and Annie's birthdays within a week of each other. Maggie's idea of a celebration for them had been met with enthusiasm. Even Edna had entered into the spirit of it, encouraging anyone who entered the shop to make a small donation for their oldest residents.

The Major and his wife had arrived and watched in amusement as the two old ladies puffed as hard as they could on the large candle flame. Overwhelmed by the cheering and clapping, they held each other's hands tightly, shocked to see so many villagers gathered around. The Major followed the cake cutting with a short speech of thanks to those involved before Dawn Creasey handed over two large birthday cards signed by everyone. Angela and Tom's daughter, Rosie, giggling with shyness, was helped by James as she presented them both with a small bouquet. The Major, still holding the microphone, spoke again, keen to remind people of Annie's and Ethel's years of service locally, paying tribute to them and their deceased husbands.

With the formalities over Tom started up the music and Edna and Dawn encouraged everyone to finish tucking in. The twins now fast asleep and watched over by Elizabeth and Frank gave Maggie a chance to talk to Doctor Southgate.

"I miss you, young lady," he said, grasping her hand tightly, "but I'll let you into a secret. I'm retiring after Christmas."

"You can't do that."

"Yes he can," his wife said, smiling. "I finally managed to persuade my husband to retire and we've been talking to your mother about the cruise she and Frank went on. We're planning to do the same."

Maggie missed her job despite her growing family and felt upset at the thought of not working with the doctor she admired so much. She herself would not be returning to work for some months; they would certainly miss each other.

"I can let you into another secret, though," he said. "I've been given permission by a young woman we're both rather fond of."

"Come on, then, spill the beans!" Maggie laughed, unsure what might follow.

"Young Alice is pregnant."

"No!" Maggie's mouth dropped. "She's been helping me with the twins for the last three months. She never said she was trying for a baby again."

"Yes. She knew this would come as a shock and wasn't quite sure how to break the news so I offered to do it for her. I don't think she'll complete her training now but I think we'd both love to see her with her own baby again."

"She's not shown any signs, no sickness or anything."

"It's very early days," Doctor Southgate said. "She wasn't sure."

"Well, I'm amazed," Maggie said. "It's wonderful news. We'll never forget dear little Honey but I can't think of a better birthday present for Ethel."

Doctor Southgate smiled as he turned to his wife. "You see what I mean, dear, we'll miss each other. We've always been a good team, Maggie and I."

Maggie turned away, not wanting him to see the sudden tears in her eyes. Robert was coming towards her with Woody, waving and laughing at something Frank had told him. She could hear the sound of her babies, happy and gurgling with delight as Elizabeth passed them, proudly, from one villager to another. Tom and James were distracting Charlie with a football and some fancy footwork. Suddenly the donkeys brayed in the background and Maggie breathed deeply, overwhelmed by her own good fortune and hope for young Alice, who had suffered so much.

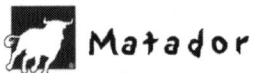 Matador